Field of Blood

Wayne Allensworth

This book is for my mother and father.

But what if Juarez is not a failure? What if it is closer to the future that beckons all of us from our safe streets and Internet cocoons?

Charles Bowden, *Murder City*

The struggle of man against power is the struggle of memory against forgetting.

Milan Kundera, *The Book of Laughter and Forgetting*

How shall we sing the Lord's song in a strange land?

Psalm 137

And he cast down the pieces of silver in the temple and departed...

Matthew 27:5

Prologue

A fire in the land... Connelly makes a stand... Rodriguez says goodbye.

*

In those days, there was a fire in the land and the people became dimly aware of a terrible judgment being visited upon them...

They had come for Connelly on a November afternoon, when the air had turned cool and calm and the sunlight slanted and softened itself as it hit and colored the Earth, bringing out the hues of fall that did not exist in summer.

Connelly lived just outside of what was called "Old Town," near the main street that had once been the town's center, but was now an array of mostly closed-up antique shops and barbecue joints marked by the old water tower that read "Home of the Rangers" on one side and "Parmer" on the other. There was a faded depiction of a mustachioed Ranger with Stetson and badge facing the street.

Connelly had sent his wife and two children to Fort Worth. He didn't explain everything to his wife. He just sent them to his mother's house. But she knew. They were coming for him and he knew he couldn't get away. So he waited for them. He couldn't think of any other way for it to be.

What if I killed them all? Could I get away then? Stop it. Thinking too much is bad for you. It gets in the way. It gets in the way of what you have to do.

And you can't kill them all.

Connelly had set himself up on a small ridge southeast of his house. He left his Jeep near an old barn and took his rifle, a 12-gauge pump shotgun, a .40 caliber Glock handgun, some ammunition in a shoulder bag, and some sandbags to the ridge. He set himself up there. He was prone, the .30-06 resting on the sandbags, the Glock in a holster at his belt. The shotgun was resting on the ground beside him. He pushed his sunglasses up on his forehead and adjusted the rifle's scope, looking at a spot just outside the gate and the cattle guard. Then he took off the glasses, set them on the ground, took a breath, and waited.

It was like in Iraq. You wait for hours and days until the boredom almost overcomes you — and then it happens, and there are those short bursts of adrenaline and your heart is pumping. He had never had time in those moments to think or to be afraid. And some part of him had liked it.

Connelly glanced over at his right forearm, the one that had had a tattoo of a swordfish on it. He'd had it removed. Natalie didn't want the boys seeing that thing, getting ideas, and he guessed it was ugly. He couldn't remember why he had chosen the swordfish. He had never seen one, not a live one, anyway. And he had lived most of his life near this ground. Lots of cattle. Horses. But no swordfish. He was drunk when he did it.

That's what they had called him over there: Swordfish. And that's what the men coming to kill him had called him, too: *pez espada*. He liked that better than them calling him *sicario*. But today, that's what he would be, with any luck.

Connelly didn't drink any more.

He watched the gate and saw two crows fly out of some brush. Then he saw a turkey buzzard flapping up into his line of sight, herky jerky like they do. There was something dead out there. He tensed up, then took a breath and watched through the scope.

He heard the motor of the SUV before he saw it. The SUV came up over a hump in the dirt road not far from the gate and stopped. The doors opened and four men stepped out. Connelly watched them through the scope. Two of them had shotguns, the other two carried M-4 carbines. The driver gathered the men around him. They were talking and gesturing in the direction of the gate and Connelly's house.

They had not spotted him.

Connelly aimed at the man doing the talking. The man's back was turned toward him. Connelly shot him in the back, chest high, and watched him hit the ground on his knees. He chambered another round and shot the second man in the chest. Only the shotgun men were left and the one nearest him made the mistake of running toward the gate and Connelly shot him through the head.

It was a good shot.

Connelly couldn't see the last man. He'd be calling for help.

He reloaded the magazine of the .30-06 and squatted on his haunches and looked out over the scene in front of him. He looked through the scope at the road and saw nothing.

He wanted their weapons.

Connelly squatted on his haunches and waited.

He gingerly scooted around to look behind him and then to each side.

He didn't see anything.

Maybe they wouldn't come until dark. But maybe not. These shooters didn't think too much, either. Maybe he had killed a brother of one of them, or a friend.

Now you are thinking again. Only think about setting up.

He needed another spot, one with his back protected. And he needed those weapons. But it was too soon to move that way. Connelly decided he would move to a spot with the barn at his back. He could set up in some mesquite down there.

He waited until near dusk. Connelly was preparing to move to the new spot he'd picked out when he thought of Natalie and the boys. At least he could see if they had made it to his mother's alright. He thought of where they might go from there. Swordfish decided to go to the house and try and call them before he made his way to his new spot. Then he might go down there and get those weapons.

When he walked through the screen door, it was near full dark and he could feel the cool snap in the air. He walked inside the white frame house that had belonged to his grandparents and it was dark inside and very still.

He propped the shotgun and the rifle against the wall and was making his way through the living room to the kitchen phone when a light snapped on and just to his left he saw a man in a khaki uniform sitting in an easy chair and pointing a pistol at him.

"Hello, *amigo.*"

The man was of medium height and stocky. He had a black mustache and hooded eyes. And he motioned for Connelly to sit on the couch across from him.

Rodriguez didn't say anything about the Glock. Connelly thought maybe he didn't see it.

But he did.

Rodriguez smiled. He had little pockmarks on his cheeks.

"*Amigo*. Just lift your hands up a bit. A little higher. That's enough. And sit down. You must be tired."

Connelly silently stared at Rodriguez.

Rodriguez sighed.

"*Amigo*, you will get your chance. Consider it a promise."

"I'll stand."

"Okay, stand. If you are thinking of making a move, just wait. But lift your hands up, they are slipping a little."

"You go to hell."

Rodriguez shot him through the left shoulder. Connelly grabbed at the shoulder and fell to one knee, his face a mask of pain. He sat on the floor and leaned against the wall. His breathing was in short, sharp gasps as if the oxygen was thin and he was stranded on a high mountaintop, and not in an old house on the prairie facing a man with a gun.

Rodriguez had a quizzical look on his face. Connelly was wondering if he could get to the Glock.

"*Amigo*, you are thinking of two things. I know this. You are thinking of whether you can get to your gun. You'll be killed, but at least you will make a stand. Like today. There is no way you can escape. And the best thing for your wife and children is if you die now. You know that. But you want to make a stand. Impossible odds, *amigo*. So, it's like the Alamo."

Rodriguez paused. He grinned a little and cocked his head to the left as if he were studying a specimen in a jar.

"It seems that there are so few opportunities for a man to make a stand. And to die with his boots on, just like in the old movies."

Rodriguez was grinning and watching Connelly closely.

"But times change, *amigo*. It's like the frontier days now, all over. But wilder, no? Crazier?"

Rodriguez shrugged. "A man can start over, make something of himself. You don't have to be held back. Everything's wide open. Wide open spaces, no? They say the country is in crisis, but in that crisis is opportunity. The land of opportunity."

Rodriguez smiled. He was pleased with himself. He wanted to save this moment.

Connelly's right arm inched down his chest. Let him talk. Let the crazy bastard talk. Connelly was bleeding badly. The pain was keeping him from seeing this clearly, he knew. What to do and when.

Connelly gasped and said, "What was the second thing?"

Rodriguez looked sad.

"You are wondering what you are guilty of. You are guilty of doubt. Guilty of being here at this moment. In this place."

Rodriguez shook his head.

"You stopped taking the money."

He looked intently at Connelly, like a man pondering a complex metaphysical problem. A problem of being and meaning. It was an existential issue.

"You didn't take the money."

"No."

"Your share."

"No."

"Did you talk to the Rangers?"

"I haven't told them anything."

"What's it like knowing you have to die?"

"Everything dies."

Connelly's right hand was almost at his waist.

"You broke the rules, *amigo*." Rodriguez paused for effect. "You violated an ordinance."

"You go to hell."

"Hell is where you are at. I am hell."

"Shut up."

"You wish me to stop talking. Then you die. Like you say, everything dies. Some things sooner than others. But you need to know why. You broke the rules."

Rodriguez paused for effect. It was important that Connelly understand. That was the Rodriguez ordinance.

"I've given you a chance, *amigo*. A small chance, but a chance. I'm going to shoot now. Do you go for it? Or do you want to shut your eyes?"

Connelly rolled to his left side and grabbed for the Glock. Rodriguez shot him in the head before he got it cleared from the holster. Swordfish slumped over on the floor.

11

Rodriguez turned out the light and stood up in the dark.

"I always liked you, Swordfish. Why did you do such a stupid thing?"

He walked over to the body, reached down, and patted the dead man on his shoulder.

"Goodbye, *amigo*."

And he walked out into a cool, crisp night.

1

About a boy... The disappearers... The informer... The raid... The informer tells Rodriguez a story (the head man's bargain; the drug runner's vision)... Rodriguez contemplates the new world (the taking of the informer)... Rodriguez begins

A boy is born to a mother who dies in a car accident when he is ten years old. His father is a simple man who works in his garden, attends Mass, and delivers the mail in their town. At night, he sits in his chair and says little to the boy, as if the death of his wife had cut off something inside him. Sometimes he leaves and the boy does not know where he is and the boy's uncle returns to him a staggering man, drunk and incoherent, and the father sleeps. The uncle looks at the sad boy and tells him he should be glad his father is kind and does not beat him. He was not a drunkard before. Life has taken a turn. Go to bed and say nothing of this. He will forget. And so will you.

Sometimes the boy and his father visit relatives in Mexico. The father leaves the son, vanishing for days at a time, and the boy and his cousins wander the dry and dusty streets, watching the army pass through. Wary men leave town or lock themselves, and especially their wives and daughters, behind the barred doors and windows of their houses as they wait for the soldiers to leave. They see the new pickups and SUVs of the narcos and they listen to their ballads, the *narcocorridos.*

The narcos give money to the poor and to the padre at the church. The patron saint of the narcos is a miraculous bandit. There are murals in the town, depictions of the sainted bandit painted in bright colors, the Holy Virgin gazing at him, a simple man with a black mustache who sees us from his mural and his place in heaven. They say he was a great man who robbed the rich and helped the poor. They say he was betrayed by a man in his own band who took blood money and delivered the blessed bandit to the authorities, who hanged him and left him to rot, an example for all to see and learn. The people made a shrine to him and came from near and far to ask his blessing. And the miracles of the bandit saint were heard of across the land.

The boy watches people leave notes at the shrine, some of thanks, some asking for the intervention of the sainted bandit. They are addressed to the holy and miraculous one and they thank him for saving them from death and disease. Some ask for help with a wayward son or daughter. And the boy hears stories of visions and dreams that change lives.

One man tells of a vision or dream he had. He is not certain if he was awake and walking or sleeping when the thing happened. We are all sleeping until touched by a miracle. The man sees a great panther stalking the streets and the panther follows him. It is a demon hungry for a soul, the man is sure. But the face of the blessed bandit appears and guides him to safety.

The people leave pictures of themselves at the shrine, giving thanks. There are baby pictures and pictures of smiling men in straw hats and pictures of weddings. The people name cafes and tire shops after the miraculous bandit. A barber praises the bandit for his son's release from an American prison. The shrine is built near the spot where they say he was hanged and the miracles and visions began.

Yet the boy's mother is dead.

The question is one of purpose.

The boy asks pilgrims at the shrine to explain this to him.

Does everything have a purpose?

"Yes, of course," they say.

Then what purpose was behind the death of the boy's mother?

That's a mystery.

It's so simple to say, "It is a mystery."

One late night, the boy wanders with his cousins. His father has been gone for many days. The air is hot and dry, and they encounter the somnambulant man of the visions. He swears he has seen the panther demon wandering the streets of town, aglow with evil intent. The boy's cousins are frightened, but the boy insists they find the panther demon and see it for themselves.

The cousins walk slowly behind him as he stalks the panther. The boy says he will grab it by the tail. The cousins say he is toying with hell itself. We will see. The boy wants to grasp the demon, to see whether it is real or a vision. He wishes to test its strength.

14

One of the cousins drops away and shouts that the boy is asking to be cursed. Another wonders if the curse would fall on them all, and he, too, drops back. And another doubts him and they all fall back and fade away like apparitions vaporized in the hot air. But the boy's determination is adamantine in its resolve and soon he is alone.

Where is the demon? Let me see you.

If there is nothing, then one makes one's own mystery.

*

The boy's father quits his job. He has his own business now, special delivery and high priority mail. He keeps the boy busy when he is not in school.

But the father is negligent and incompetent and the business is in danger of failing. So, he leaves the boy and once more goes to Mexico.

The boy takes care of himself. He has few real friends, but has learned to cultivate people around him, to make them believe he is a friend and close to them in the way these people are close, which is not very. He makes his lunch and goes to school. What else could he do? He is making his own way. There is no mystery to this.

He does well in school and is bright, unlike his relatives, who cultivate the look of the gutter. This boy has made some decisions and one of them is to *be* something. To cut through the veil.

He walks between the worlds. He is no Anglo, but is accepted by them. He is not exactly a Mexican, but can move in their world and is accepted by them. This is the way. He thinks his tribe superstitious, and does not idealize them as others do. But he can use his connections. He does not exactly resent the Anglos, but knows that keeping one foot in the other world is an advantage, while he can use the Anglo world for his own purposes. Anglo organization. Mexican guile. The objective and the subjective. He knows the mysteries of both and this gives him power.

His father comes back with enough money to keep his business. He says he has sworn off drinking. But the man lies and soon falls back into his binging habits. The father remains largely silent, at least to the boy, to whom he is a puzzle, like a sphinx. The boy thinks the man has nothing inside, so maybe there is no puzzle after all.

When his father dies, the boy moves in with his uncle and his family.

At the funeral, he sits and watches the ceremony as an observer of foreign rituals, eyeing the events closely and taking mental notes. The boy looks at the mummy in the coffin and thinks, *you made me this way. I am your creation.* He looks at the figure on the cross, then again at the pale mummy of his father. *I am your creation. What I am is you. But I will make my own mystery.*

*

In the days of the great cross-border raids, Deputy Sheriff Rodriguez was part of a delegation sent by the American side to train the Mexican police. Rodriguez was a rising star in policing circles around the state.

They called it a war. A drug war.

Rodriguez understood the events in a different light. And that light removed the veil obscuring what he knew to be a new world and a new reality that at the same time was very old. But the world had given it new context and new direction.

Whole villages and towns had emptied out in the heyday of the trek to *El Norte.*

Then the army had swept through, in its battle for controlling the drug trade.

Were the soldiers agents of rival cartels? A cartel of their own? Which cartel was dominant? Nobody seemed to know.

Whole villages emptied out again as the army disappeared people, vanishing them, never to be seen again. This was not kidnapping, which had grown to be a separate industry. If a crew kidnapped someone, they wanted something for them. Money. Drugs. Something. They kidnapped women to gang rape them. Sometimes the women were left alive, shattered and dismembered in their souls, but physically alive and in the here and now. But to vanish them, to disappear them, that was to remove them as if they had never inhabited the face of the earth.

There were signs of what became of the vanished. Heads lining the rails of bridges in major cities, so the people could see them and learn, the brooding and contorted masks watching them pass on their way. Bodies dangling from flagpoles with signs on them. YOU WILL LEARN. LIKE HIM.

Mass graves were uncovered and people lined the streets to watch the police and medical officials bring out the bagged remains of nameless victims, the waste removal of the new world.

Killing was casual and offhand. And professional, achieved like a precise surgical operation. The crews prided themselves on professionalism. They kept their groupings tight, concentrating the wall of fire on the target inside a moving vehicle.

There were death houses, where the vanished were tortured in unspeakable ways before being shot in the head.

Internet videos appeared of the condemned on their knees before masked men, who sometimes decapitated the victims for the viewing audience. It was meant as a warning, but became a ghastly form of entertainment. The videos were watched repeatedly by many people.

The sun is bright and piercing here. But this is also one of the world's dark places.

Death is a glowering monster, malevolent, a great beast. It hangs over the people like a great cloud, but peaceful like a mist, the only peace left in the places of dust and blood and guns and drugs and money, a place of inhabited desolation.

*

Rodriguez sat at the table and made damp circles on the smooth wooden surface with the cool, wet glass in his hand. He was listening to the story of the walking dead.

The dead man walking was tall and had a scar on his chin. He did not drink. He had stayed clean all these years, even when he worked for the cartel. He watched others destroy themselves on liquor, cocaine, and whores, he said. He visited the shrine to the holy bandit at some point in his wayward life and became a believer. This dead man walking, this informer, carried a Bible with him and quoted scripture with great authority and rectitude.

The informer read a passage about the plagues visited on Egypt. He turned the Bible towards Rodriguez and told him to read. Then he turned it back around and flipped the thin, translucent pages. And he found another passage and turned the Bible again and asked Rodriguez to read aloud.

And Rodriguez read:

"And I looked, and behold a pale horse: and his name that sat on him was Death, and Hell followed with him. And power was given unto them over the fourth part of the earth, to kill with the sword, and with hunger, and with death and with the beasts of the earth."

The informer had been a university student and studied martial arts. He was very good. This caught the attention of one of his cousins, who introduced him to high ranking officials in the state and city government. He became a bodyguard to the city's mayor. He wasn't sure at the time, but he was working for the cartel even then. An allotment was made for the mayor from the leading cartel of the city.

One day, the former university student, now a bodyguard, entered the mayor's office and saw a small, scarred man with a scraggly beard sitting across from the mayor, turning a pencil in his fingers.

The mayor introduced them. This small, unassuming figure was the top man of the cartel in the city.

The cartel boss watched him and rolled the pencil across the desktop. He asked indirect questions. The city's cartel boss wanted to know about his family, where he was from.

Soon this former university student was in the business himself. He moved tons of drugs across the border. He was very smart, very cagey, and found ways to confound the Americans. At one point, he employed deaf and mute people as mules. It was a very successful ploy. The Americans were embarrassed to bust these poor unfortunate people. They were touched. And gentle. And the mules revealed nothing. So the former university student and martial artist has been very successful.

The informer said he was in the business, but not in the life. He did not consume drugs himself. One of his jobs was to protect a cartel business manager. This man was an addict and had to be watched closely. The cartel managed its affairs very carefully and all shipments and allotments and *sobre*, the payment slipped under the table, had to be accounted for.

There were bribes and payoffs to journalists, army officers, police, politicians. It was not a simple matter to divide the corrupt from the incorrupt.

"You see," the informer told Rodriguez, "they must take the money."

The dead man walking's hands were on the Bible as if he was swearing an oath in a court of the highest jurisdiction.

"This is business. No one can be outside of it, you see? Outside is their outer dark. You are alien."

There are other inherent difficulties for those who would be outside, this dead man walking said. "If you go to Mass at the shiny new church, you may find a plaque there thanking the donor, and the donor is a narco. Your brother or son-in-law works for the narcos. The construction company you work for is financed by narco investors. The hotels and

18

clubs and restaurants are run by them, or they are investors in those enterprises. The mayor you voted for — and he is a good mayor, as mayors go in this country — he works for them. Maybe he does not steal. At least, he does not take more than he is entitled to. But he works for them. Or maybe you own a business. You must pay. It is protection. Security. You see the difficulties.

"It is hard to remain outside. This thing is an absolute thing that demands all. It cannot be satisfied if there is one other thing that remains outside it and diminishes its totality.

"For we wrestle not against flesh and blood, but against principalities, against powers, against the rulers of the darkness of this world, against spiritual wickedness in high places."

This former university student, martial artist and narco, now a dead man even as he spoke, told Rodriguez he must read this passage again and again.

*

Rodriguez takes part in a raid. He rides in a Humvee and wears body armor and a mask like the police.

The target is a warehouse. The information is sketchy. But the narcos have used it. Who is the source of this information? The air, the wind. Everybody knows. They see the SUVs and shiny pickups of the crews come and go.

A policeman was tortured to death, his body found not far from the warehouse. Maybe he was too inquisitive. Maybe he insulted a narco. It is easy for this to happen. One of the narco songs, a *narcocorrido*, played over the police radio and then the body was dumped.

Rodriguez carries an AR-15 and follows the first wave into the warehouse. The police kick in the door and cordon off the area.

There is a strange smell in the rank air inside. There are pallets, but no crates. Barrels that are empty, but the floor has been torn up. It is dank and dusty. Deserted. Musty.

They bring in a backhoe and the cadaver dogs.

It is less a warehouse than a crypt.

The digging begins and they find dozens of bodies, plastic bags over the heads, hands tied behind their backs. Why were they killed? Nobody knows. The police do not bother identifying the bodies or notifying anyone if they do. What would be the point? They have been disappeared. Vanished. Forgotten except by some family members with little shrines to them. A warehouse and quicklime. A mass grave. The cadaver dogs are highly valued.

Police officers are quitting in great numbers. Some members of the group Rodriguez is training in American police methods and procedures quit, too. This is lamentable, says the captain, but it happens. They will be replaced.

Rodriguez is very observant. He notices the big things and the small ones that the others have grown used to and no longer absorb. The brightly colored narco mansions. The strange tranquility and indifference. The barely masked fear that is subsumed in fatalism and drinking.

There is a ritual. The police and army pretend to fight the narcos. Often, they are working for them, too. The mayor, who receives his allotment, issues outraged press statements about the violence and probably thinks he is telling the truth.

At one point, a number of journalists issue a plea that is printed and posted around the city. What do they have to do to be safe? They learn. Journalists write about everything except the killings. Those who violate this ordinance may be killed or they simply flee across the border.

Businessmen and police officials live across the border, too, as do many narcos who feel more secure there.

There is a dual life here. One life is put on for outsiders. And another for family or a few trusted friends. Crews. Contacts. If you are foolish enough to move outside, you will pay the price. One learns to live with the deficit of trust. But the passion and trust invested in a close circle can be dangerous, too. Each friend is a weakness. Every attachment a vulnerability.

Rodriguez knows this. He has learned.

*

"There are mostly two kinds of people in this place."

The dead man walking patted his Bible and looked at Rodriguez and shook his head. A lamentation. A sad acknowledgment of immutable facts.

"Those who bow to the powerful and fear them. And those who have power and wield it without mercy. It is easy to see. And if given the opportunity, the submissive will become the merciless rulers. There is a deep desire to be punished. Many long for the strong, harsh hand. The *mano dura*. You will find that it is always 'they' behind everything here. Nobody knows who 'they' are. Maybe the soldiers and corrupt police do not know who their real employers are. It is very confusing, but accepted. Fate is accepted. If you have money, you spend it. I saw many narcos gain millions and spend it all on drugs and whores and parties."

He paused.

"The narcos are seen as striking out at the rulers of the darkness of the world, even as they are the rulers themselves. This confuses the people, who want another holy bandit. It is best to lead a quiet and private life. To turn inward. You have a close circle and that is your life. It is a refuge. Outside of it is danger."

The informer tapped the Bible with the fingers of his right hand.

"I have a refuge in this."

He picked up the book and looked at it with longing. He held it to his chest, then slowly set the book down.

"I walk in danger. I will be betrayed and killed. You know, and I know, that the police are part of this world. But I must follow my conscience. You understand?"

He looked sadly at Rodriguez.

"Ours is a strange country. It was founded on blood. The blood of human sacrifice. And the blood of the conqueror."

And the former narco turned informer told Rodriguez a story...

There was a man who was very successful in trafficking drugs. He had contacts in high places on both sides of the border. But he lost a load. This happens sometimes. It means you have to pay off the load at full value. He owed the cartel lots of money. They might kill him and maybe kill his whole family. This is part of the risk involved in such a business. It is understood.

For some reason, this man decided to go to the head man and tell him. To tell him what had happened. This is very strange behavior, but it happened just the same. This is true.

This man who had lost a load approached the great house. He was stopped, frisked, and questioned by the security men at the gates. The great, many-storied house was like a castle built in the desert or an obelisk of an ancient religion, a mysterious rite. It was like a narco pyramid. And this was the home and headquarters of the head man, so far as this man who lost the load was aware, at least. But these things are mysterious also.

The head man was impressed. This man who had lost a load stood before him and told him the truth. So the head man walked over to him and looked him in the eye and said that he liked him. He had balls. Great ones. This was really a rare thing, despite all the pretending that goes on. Give a man a gun and some money and he thinks he has balls, too. But that is not the case. This is what the head man said.

And the head man took this brave one who had lost a load and they got into a Hummer and drove to the top of a steep ridge that faces the vast estate. The brave one was not sure what would happen. There were bodyguards nearby with Kalashnikovs and they could kill him at any time. Maybe they would push him off the cliff. Maybe he would be tortured first. He wondered what expression would be on the face of his severed head.

There were vultures flying nearby. Perhaps they sensed that there would soon be carrion.

The head man led the brave one to a point near the edge of the ridgeline. The head man stopped and spread his arms out wide. Before them was a vista of his vast estate, the fields of marijuana all around. And the head man said, "This is all mine. I offer it to you. It can be yours. Someday.

"But first, you have a job to do."

The head man said the brave one must move a huge amount of drugs into the United States for him. He must not lose anything or he will die. If he is successful, then someday, perhaps, he can have *all this*. Maybe that is the brave one's fate.

So says the head man.

So the brave one moved a huge amount of drugs into the United States. Vast quantities that he had never before dreamed of. He was very successful. The head man was pleased.

Then one night the brave one had a dream, a dream that was a vision.

In this dream, he was awakened by a large figure in a flowing white hood that seemed to glow with a mysterious light. The figure took him by the arm and led him to a high mesa overlooking vast cities and fields of marijuana. The arm of the great being extended and swept the horizon and then pointed at the brave one. There were no words spoken but a message was conveyed. This man was serving the devil. The brave one was an agent of his own country's damnation.

The brave one was transformed. He changed his life and stopped his work for the cartel. He walked with Christ and began to see the terrible suffering and violence for what it was. A cleansing. A scourge. Maybe others will see.

He changed his ways and tried to fight the cartel. But in the end, the brave one was murdered. His mother found the mutilated corpse of her son on the town square. The townspeople gathered and viewed the body. Then, vast storm clouds covered the sky above the town, and lightning and rolling thunder followed. Some of the people saw a vision of an angel in the clouds and they ran to tell the priest of what they had seen.

*

Rodriguez walks outside the house into the compound. It is like many houses here, with gates and barbed wire and cut glass on top of the surrounding walls. He watches a hawk overhead. It floats in the air as if suspended in time and space, only the barely perceptible flutter of its feathers indicating that this is real and not one of the visions he has heard of. It suddenly dives to earth, aiming for prey that is beyond his field of vision.

*

"I have killed. I have worked with the *sicarios*, the assassins."

The former narco walked beside Rodriguez in the compound. They were like pilgrims sojourning in a strange and holy place. They were very serious, as if they had encountered something vast and inscrutable. Evil or truth.

"I had wondered all my life. What was the great and terrible secret? The secret of life and death. What was behind the mask of the world? What was the power of the gods?"

The informer described the work of killing.

"You understand that at first I did not think of this as murder. These were not my people. They were outside or had betrayed us. At least, that was understood. I did not know them. There was no ordinance against this."

He went on.

"The crews had different sets of uniforms and official documents for different jobs. Some of them were active police officers. Most were former police or army deserters. They could stop you and arrest you. They could take you away and nobody would ask questions.

"Their basic tools were guns, plastic bags, duct tape, and plastic ties for the hands and feet. It was important to use the duct tape on the mouths of the victims and secure their hands and feet. Put the bag over their heads quickly. When they realized what was happening, they would begin to flail about, making the job more difficult, so it was better to secure them quickly.

"You could feel the power," he said.

That power intoxicated and frightened him. The informer explained how he began to avoid this aspect of his work.

"The victims' eyes pleaded for mercy, but there was none in the killers."

Rodriguez asked him whether the professional killers enjoyed their work.

"At first, yes, I think so. But later many of them became hollow men who found it hard to feel anything. They found a release in drugs."

The informer, this dead man walking, said that he thought some of the worst of them, the experts on torture, were damned souls who sought a revival of sensation in themselves by devising and carrying out ever more elaborate and fiendish tortures on their victims. The beatings brought no more sensation, so you used a knife. When that became boring, you used a blowtorch or pliers. A sort of impotence set in otherwise.

"You have to choose," the informer said. "You can indulge in murder and torture as a drug. But the same amounts yield diminishing results, so you either stop or move on and become engulfed by it. Then the consuming of the soul is complete. When a killer has reached that point, he has lost all ties to humanity. He cannot be trusted and does not trust. Then the fine, invisible lines that hold this thing together become frayed. Often, a burnt-out killer is then killed himself. He becomes reckless. You can see it in the deadness of his eyes."

He looked at Rodriguez gravely.

"So you have to choose, *amigo*."

*

Later that very day, Rodriguez crossed the square, read the plaque, and surveyed the great new church before him. It was paid for by the narco bosses, invisible men with names and sometimes without names. Men unseen. Known and unknown. Smiling and kindly vampires and anti-saints of the Pit, their hand made manifest in the mounds of bodies and severed heads and piles of cash and cocaine, sacrifices made to a god or devil none worshipped officially but sacrificed to in howls of laughter and screams of despair and the mournful silence of death, the only release from Moloch. It was a deadly embrace that had its own reasons, its own inscrutable calculus.

Rodriguez noted the cartels openly advertising for new recruits. A huge banner was hung across a central boulevard of the city. Soldiers and ex-soldiers were wanted, with good salaries and benefits offered for recruits and their families. The banner read "Don't go hungry. Don't suffer." There was a cell phone number to call. Another appeared a few days later. It offered life insurance for recruits and a house for each recruit and family, a new car or truck. "What else do you want? The world is our territory!"

The cartels operated training camps and their troops had the best equipment, automatic weapons, explosives of every kind, even armored vehicles and rocket launchers. Many of the leaders were former army officers trained in the United States.

Rodriguez saw that there were simply no external checks. No restraints of passions and hatreds and violence great and small. They killed because they could. Because it gave them power. Because it made them gods and devils. Before them was the limitless expanse of a new world both external and internal, an inner life devoid of content that was filled by naked power. The end of man's existence exposed in the death houses. The bewildered gaze of the victims. The gawking, glazed eyes.

Rodriguez watched the birds of prey, and he saw the whole history of that country in a fleeting slash of time. Grasping, rolling death. Predators in the silent hum of the universe. A door to darkness. The passive, resigned prey.

You thought you had seen things. And now?

So unreal. But there was nothing more real than the redeeming power of the AK-47 and the ultimate reality of temporal existence, which is death.

Back in the compound, the informer was reading his Bible at the table. He was reading the Psalms.

Plead my cause, O Lord, with them that strive with me: fight against them that fight against me.

The informer heard the gate open outside and the noise of a motor. A large truck was entering the compound. Maybe a Hummer.

He closed the book.

The door opened and a group of masked men entered. They wore black uniforms and were led by a stocky man of medium height. This one walked to the table. He waved his Armalite rifle and motioned with his head. *Outside.*

The informer rose and faced them.

"So, you have come for me."

The informer looked into the eyes of the leader. He looked at him with the clarity and knowledge of a man looking at his own life.

A voice crying in the wilderness.

And they took him away.

*

Rodriguez concluded that one could not judge the cartel boss as other men. He has his own psychic rhythm, an ethical stance fit for a man who is both misanthrope and philanthropist, easy killer and extravagant, lavish angel, showering followers with temporal gifts. He is lawgiver and executioner. And a willful and jealous god.

Rodriguez moved into that realm as a disciple and emerged an apostle of a new world both gleaming and of interminable darkness, eyes gazing into the abyss. A cosmic speck. A touch of stardust gone to ground. A vapor. But real. *Now do you understand?*

They had tortured the informer, though there was no real reason for it. They didn't try to make him talk. Rodriguez already knew everything that he had told the DEA. And the highly placed police officials who received reports based on his information had passed them on to the cartel. The torture, in this case a man stripped naked, beaten severely, then set upon with knives that slashed and cut, but left him alive for some time, was part of a ritual. The crew would have felt they had committed some sacrilege if they had merely shot him.

The victim screamed, but said nothing. There was no special pleading. The walls were covered with plastic trash bags because of the blood. The men that tortured him wore overalls.

Rodriguez punched the informer first, coiling up and releasing into his solar plexus, then he stepped back and let the crew take over. He pulled up a chair, turned it around and sat watching the proceedings. Rodriguez looked on it as a learning experience. He did not allow himself to flinch or turn away. Or to feel any compassion for this man who had taught him so much. Yes, he had been a great teacher.

*

The day before he was taken, the informer had been on a walk with Rodriguez, inside the compound walls. There were police with body armor and Armalite rifles casually leaning against the gates or walking around the house. One man was checking the surveillance cameras on the walls.

The informer stopped and looked over at the policemen and nodded his head toward Rodriguez.

"Any one of them could suddenly turn and open fire and kill us both," he said.

He looked at Rodriguez, then continued the stroll.

"My parents are dead. Before she died, my mother was in a hospital. I knew she was going to die. So I prayed that her death would not be a lingering one. She died within a couple of days. I was able to speak to her near the end. I told her that she had not given birth to me in vain. This was my hope. My brothers and sisters? Several of them were in the United States. But they all came, as did people from her native town. She knew these things. I felt my prayer was answered."

The informer paused and gazed up into the vast expanse of pale blue sky with a piercing look that seemed to penetrate the thin clouds.

"We think of God as above us, but on this sphere, there is no up and down. That is an illusion. God is within us or without. We can push Him away. I no longer pray for myself, I mean in the sense of praying for an end that relieves me of anything."

"Why not? We are taught to pray. For ourselves and for others."

The informer paused, hands in his pockets, then he cocked his head and looked away and said, "I began to wonder about the nature of prayer."

"How so?"

"Look around you." He swiveled his head around in a symbolic gesture of gazing on the murderous city.

"In this city, the bodies are piled high, and buried in shallow graves, and we are tortured and raped. When I was younger and had forgotten God, sometimes I would want something or need something. My mother would tell me I could pray for things, just not only for myself, or merely for a prosperous temporal life. What could I pray for? Health, maybe. To meet a woman and have a good wife. Maybe something like that. To be spared pain and suffering. But there was a problem."

"And what was the problem?"

"Why should I be granted these simple things, when others, many of them much more deserving of mercy and consideration, had died terrible deaths, seen their children dismembered, their lives destroyed by the narcos. So why should God give me consideration?"

Rodriguez shrugged and looked back at the informer.

"It is a mystery," said the informer. "If God can forgive me, then anyone can be forgiven. But no man can forgive what I have done."

He turned and walked back toward the house. The informer paused and without turning around said, "I only wish to be an instrument. An instrument of God's will."

Rodriguez watched him enter through the door and shut it.

*

The informer's naked and disfigured body was hung upside down on a memorial to fallen police officers. A sign was draped on the monument that read: NOW DO YOU UNDERSTAND?

*

Back at home, Rodriguez started with his Sheriff's Department computer. He checked for outstanding warrants, DEA chatter, anything he could find that might be of use to the cartel. He passed the information to a cousin of his who acted as a conduit to cartel cells in that part of the state. In time, Rodriguez and the cousin expanded their network of relations and friends and a stream opened.

It was a beginning.

2

The base camp... Hearts and minds... The red zone... The captain's calculations (on patrol)... Opie and Houston talk over the war (Houston's history lesson)... Connelly makes a joke (the philosopy of a man-killer)... Connelly and the indigenous allies... Connelly in his element... Meyer's sacrifice

The base camp was about the size of a big box store back home, including parking lot. It was surrounded on all sides by the city. The minarets of the mosques acted as watch towers and positions for snipers, and observers could estimate distance and range and call in a mortar strike on the camp. Haji was all around.

They could not raid the mosques or target them. That was not in the win hearts and minds plan. The bad guys knew this. The colonel said that cultural sensitivity had to be maintained in order to legitimize our indigenous allies. He said that.

So you kept your head on a swivel, looking for the glint of the sun on a rifle. That way, maybe you wouldn't get dead out there.

The captain was taking a smoke one day outside his headquarters and snipers began taking potshots at him. A mortar round followed. The captain headed for cover and made it, but Spc. Jensen didn't. They had to take his right leg off at the knee. From then on, it was ordered that all personnel wear helmet and body armor when outside a building with a reinforced roof.

Local Haji was a crappy shot. But some of his foreign counterparts were better. You learned these things in the red zone.

Convoys had to bring in supplies. Each convoy was preceded by an explosives ordinance disposal unit, on the lookout for improvised explosive devices. Most of the men killed had been taken out by IEDs. So the colonel had observation posts set up around the base camp to watch for the bad guys trying to place them. A base camp sniper could zap them while they were digging holes in or beside the road. Zapping them was doing them a favor. Those zapped would be suitably blessed, ascending to their paradise to service a perpetual stream of willing virgins. Maybe that explains something.

One day, a disposal unit dug up maybe 20 IEDs on a stretch of road outside the compound. The next day, there were 20 more. Haji was determined.

You had to drink lots of water. The dry, dusty heat could sap your strength, striking you with sudden alacrity like a stealthy ambusher. And down you went.

Sometimes it seemed as though the country itself, that corner of the universe, that spot of ground, was an enemy. It seemed as though Haji sprang from it as the natural spawn of a deadly and malevolent climate that had a personality and aim of its own. A different world. Some world.

The men were very young. The captain was in his twenties.

The colonel said it was like this: carry out another surge of forces and the bad guys would leave the city and go somewhere else. So the plan was to try and draw them in, engage in a firefight, and destroy the enemy.

Patrols were sent outside the wire, looking for the bad guys. Groups of men in body armor with night vision equipment, looking like aliens from a science fiction movie set on a desert planet. The bad guys learned and avoided them at night. So the colonel decided that daytime patrols might be more productive.

Haji was a guy in a t-shirt and tennis shoes with a Kalashnikov. The men at the base camp killed lots of them, often taking down more of them in a day than the unit had lost on the entire deployment. But they kept coming. Nobody gave much thought as to why they did. But in the red zone, most didn't give much thought to anything outside of operational practicalities when the time came. This was the logic of war, the calculus of survival.

The soldiers went from house to house, looking for bad guys and confiscating weapons.

They were very polite. First, they would knock and announce themselves, then step back and wait. If there was no answer, they would kick the door down.

One day, a large, sturdy door would not yield, so the biggest soldier in the patrol ran at the door like a battering ram, slamming the structure with his boot. The whole door, frame and all, broke away from the cracking, flaky walls and tottered and fell, crashing with a *boom*.

Then a little man, looking very perplexed, approached the patrol, holding out a key in his hand.

The patrol entered and they went through every room, many of which were also behind locked doors. Nobody liked smashing up these people's houses, but if there was no key and they just stood there, looking at you, you kicked the door in, hoping there was nobody waiting for you on the other side.

A few of the men read the Bible, and if there was somebody waiting for them on the other side of the next locked door, they said they knew where their next stop would be. The others said they didn't know and didn't think about it. But they were pretty sure there wouldn't be a bunch of virgins looking to get their cherries popped wherever they wound up. They would go back to cleaning their weapons. Maybe that explains something.

The captain complained that his men weren't getting any news coverage. So a press photographer came to the compound with the next convoy. He was with one of the hunter-killer companies. The photographer went out on patrol and was told not to take photos from the middle of the road, but he made a big mistake and forgot himself and did. His femur was shattered by a sniper round. Sgt. Jackson tried to drag him off the road and caught a round in the leg himself, while the photographer had his ankle ruined by another round, then a third. They say he got a rod in the thigh and a plate in his ankle. You couldn't forget yourself out there.

The men at the base camp learned what was true and what was bullshit. Like they told you that you had ten seconds to take cover when there were incoming mortars. That was bullshit. It was more like three. Anyway, there were lots of places out in the compound more than ten seconds from cover. Three men had learned the truth too late. You could still see the depressions in the compound from the barrage.

At first, there were no portable toilets at the base camp. So the men had to take a leak in one spot and a shit in another. They burned the shit. The mess hall didn't have a reinforced roof and early on, the men stopped going there after a couple of mortar rounds landed on their dinner. They bitched about the food whether they tasted it or not.

One hunter-killer company was short about 30 men, but they went out on patrol anyway.

One night, an IED flipped a Humvee and a tank went out after it. The tank was disabled by another IED. The fuel line was cut and the tank caught fire. The men couldn't leave a tank out there. The bad guys could check it out and figure out how to attack it. Or they could pass on pieces to other interested parties. No air strike. It would just scatter the pieces. The rounds from the tank's main gun and machine guns started going off.

So the men had to set up a perimeter to guard a burning tank that was belching rounds, spewing out fiery death in the ink black darkness. Haji knew they had night vision equipment and laser pointers, but he came just the same, the tank acting as a beacon, then a funeral pyre for the faithful. The bad guys tried throwing IEDs at the perimeter. They were picked off, then mowed down in waves, the scene illuminated by the tank's bonfire like a hellish nightmare. How many bad guys killed? Confirmed, 30. The company lost two men to an IED.

*

The captain has things figured out. From the time the men leave base camp, it takes the enemy about 45 minutes to set up an attack. "It's a science," he says. So they begin clocking the bad guys.

The patrol starts out in a convoy of Humvees and armored vehicles fixed up with what they called cheese graters, metal cages around the vehicles to stop rocket propelled grenades from striking them broadside. The indigenous allies join them.

The captain reminds them before they go out that those people — ours and theirs — shoot high. That was a good thing when it was the bad guys. Maybe not so good when the indigenous allies were supposed to be helping. It was a small sacrifice to cultural sensitivity.

They kick in doors.

There's another photographer with them. He follows them into a house and an old woman sternly admonishes him. He says he didn't kick her door in, but she figures maybe he is important because he has a camera. He takes her picture. The old woman shakes her fist at him. She admonishes him in her tongue. The photographer smiles and says he does not understand Arabic.

A girl steps into a hallway with a baby in her arms. She sees the photographer, smiles, and holds up the baby so he can get a good shot. The old woman is still shaking her fist. The photographer steps back for his shot and bumps into her. "Pardon me, ma'am," he says. She watches in resigned silence. The old woman shakes her fist when the men march out the shattered door. The girl is watching, her face showing awe and deep curiosity as they leave, as if she had just witnessed a supernatural event.

The photographer wonders where the men are. There are plenty of girls, children and old ladies to be seen. But no men. Where are they? Maybe they were killed at the tank bonfire. Maybe half the fucking neighborhood was finished off there. Who knows?

The captain is clocking this. Within 15 minutes, he says, the spotters have come out. By thirty minutes, the weapons have been brought in. He tells the patrol they'll be shot at by the 45 minute mark. Check your watches. You can bet on it.

At 44 minutes, a beat-up sedan approaches and the passenger window goes down. A man in the backseat opens fire. Within another minute, the vehicle is a smoldering heap, blood splashed on its shattered windows. The captain smiles. *What did I tell you? That'll get your pecker hard.*

The men take a position on a nearby building top. It's a good spot. A flatbed truck with four bad guys riding with their AKs approaches. A hail of gunfire through the engine block halts the truck and a grenade launcher takes out the rest. Six confirmed kills. We're on a roll, says the captain. Bring it on.

The men fight like a machine.

More bad guys on the way. The captain calls in air support and two helicopter gunships dismantle the oncoming trucks in a whir of buzzing machinery that has an effect like a tornado called up out of the ether. The streets below are a bloody junkyard.

The enemy has pulled out and the patrol does not pursue. We wait and make the bad guys come to us, says the captain.

The patrol rides out in Humvees. The captain is pleased, saying that he has been soldiering for a while now and it isn't enough. He wants more. The patrol has been like a buzz saw loosed in the streets. The captain looks at the photographer, who is an educated man, and says that somebody named Johnson once said that every man who has not been soldiering thinks meanly of himself, but we are not those men. He thinks maybe the photographer understands this, or at least knows who Johnson was. But all the men understand in their way.

Some of the men look like young boys. The captain christens a soldier named Taylor "Opie," but few get the joke until he tells them. Then some of them still don't get it. The captain says, "you never watched classic TV? You guys are culturally deprived."

Lt. Hansen says he feels pretty deprived in this shit hole. Then he looks around as if surveying his drought stricken holdings and says, "Well, at least we got something to go back to. These people got nothing."

The captain says there are no convenience stores in Haji's neighborhood. "That's for sure. Think about that a minute. No convenience stores. No supermarkets. No laptops or multiplex theaters for Haji. And look at these crappy cars. These people got nothing."

*

The men are eating. Opie says something about the Iraqis this and the Iraqis that and one of the men, who is studying a Bible, looks up and asks Opie "Where have you been," as in, haven't you been paying attention? "We ain't in Mayberry, Opie." The man with the Bible is Houston.

"Opie," he says, "there is no such thing as an Iraqi. An Iraqi is what they call a 'social construct.'"

Opie looks puzzled, so Houston continues: "There are Sunnis and Shiites in Mesopotamia. There are Kurds and Chaldeans. There are tribes and clans and the people from your home village. But there are no Iraqis. That's an invention."

Opie grins and says, "Then where are we, *Reverend* Houston?"

Houston adopts a serious and scholarly pose and says expansively, "The land between the rivers. Cradle of ancient civilizations. Sumerians, Babylonians, Assyrians. The beginning of recorded history. Cuneiform writing. A stylus on wet clay about 3000 BC. The land of Gilgamesh. Astronomy. Hammurabi and his code. The birthplace of Abraham. Terraced step pyramids, the ziggurats, the tower of Babel. And of Ishtar, the goddess of love and war."

Houston looks reflective, as if he has unearthed a rare and fundamental object from the lowest stratum of an excavation.

"Maybe she was related to that bitch I was married to."

It's Connelly. He is still eating. Houston is surprised.

"Swordfish the Man Killer speaks."

Connelly leans back, crosses his arms and eyes Houston.

"So, what happened to all those people? Babylonians and the rest."

"Swept away. Conquered. Collapsed from within. Maybe they poisoned themselves."

Spc. Meyer wipes his mouth, clears his throat, and says, "What the fuck? No space alien invasion?"

"Wars and internal collapse, maybe helped along by man's failure to grasp what he thought he had mastered."

Houston's voice takes on a special balance of tone and pitch. He is aware of the gravity of his pronouncements.

"Take irrigation. If the water is allowed to sit in the fields and evaporate, it leaves mineral salts behind. If this continues, the mineral salts concentrate and destroy the soil. It becomes toxic, so that nothing can grow. They did not have an effective drainage system, so the toxins accumulated in the soil."

Opie sighs and says, "This is all way above my pay grade, reverend. Just a circle jerk. I'm here because of weapons of mass destruction and freakin mushroom clouds that coulda been over our cities."

Houston gazes on earnest Opie as he might a dull and recalcitrant pupil.

"In theory."

Opie, sensing he is being challenged, frowns and continues, "I'm here because'a 9/11."

Houston stares past Opie, as if he were receiving signals from a transmitter deep in space or from a being unseen.

"Didn't have anything to do with it."

Houston is still staring into space, not looking at Opie or at anyone. He is self-contained and unattached. A visitor in this strange compound, sojourning in a strange land. He is both traveler and messenger, admonishing a stiff-necked people.

"No WMD?"

"Nope."

"No Osama?"

"Not here."

"No?"

"No."

"Then *what*, reverend?"

Houston sighs. The signal is complete.

"Somebody wanna try that?"

Opie smiles. "You're full of shit, Houston. Always full of shit. Always actin like you know somethin nobody else knows. Always preachin to us."

Houston glances at Opie. "No. Just trying to tell the truth."

"Well, then, we liberated these people. We liberated the Iraqis."

"Try 'indigenous allies.' I told you, dickhead, there's no such thing as an Iraqi."

Meyer shakes his head in disbelief at the course of the conversation.

"Shouldn't we be talkin about, oh, maybe some bush." He says "bush" in all caps. Meyer does not care for questions.

"Poppy or Dubya?" It's Houston making the inquiry. Meyer does not catch the joke.

"Shit, Houston. Bush as in poontang, snatch... "

"'Bush' dear boy, is an archaic term for female private parts. Where did you pick that up, from your grandpa? I guess Haji's got Allah and his virgins. We've been recruitin for em. Right, Man Killer? Makes your pecker stand up, like the captain says."

Houston glances at Connelly, still sitting with his arms crossed. Connelly raises the middle finger of his right hand, then drops it, and pats his left arm.

"Man Killer. That's what my ex said, too. Said it was killin her soul to live with me."

The voice is a matter-of-fact monotone.

The men laugh.

Meyer says, "I heard that."

Houston taps the table and says, "Then I guess she's alive now."

Houston closes his Bible and gets up to leave.

Connelly, without addressing anyone in particular says, "There's no gods here. No allahs. Just men."

Houston pauses and without looking at Connelly says, "Why are you here, Man Killer Connelly?"

"Get away from that bitch. Somethin to do."

Houston walks out mumbling about some reason to be here. And Connelly says, "Fuck you very kindly, reverend."

"Oh, I'm fucked, alright. We're all fucked."

*

The next day finds the men on a roof, a bright yellow fluorescent banner hanging from a railing. That's in case air support is called in. Nobody wants to be the target of friendly fire, so you mark your position. Connelly is manning a light machine gun when he sees a Haji on a bicycle toting an AK, so he whacks him. By the time they quit that day, he has four confirmed kills.

The captain is ebullient. He says something about unleashing the dogs of war. Opie says that would be us, correct, captain? The captain nods his head.

A sniper round zips past, close to the captain's head. He shouts "Motherfucker!" Connelly swivels and sends a couple of bursts in the direction of the sniper's location. Opie uses binoculars to confirm Connelly's second kill of the day.

The captain dubs the hunter-killers "war dogs" and everybody seems to like it except Connelly, aka "Swordfish" and "Man Killer." Connelly seldom shows any emotion. Opie notes that Swordfish doesn't talk much and the captain says that's OK. This Swordfish is a man killer. He doesn't have to talk. Our Man Killer is in his element. Connelly nods and says he guesses he is. In his element. The Man Killer speaks.

The captain turns to the photographer and wonders if he got a picture of Connelly's last kill.

When the men exfiltrate two houses that back up to each other, the bad guys have zeroed in. Small arms fire comes from all directions. They could stay and shoot the place up for the rest of the day, but the captain says there are too many civilians around, so they have to get out of there. They zig zag through the narrow streets. Connelly lays down some fire and the men run like hell. Then, when they reach a new position, they open up and Connelly runs like hell. They come to a wide avenue, so they toss smoke grenades and all of them run like hell.

The photographer is shouting his blood type in case he gets hit. The men press themselves up against a long wall on the opposite side of the avenue and prepare to make the corner. The pickup area is nearby.

A group of indigenous allies manages to cross the avenue with Connelly laying down fire to cover them. Opie turns and sees one of them with blood streaming from his nose. Holy shit. The guy took a round through both nostrils. His nose is bubbling with every breath he takes. Some clusterfuck this is.

Connelly and a couple of others start firing and the men turn the corner running for the pickup area. A tank and armored personnel carriers are there. A rocket-propelled grenade pings off the tank, exploding in the dusty street. Heavy machine guns open up from the armored vehicles.

No air cover shows up until they are out of the area. The combat zone is too small and dense for the planes to attack, there is too great a risk of killing friendlies. The indigenous allies do not understand this.

One of the Iraqi soldiers sits next to the man with the bubbling nose, and he eyes Connelly. He points in the general direction of a fighter as it fades away in the burning air over the land between the rivers and says, "Amerika no good." He shakes his head for emphasis.

Connelly gazes at the man with the ruined nose impassively.

*

Two days later, Connelly nails a bad guy planting an IED. Opie is his spotter. Opie focuses his binoculars, confirming the kill. "You got the bad guy. Another one for the virgins." He switches gears and says, "That kid was probably a virgin himself. But I guess you popped his cherry."

Connelly takes a deep breath and says, "I need some water. Damn this fuckin heat."

The next day, Meyer jumps on a grenade, saving the lives and limbs of several men on his patrol. All the men are shaken, Opie in particular. He keeps saying, "I shoulda done somethin. I shoulda." And the captain tells him to stop it. Meyer reacted. We do our jobs. We do our best. Not all of us will go home.

Meyer is posthumously awarded the Medal of Honor.

The captain eyes a reporter who has asked when the victory will come. And the captain answers that his men achieve victory each day. The experience here will live forever. The stories can only be understood by us. The men do this every day and without question. They love the victory over our enemies that we share. The captain eyes the reporter and says, "Now do you understand?"

3

Rodgriguez and the big man (Rodriguez solves a problem)... The raid on Parmer... The informer poses a question... Sunday afternoon in Big D (the procession of death).

Rodriguez had waited for this meeting for a long time.

He met his contact on a San Antonio street corner near the riverwalk. They nodded at one another and walked in silence to a pickup, then drove to the Menger Hotel parking garage. The two of them walked past glass cases displaying old uniforms, into the bar and up the stairs.

The cartel big man was expansive that night as he sipped a drink and patted Rodriguez's arm, telling him of the bright future they had together. There was the problem of Espinoza and of his boys, the *puta* Vega and his brother-in-law. But these problems can be solved. With your help. The big man smiled and Rodriguez was wondering why this big man did not get his teeth fixed.

Rodriguez was always a bit impatient with these people, who seldom spoke directly of anything. A meeting with one of them would often come down to interpreting signals, which could be tricky. The big man made mention of the *puta* Vega, Vega's brother-in-law and of the son of a whore called Espinoza. This was one signal. The others would come. That's how these things played out.

After two hours of smoking thin cigars and sipping drinks, the big man edged up to the point. Elections in Parmer. The *puta* Vega. He should win. Yes, let him win. He deserves this. The big man taps ash from a thin cigar into a tumbler. Espinoza makes trouble. He fucks us over in Dallas. So we move some of our operations west, to Parmer, maybe. The *puta* Vega has an operation. For guns. Armor. You know, yes? That is good. So maybe our friends in the DEA find out about this operation.

The big man grinned. He made a motion like driving a knife into a man and he twists it and growled. And then the big man looked across the table and what do you do? You grin back.

Rodriguez did not go back with his contact man. He was to walk to the Alamo and look for a tall Anglo. The big man said he would know him. He is very tall.

It was dark, the old chapel lit up with floodlights. There were a few people milling around. An angular figure emerged from the shadows just out of range of the lights and walked right up to Rodriguez. The tall man with blue eyes wore a windbreaker. The two of them walked off together, out of the light.

The tall man said his name was Posey. They should know one another.

Rodriguez knew that the Anglo approach was different. It was more businesslike and straight forward. Posey thought of the meeting in cold, economically rational terms.

Rodriguez was thinking, *yes, in a way I do know you. Already. I've met you before. And I know what you are after.*

*

Ida was in the kitchen when she heard Emmit yelling at the TV. He was watching a football game.

She told Emmitt to calm down, it was just a football game after all. Not life or death. "Have you taken your medication?"

Emmitt said, "Yes, dammit, when I can afford to."

Ida said, "I'm fixin to head to the store before it gets late. You want anything special?"

Emmitt tuned the sound down on the TV. It was a commercial, anyway.

"You oughta not be drivin at dusk, Ida."

"Well, are you wantin to go?"

"Oh hell. I guess so. Let me get my gun."

"You best be careful with that thing."

"I am. Being uncareful these days is not havin one. I'm careful cause I ain't got any choice."

Emmit paused. "What am I goin for, anyways?"

"We need some milk and bread, else I cain't make breakfast tomorrow."

"You sure they got milk and bread? Distribution's been spotty out here. We only get five TV stations. The damn cell phones don't work all the time, least mine don't. I'll have to check and see if I got any money."

"Quit your bitchin. I reckon they got it. And I ain't so sure about your drivin either. Both of us too damn old... Myself, I got the CRS."

Emmit was heading for the closet and said, "What's CRS?"

"Cain't Remember Shit Syndrome."

"That's CRSS. But you got that right. I got it, too."

Emmitt retrieved his gun, a 9mm Sig Sauer, slipped it into a holster and clipped the holster on his belt before putting on a jacket.

He was reaching for the lock when somebody knocked on the door. Emmitt looked through the peephole, squinting to see through the bars, focusing on the spaces between them.

"Who is it?" Ida was whispering.

He squinted hard. It was a tall white man. He was holding up some sort of ID. He wore a windbreaker. Emmit focused on that.

"He's white. Tall. His windbreaker says 'DEA' on it." He was whispering back to Ida.

Emmit slid back the high and low bolts to unlock the reinforced door.

The tall man said his name was Posey. They wanted to use the house. "For official purposes, you understand."

Emmitt nodded and eased the door closed. He hadn't opened the bars yet.

"They's somebody with him. Mexican in a uniform. I seen him before, I think."

*

[*News item for posting on Channel 12 website/Video for nightly news broadcast embedded in Internet story*] The city police force of Parmer, Texas has been disbanded. Police Chief Eddie Vega was led away in handcuffs after a pre-dawn raid led by agents of the Bureau of Alcohol, Tobacco, Firearms and Explosives. [*Video shows Vega in handcuffs*] The raid included officers from the Drug Enforcement Administration and Customs and Immigration officials. [*Video clip of officers rushing the door of the house*]

DEA officer Leland Posey [*Cut to video of Posey*] said, "This is a special joint operation mounted by several federal agencies aimed at the interdiction of a weapons smuggling channel to Mexican-based drug cartels. The cartels are increasingly expanding branch operations inside our borders. This action is part of a sweep designed to curtail those operations." The Parmer scandal follows on the heels of a series of unsolved murders of prosecutors and judges across the state, underscoring the urgency of combating the drug cartels. [*Video of the crime scenes; cut back to video of Parmer.*]

[*Video cut to eyewitness*] Jeanie S. Thompson of Parmer was awoken by the commotion. "I was sleeping. I heard a commotion outside, a very loud bang, lots of shouting. There was someone yelling through a bullhorn, red lights flashing, lots of men with guns and a helicopter overhead. I thought I was in a war zone."

Police Chief Vega and his brother-in-law, town controller Mike Villareal, were arrested for allegedly managing a weapons-smuggling operation connected to a Mexican-based drug cartel. [*Video of Vega and Villareal being led to arresting officers' vehicles*] Vega and Villareal used police vehicles, driven by officers from the Parmer police force, to transport body armor and weapons to San Antonio, where a cartel contact paid them in cash for the equipment. [*Video cut to stock footage of downtown San Antonio. Cut to Texas National Guard vehicles on the move*] Vega and Villarel had used channels in the Texas National Guard and other Texas police forces to acquire the weaponry and equipment, according to BATFE officials, who would not elaborate.

In addition, Vega and Villareal stand accused of providing false documentation, acquired from corrupt Customs and Immigration officials working with the Parmer operation, to illegally bring in migrants under Washington's new guest worker policy, evading control and regulation by federal officials. [*Video of guest worker program processing center. Cut to video of trucks passing through trade zone centers*] Washington has advanced the controversial new policy in spite of popular opposition in border states, with the White House, under its slogan of "America is a continent, not a country," standing by the guest worker program as a way to facilitate a recovery throughout the North American Free Trade Zone.

[*Video of Parmer Mayor Doolittle*] "It's hard to believe this is happening in Parmer," according to Mayor Benjamin J. "Buddy" Doolittle. Doolittle has disbanded the police force and contracted with the County Sheriff's Department under Sheriff Manuel "Manny" Rodriguez to provide police protection for Parmer.

Parmer has been the scene of tensions between Hispanic and Anglo residents recently, tensions sparked by the bitter election campaign for police chief just last year, when Eduardo "Eddie" Vega challenged longtime Parmer Police Chief Robert R. "Bobby Ray" Tinsley. [*Video of voting stations and vid caps of Vega and Tinsley*] Doolittle backed Vega, sparking controversy in the community. There were altercations near polling stations following the as yet unsolved shooting of Parmer police officer Jimmy Longoria. The shooting followed a public disturbance call at an unregistered Hispanic nightspot one block off Parmer's old town district. [*Video of Parmer downtown area and of the Jaguar Club*] The Jaguar Club had been targeted by complaints from an association of city residents, the Parmer Citizen's Watch Committee, who found themselves entangled in a lengthy lawsuit with a Dallas-based civil rights organization.

[*Video of Sheriff Rodriguez at the press conference*] Sheriff Rodriguez, who is often mentioned as a potential candidate for a state-level office, said that the arrests of Vega and Villareal presented "an opportunity for healing," at a joint press conference with Doolittle earlier this week. Rodriguez, who is seen by community leaders as a bridge between Hispanics and Anglos in Parmer, said "We can now move forward. This cleansing can unify us." [*End*]

*

On the day they took him, the informer had been in a pensive mood. Rodriguez poured him a glass of water and the informer drank, then got up, walked to the barred window and looked at the high, pale sky outside.

"Is this the only world?"

Rodriguez was sitting at the table. He turned to look at the informer.

"What do you mean? Do you mean is there heaven and hell? I thought we had established your position on that."

"I mean the only world, the only planet with life."

Rodriguez shrugged.

"You are a curious man. I once asked myself those kinds of questions."

"And?"

"I stopped asking."

The informer squinted at the sky as if he were eyeing a puzzle or contemplating a problem of advanced mathematics.

"It is a question of destiny or fate or material determinism. Or God's will."

His hands were in his pockets. The informer closed his eyes for a few seconds.

"It is a question of purpose. Do you see?"

"I asked the question of purpose when my mother was killed."

Silence. Rodriguez continued. "So, what is the question of purpose in the knowledge of the existence of other worlds?"

The informer said, "Is there a special purpose for this world? Do other worlds share in the same purpose or have they their own? Perhaps one we have not fathomed and cannot."

"That depends on whether one believes in God, and if you do, what you think about the nature of God."

The informer nodded his head silently.

"You once asked the question of purpose. And what was your answer?"

Rodriguez sat at the table, his hands placed palms down on the table top. A witness. A man giving testimony in a court of the highest jurisdiction.

"That a man makes his own purpose."

"And how was that related to your view of your mother's death and of God?"

"Either there is no God or what there is, is a terrible malevolence. One that gives us no purpose or one that tricks us. His offers are arbitrary, as are his rewards and punishments, which have no meaning beyond his own caprice. A whim. He defies us to defy him. If he exists at all, if that something, that terrible malevolent whim does exist."

"And the devil?"

"Maybe they are the same."

"God and the devil, you mean?"

"Yes."

Rodriguez continued, "A man's life is his own. He can make it something or watch it slip away one second at a time. We all live and die. No one escapes. But God, or the devil, or the something that sets the play in motion, does not make it. A man's life. It may confound the man. It may lay traps for him. But whatever it is. That something. It does not make what the man can become, something greater than what he seems."

The informer shrugged. He turned and leaned against the wall of his enclosed and encapsulated world and said to Rodriguez, "Our positions are not all that different. We see many similar parts. But we reach a choice of paths and you say you will take one and I say I will take another."

"How do you mean?"

"I say a man's life is not his own. And in embracing that, he lives. He becomes himself truly. You say that God sets traps for us. That this malevolent or capricious something does. But that which is, is a sum of many parts. God and His will. Man and his nature. Material determinism. The devil. But a man's life is not his own. If he gives it up, he gains it. To cling to it is to die."

"So you are… what? Christ?"

The informer shook his head.

"No."

Rodriguez paused. He looked at this man before him. Was he defender or prosecutor? Father or child?

The informer's eyes seemed misty as if he were about to be overcome with emotion or an overwhelming sense of transcendence. And then he was here again. In this place. And he looked at Rodriguez with compassion and disgust and hope and despair.

His voice trembled and the informer said, "What would a man give in exchange for his soul?" He turned again and looked out the window, as if he were seeking guidance.

"To submit is freedom. This is the paradox."

"I choose not to submit. And this is freedom." Rodriguez slapped his hands on the table and said, "I choose freedom."

"So, you will reign in hell."

Rodriguez got up from the table and walked over to the informer and placed his hand on his cheek. And he nodded his head and walked to the door. He opened it and the informer said, "When will you come again?"

And Rodriguez looked through the door, turning his back on the informer and said, "It will be soon."

Later, as the crew tortured him, the informer sometimes looked directly at Rodriguez. At first, the look was not merely one of agony, but of longing. Then a strange look of passive submission. Then peace. And then he was dead. He chose peace. The peace of the grave. And that, thought Rodriguez, is not what I choose.

The last thing Rodriguez had said to the informer before he left was, "I could take you away from this." But there was no answer, and he walked out and shut the door behind him. Rodriguez left the compound in his truck and reached for his cell phone. He had a call to make. And then all paths had been taken. All worlds would collide.

*

A pickup truck pulls into a dead-end street in South Dallas. It carries a load covered by a canvas tarp. It is midday on a Sunday afternoon in Big D. The street is lined with little wooden houses, the yards packed with pickups and low rider cars. At the end of the street is a cul-de-sac where there stands a large brick house behind a gate. The house is in a walled compound with cut glass on top of the barrier walls. Surveillance cameras are mounted on the walls, looking like alien robots surveying the surface of a distant planet. Scrutinizing life forms, primitive and ready to be taken as specimens. The brick house is painted a bright blue.

A little boy rides by on a bike, watching a man walk to the back of the truck. The man climbs into the truck bed and removes the tarp and the little boy stares in awe and wonder, experiencing a sense of foreboding he has never felt before in his short life. The man wears a T-shirt and his arms, shoulders and even his face are covered in bizarre tattoos depicting strange lizards and feathered gods. His head is shaved close.

The truck moves slowly down the street and he begins dumping out a mass of naked, and almost naked, bodies that are bruised and scarred and covered in crusted blood. Many of them have plastic bags over their heads. Their hands are tied behind their backs, their ankles cinched together. The tattooed man or Aztec god or devil has on yellow rubber gloves and he smiles at the boy. The truck and the devil-god man leave a trail of bodies that proceeds right up to the gates of the blue house. The boy is trying to count them and he counts ten, no, twelve bodies, the last bundled up against the gate like a sack of waste. Then the truck turns, and the man re-enters the cab, and the truck with its bright aluminum wheels tears off down the street in the opposite direction, sometimes running over the bodies that make strange noises like bursting balloons when the truck hits them.

The boy rides slowly down the street on a cracked and broken sidewalk and looks closely at the bodies. He wants to see if he knows any of them. Maybe his brother, missing for a week or more, is there, but he cannot find him. The boy stops the bike and vomits on the sidewalk. There is a smell in the air that will linger on that street, as will the story of the macabre trail of the dead. The devilish man has left a sign on the gates of the blue house that reads THEY NEVER LEARN in Spanish, and the same in English.

It is one week after the raid on Parmer.

4

Cole (two years after)... The highway of death (desperate men, joyful killers)... The Iraquis put up a fight... The return... The Refuge (Cole and his mother)... The sighs of Laurie Anne Grace.

Two years had passed, and the Gulf War had come and gone.

Everybody had been hyped-up about nerve gas attacks that never happened.

Cole had marched with his men into the droves of surrendering Iraqi soldiers.

He saw a stretch of what they later called a "highway of death," where the vehicles of the retreating Iraqi army had been rendered into odd sculptures of smoldering metal. Dead men charred and dead men whole and dead men in pieces. They lined that highway like sacrifices to the ancient gods of the land between the rivers.

What to call this? The mother of all battles it was not. The mother of all slaughters it seemed only at first glance, for Cole knew that the world had seen much greater debacles on battlefields far more vast and bloody. Maybe they were all part of one ceaseless battle, a perpetual demonstration of the depths of destruction that man had reached and would reach again for it was in his nature to make war.

To create and then destroy.

What would come after?

That which had gone before.

The highway had an official number, but such a designation faded beside the reality of what it had become.

The planes had come and blocked the highway with anti-tank mines. The rear of the Iraqi column had been bombed, and the stretch between boxed in. Air strikes reduced the highway to rubble and the tanks and other vehicles to scrap. One stretch was packed with abandoned cars and even buses that the Iraqi soldiers had commandeered and packed with booty from the great raid. When the bombing began, they left their cars and buses in panic, running into the desert or into the swamps.

Cole walked past trucks overturned. A wheel was spinning on one of them, as though a ghost was playing a bizarre game of roulette in a wasteland that had become a scrapyard and a monument to folly. A radio emitted a jarring cacophony of their music that drifted across the scattered column like a dirge or maybe it mocked them.

To the east, a Republican Guard division had been destroyed, vehicles and abandoned tanks scattered along a road and in the desert. Remnants of the remaining Iraqi units had attempted to reach safety a few days later, and they, too, were destroyed.

Cole could tell that a particular destroyed vehicle was a tank by the long barrel of its main gun. Behind it was a row of unidentifiable vehicles, burned into heaps of charred matter resembling mounds of industrial excrement.

No one guarded the wreckage. Looters would come to search for weapons that remained operational, selling them across a region of desert wastes, elaborate rituals, tribal wars, desperate men and joyful killers.

Cole came upon one truck and saw a man sitting in its cab. The man was burned black and his teeth were clinched in a macabre grin. The eye sockets were hollow. There was a small patch of hair on his skeletal dome.

Cole wondered whether the man had had a brother, or a son, or a daughter, and how old he had been, and whether his mother and father knew of his fate. Or would ever know. And in that very dangerous and terrifying moment, Cole understood that each one who had died in that place was a universe unto himself, each life lived out in a parallel world of which he was now seeing but one corner.

The charred remains of the man in the truck were merely the hollow shell of a vessel that had contained a spirit that was the man himself. That spirit could make contact with the world only through that particular vessel, which was no longer in a condition to contain anything, much less a small universe.

Cole knew of battles and invasions and conquests and slaughters in this land between the great rivers. Violence spanning tracts of time daunting and barely imaginable. Scrapheaps from past battles had vanished, but others had followed like flotsam left by tidal waves on the shores of a desert island.

The roads looked like junkyards or a parking lot at a boarding house for lunatics, the vehicles parked one way and then another, doors open or off. Shells of cars and trucks and buses overturned.

A small war about oil. And all these cars.

Hendricks, a tall Californian whom everybody called "Birdman," asked Cole, what did they think these camel jockeys was gonna do with all that oil? Eat it? They got to sell it to somebody. Right, Pappy?

The men called Cole "Pappy" because he was older than the rest of them, quite a bit older in many cases.

Cole, for instance, had mentioned that Red Adair was in Kuwait to put out the oil fires. The others looked at him with blank stares, not knowing who Red Adair was. Cole shrugged and noted, "You boys ain't from Texas. Don't ya'll watch John Wayne movies?"

Cole sighed. "What's the world comin to?"

The Iraqis surrendered in droves. They came to the Americans like frightened schoolboys, lost and looking for a teacher. A skinny man with no shoes ran headlong toward them, frantically waving his arms, pleading in his unintelligible tongue. Martin turned his head to spit, then looked over at Cole and said, "These guys think we're gonna kill em." Cole motioned for them to get down on their knees. He kept telling them it was alright, looking at them gravely, nodding his head affirmatively as the skinny one continued to plead for mercy. One of them was no more than a kid. He had tears in his eyes.

Martin was disgusted. He told Cole he wished somebody would put up a fight.

He soon got his wish. Some of the Iraqis *did* put up a fight, a running fight amid charred frames of burned out vehicles, a junkyard-turned-shooting-gallery. Small arms fire lit up the dusk as Cole and his men positioned themselves, then advanced on the enemy. The Iraqis kept firing and retreating, Cole and his men firing and advancing. Cole's men found three bodies and took three more prisoners. The other Iraqis had melted into the advancing darkness. Cole didn't know if he had killed any of them or none of them.

Cole's men were jubilant and scared at the same time. They had been in a real fight, so maybe this trip was worth it, after all. That's what Martin said, anyway. Their fear had been that this thing would end too soon and they would not see any action.

They sat that night and ate, talking about the day's events. About who had been where and what they had seen and done. They had been in a war and not lost a man. Then they stopped talking for a while and Cole began again. He said that anything and everything in this world came at a great price. Whether that price was worth it or not depended on what the thing was and on circumstance. On whether you were compelled by something inside or something above and beyond yourself to do this thing. But once the thing was achieved, it often lost its substance and you were back where you had been before, the thing having left its mark on you.

It took about 30 seconds for Miller to ask Cole what the fuck he was talking about.

And Cole told Miller that he was not a thinking man. But out here, maybe that's best. Leave the thinking to me. And Miller said that he was glad to do it, Pappy, but he still didn't know what the fuck he was talking about.

Miller surveyed the darkness and wondered who was going to clean up this damn mess. He stretched out and said, "Well, it ain't gonna be me."

*

That was two years ago and it seemed like longer.

It was near on to dark when Cole got to town, a town he had not lived in for years. And it was towns like this one that many of the men who had gone to war would not come back to. Others had left for big cities and jobs that didn't exist here any more or to pretend that they were not rednecks but ironic and worldly types like you see on TV shows, people from nowhere who speak global American, the flat and accentless verbiage of mass media and chain store ads.

Cole pulled into the Sac'n' Pac, stepped out of his truck and looked up and down a dusty street. A dog trotted across the road. The electric sign at the carwash was out. He could make out the Dairy Queen sign but the storefronts seemed deserted.

He walked up to the corner where a live oak acted as a canopy for a sign declaring that you were entering the Parmer County, Texas, town of Ely. At one time, the sign had indicated the town's population, but somebody had scratched that out. Another sign showed a cartoon Texan in a ten-gallon hat smiling and saying WELCOME! The sign declared that Ely was a good town for a visit, a great town to live in! Cole kicked an old newspaper off his legs that had blown up the road and wrapped around his boots.

The garage-style doors were still pulled up on the Sac 'n' Pac icehouse that stood just outside the town limits. Cole walked into an empty hall of pool tables. There was nobody playing shuffleboard or sitting at the flimsy card tables, either. The faint sound of country music wafted through. He walked past coolers with nothing in them, decorated with old Pearl beer signs, toward the lights in the grocery and lunch counter part of the Sac 'n' Pac, past the refrigerated rows of canned beer and soft drinks and the rows of snacks. He stood at the counter and looked at a tray of homemade cookies and slices of pie with a glass cover over them. There was nobody at the counter. Just a radio playing from somewhere in the office, the door standing open. When the music ended, the disk jockey said the farm and ranch show was up next.

Cole walked back to the soft drinks and got a Dr. Pepper, then grabbed a bag of salted peanuts, walked back to the counter and set them on it and waited.

A white-haired man in suspenders stepped out of the office. He seemed startled to see a customer. For a moment, he just stood there and had to search for the right words.

"Well, hello." He shuffled toward the counter and added, "I thought I heard somethin back at the drinks."

Cole said, "Hidy" and the old man approached the counter and eyed the items as if they were artifacts from an archaeological dig.

He picked them up, examined them, pecked on the cash register, looked again, then pecked again. Cole fished some money out of his pocket and slid it across the counter and waited while the old man, who was Mr. Eb Longtree, retrieved it and made change. Eb looked closely at him through thick glasses, then smiled and said, "Cole" and then smiled more broadly still.

"Mr. Longtree."

Cole extended his hand and Eb took it two handed and shook and patted his arm and said, "Cole, you come back," as if his coming back was itself a miracle of sorts in a world that was uncertain and chaotic in many ways. Or maybe he meant that Ely was no longer the sort of place that anybody, having left it, would come back to.

52

Cole nodded and looked back out at the spreading darkness at the edge of his hometown.

He leaned against the counter, popped open the Dr. Pepper and took a sip. He tore open the peanuts, took a handful and chewed.

Eb said, "How long ya been back? From the service, I mean, from over there…" Eb's voice drifted off and he seemed unsure whether he should have asked anything at all, but he wanted to know, so he had asked anyway. He had known this boy — a man long made now — his whole life. Cole's daddy used to come to the Sac 'n' Pac and play shuffle board, so that made it alright in Eb's eyes. And in Cole's.

Cole took another sip and swallowed and said, "Not too long."

Eb asked him, "So you're out of the service?"

Cole nodded.

Eb said, "Well" and placed his hands palms down on the counter, as if he had to give that one some thought.

"Figured you for a lifer."

Cole turned toward him and smiled. "And I figured you for one, Mr. Longtree."

Eb Longtree chuckled and said he managed to keep the place open, just barely. "The war…" Eb's voice trailed off, his head cocked inquisitively.

There was a POW/MIA banner on the back wall. And a picture of a young man in an Army uniform, barely recognizable to those who knew him as Eb Longtree. His late wife Hazel had put it there, though it embarrassed Eb a bit. All the same, he had left it after she had died, leaving undisturbed her pride and his memories. Nobody noticed it any more, anyway.

"It was over quick. I believe you were at Omaha Beach."

Eb nodded. "I don't remember much about it."

Cole raised his eye brows in inquiry. Eb, like many of the veterans of his generation, rarely spoke of that war or of what they had done in it.

Eb sighed and said, "I was kindly busy that day."

Eb's face turned serious and he nodded before saying, "Your momma."

"Where is she, Mr. Longtree? I mean, where did Aunt Evelyn put her?"

Eb didn't answer right away.

The farm and ranch report was going on about the price of beef. Cole didn't catch whether it was up or down.

"She's at that old folks' home... Oh, what's it called now? I believe they call it 'The Refuge'... I can tell you how to get there. It's over in Parmer."

"Is she that bad off?"

"Well."

"Will she know me?"

Silence.

"Mr. Longtree..."

"I seen worse, Cole. Hazel didn't always recognize me before she died."

"No?"

"No."

Eb shrugged and said, "People live a long time these days, longer and longer, or at least they keep em alive a long time. It makes you wonder, don't it..."

"Yessir, I guess it does."

Cole took another sip of his Dr. Pepper.

"The old house?"

"Now, Cole."

"What happened to the old house, Mr. Longtree?"

Eb slapped his palms gently on the counter top.

"Well, here while back... They done tore it down."

They both stood there in silence.

Cole nodded and patted Eb Longtree's right hand. He ate the last of the peanuts and wadded up the wrapper then put it in a trash can. He took a sip of the Dr. Pepper and turned and said, "I'll be seein you, Mr. Longtree."

"Come by the Veterans' hall sometime. You'll be welcome."

Cole nodded and walked out.

And Cole thought that there are some things you cannot come back from. And other things that you cannot come back to. And still other things that never leave you.

*

It was full dark. Cole drove to the carwash, then turned left over the railroad tracks and down the potholed road, looking for where the house had been. In its place was a fenced-in storage shed with a sign advertising a monthly rate. There was a trailer house inside the

54

compound and Cole saw a man come out, shut off the light in the sign and go back into the trailer. The man had paid no attention to the truck sitting out front.

Cole surveyed the scene impassively.

Then he drove on.

He pulled into a motel with a broken sign that was only partially lit. The Stagecoach Inn's sign was worn and you could just make out a faded banner at the bottom of the unlit part of the sign that read AMERICAN OWNED AND OPERATED.

Cole parked and walked into the office. The carpet was blue fading to gray, the walls white working on a dirty copper color. There was a cheap coffee table with old copies of *The Readers Digest* piled in the middle. Cole glanced around. Nobody at the desk. He picked up one of the magazines and wondered who he might nominate as "My Most Unforgettable Character." That might be a tough one. Cole tossed the magazine down, then a swinging door behind the counter opened, and a short brown man with a thick black mustache and reading glasses on the tip of his nose walked through. He raised his eyebrows at Cole and placed his hands on the counter.

He said, "Might I help you, sir?"

Cole squinted at the little man and asked him, "Is Mr. Caldwell around?"

"No longer, I'm afraid."

Cole placed the accent as from somewhere on the Indian subcontinent.

He leaned against the counter.

"You mean he's dead?"

"Sadly, yes."

"And you would be... ?"

The little man turned and pointed at a plaque on the wall behind the counter that read "S. Banerjee, Proprietor."

Cole nodded and hmmmed.

*

Cole left the registration office, entering a space behind it encircled by the motel's rooms, a few with red tape across their doors. He walked past a dried-up flower bed, a yucca plant, and an empty swimming pool to his room. He set down his suitcase and duffel bag, unlocked and opened the door, then flipped on the light. There was a print of a cowboy on a horse surveying a valley in a mythical West on the wall over the bed. He carried in his belongings, hung up some of his clothes, and walked out again, shutting the door behind him and pocketing the key.

*

Cole drove slowly through town. It was very dark. There were only a few signs still illuminated as he passed a washateria, then a small brick building marked "City Hall." He turned left down a highway that became Main Street. The old facades of the buildings were in poor condition for the most part, excepting the few shops and cafés that were still open.

He turned left, crossing the narrow bridge over Pecan Creek, drove past the old ball park, and pulled into a dirt and gravel parking area. The whitewashed wooden church had a temporary building next to it with a sign out front indicating that it was the Sunday School and Education wing. The church seemed to be fairly well kept up. He backed up and turned around and the headlights of the pickup lit up a billboard across the street facing the oncoming traffic. It was black with bold white lettering that read IT WILL BE SUDDEN. IT MAY BE SOON.

Cole drove through town and turned into the car wash. He pulled into a stall, jacked some quarters into the slots and began spraying off splattered bugs and accumulated grime from the windshield, then gave the cab and bed a once-over with the high-pressure hose. He took an old towel out from behind the seat and wiped off the windshield when he was done, then put back the hose and the spray gun.

Cole heard a grating of metal nearby and decided to investigate. He saw a 25-year-old Chevy Impala with a faded blue paint job pulled up to the last stall. The trunk lid was rusty and the car lacked hubcaps. The Impala carried a lit-up sign on top that read "El Rancho Tacos and Pizza: We Deliver!"

Cole looked into the stall and saw the rail thin figure of Charlie Bass dumping quarters into a canvas bag at the base of a metal container. He laughed and said, "Charlie, I see you are a regular business magnate around here nowadays."

Charlie Bass looked up, set the bag of quarters on the ground, adjusted his camo cap, and eyed Cole suspiciously. Then he shrugged and said, "Hell, no, I'm robbin the place."

"Uh huh."

"But I ain't gonna share." Charlie bent over, picked up the bag, and put it in the front seat of the car.

"I don't expect you would."

Charlie walked over, shook Cole's hand and said, "This is what a man's reduced to doin to make a livin around here any more." He shrugged, as if to say, "What can you do?" and continued, "I'd ask about the war and all, but I figger you to be about tired a answerin that question."

Charlie took a step back and hooked his thumbs in his belt.

"You come back to see your momma, I guess."

Cole nodded.

Charlie rubbed his palms together. "I guess you know ya'll's old house is gone?"

Cole nodded again.

"Everbody that coulda has done left, Cole. Most everbody. Some still around, but I don't know why any more."

"Yeah." Cole looked around as if surveying the scene of some terrible natural disaster. And he looked back at Charlie Bass and said, "And you, Charlie?"

Charlie Bass shrugged again. "And leave all my business interests? Anyhow, what would I do in a big city, Cole? Hell, they scare me. I hate drivin in em."

Cole nodded and turned to go back to his truck.

"You gonna be around a while?"

Cole spun back around on his heel and said, "Liable to."

"You take care, Cole."

"You take care, Charlie... And say hey to your momma and daddy for me."

"They're dead, Cole."

"Both of em?"

"Momma died a cancer. Daddy had heart problems. But he didn't hang on long after momma died."

"Yeah. Well. Where are they buried at?"

"Over at the cemetery just south of town. The one your daddy's in."

Cole nodded.

"I'll go by and see em some time."

"Yeah. You do that. Well, I gotta finish cleaning this place out and deliver a pizza to Sonny Valdez."

"Sonny? How's Sonny?"

"Not worth a damn. Like always."

"Well, that's good to know. Some things haven't changed."

"Nope."

"Tell Sonny hey for me."

"If he's sober I will. If he ain't, it ain't no use."

"He still work on cars?" Cole turned and started back to the truck again. "No, don't tell me. When he's sober, right?"

"You got it."

Cole looked back over his shoulder: "Tell that damn drunk Mexican I'm liable to come kick his ass just for the hell of it."

"You tell him."

Cole turned around again and looked at Charlie Bass. "Hey, Charlie, you ever get married?"

"Yeah. Twice. The second one ain't left me just yet."

"Well, that's good to hear. People oughta believe in marriage."

"Uh huh."

"Kids?"

"Boy, name a Ray Don."

"Is he skinny as hell?"

Charlie Bass laughed and said, "You bet!"

*

The Refuge was a pair of brick buildings with a fence around it. You had to get buzzed in and there was a camera watching the front door. They said that was so none of the guests could walk out. That's what they called them. *Guests.* They said somebody or other had found Dave walking down a farm to market road one time, so they installed this set up. To protect the guests. Dave like to have caused an accident out there involving a poultry truck and a school bus. That's not good.

Cole had to check in at what amounted to a security gate, then got buzzed into the interior of the building. A white-haired woman named Mrs. Hatfield escorted him. Mr. Hatfield had died and his lingering had inspired the Mrs. to open this place, truly a refuge and thank you for asking. When they entered, he saw a wedding dress on the wall and a marine uniform and a tuxedo. There was a flag there, too, 48 stars, and

58

pictures of sailors and soldiers and their sweethearts celebrating on V-E Day and V-J Day and there were pictures of people from the generations before them, formal and stern looking, posing with family in straight-backed chairs, images from a lost world.

Cole stopped to glance at a sepia-toned picture of a lone man on horseback surveying a herd of cattle. There was a windmill in the background. Next to it was a portrait of a doughboy looking so proud, and Mrs. Hatfield said that was her father and she smiled and said thanks for asking again. She said the man on horseback was her grandfather. She pointed back to it, but Cole did not look again. He just nodded and walked on.

Mrs. Hatfield said the flag, the clothes, and the pictures were for memory's sake, something to strike a chord with the guests, to make them feel they were in a comfortable world, one they could understand. She smiled when she said that. Mrs. Hatfield further noted that her grandmother had thought the moon landings were a hoax. Would not believe it. Anyway, she said landing on the moon was blasphemy or might have been. She was born in a dugout.

Cole walked past a billboard that included the date and a notice: TODAY IS TUESDAY.

There was a big TV set with couches around it. Early American. There were stacks of video tapes around the TV, all old movies. Humphrey Bogart was eyeing Mary Astor on the screen.

A short, potbellied Mexican emerged from the kitchen pushing a cart with plastic trays stacked on top. The little man wore rubber gloves like he was about to wash dishes. He looked very bored. Mrs. Hatfield asked Cole if he would like to see the kitchen. He told that he didn't care to.

Cole paused at a table with a toy hammer and a disconnected telephone and some pegs and squares with slots they fitted into. There was an electric bell you could ring if you could figure out which button to push. Mrs. Hatfield said that was for the old men who like to fiddle around with tools. She didn't thank him this time.

A tall man with a pleasant grin walked up to Cole and shook his hand and said "Hi, my name is Tom." He had on khaki pants and a plaid shirt and seemed alright. Then he walked away and Mrs. Hatfield said, "It's time for your lunch, Tom." He turned and smiled and came back and introduced himself and shook hands and said, "My name is Tom," again.

Then he started to cry and said he couldn't remember — had they met on a previous occasion?

Mrs. Hatfield said she would go get his mother, so Cole sat down on the couch and watched Humphrey Bogart verbally sparring with Peter Lorre. An old man shuffled by. Cole squinted, noticing that his pants were on backwards. A heavyset woman wearing a hairnet was cleaning up the place. She turned to Cole and said, "That's so they don't pee in a corner. They do sometimes, ya know." He nodded.

The lady with the hairnet drifted over into the kitchen. A short stocky man with a thick wave of white hair walked up to Cole and asked if he was a veteran and Cole said yes and the man saluted. Cole sat there looking at him and the man looked annoyed, so Cole stood and returned his salute and the man smiled and walked away.

A woman who didn't look all that old sat down next to him and he said "Hi," but she did not respond. She clung to his arm and then reached down with a rag in her right hand and began to rub a spot on his pants leg at about the knee. That seemed to satisfy her, then she sat back and put the rag over her face and went to sleep.

Mrs. Hatfield wheeled Cole's mother out and stationed her next to her son. She looked at him blankly at first, then smiled and said, "Son."

Cole said, "Momma," and reached over and gave her a peck on the cheek and patted her arm. She leaned over as if to confide in him, then told him his father was dead. He nodded and saw small tears welling up in her eyes.

Cole reached for a Kleenex and wiped them. She sat back and seemed calm.

She leaned over again and told him that "…these people are plumb crazy. But maybe that's not charitable." And Cole told her they were not crazy, just old and tired and lonely and he wished he had not said that because she looked at him and said, "What does that make me?" He had never thought of her as old. Tired, maybe. But he could see how lonely she was.

Tom walked up and introduced himself again and shook their hands, then turned and walked off, satisfied — for the moment — that he had met them. Cole's mother smiled and looked over at him. "That's old Crazy Tom. Of course, we got a Crazy Dave and a Crazy June and a Crazy Louella. I'm not crazy, am I?"

And Cole said, "No, momma, you're not."

He wheeled her back to her room. There were pictures hung at the door of every room, pictures of that particular room's occupant or occupants in their youth. One of a man in a double-breasted suit and fedora, another in a broad-brimmed hat sitting on a horse, a cloudless sky above him in the time of his strength and competence that marked men like him.

And he wound up in here.

Cole watched his mother pick at her lunch, a piece of ham they had cut up for her and some green beans and applesauce. Some kind of drink with a straw in it.

There was a picture on his mother's dressing table of Cole's brother John Thomas, more often called J.T. He was in his high school letter jacket, smiling broadly. J.T. was gone, too, killed in a power line accident when he worked for the county. His wife lived in Houston now and stayed away. Their two boys hadn't seen their grandparents much, as if the mother was keeping a distance from fear of bad luck.

Cole's parents never got over that last heartbreak. It seemed to him that's mostly what they had known. Heartbreak. And he wondered why. Why them and not somebody else. Or why anybody, if you care to tell it. He had once told his mother so, and she would have none of it. She insisted they had been fortunate, that God had blessed the family. So, he asked whether a stillborn baby, a grown son dead, and a crazy daughter were blessings and she told him that "...we cannot fathom the ways of Providence." And he said he guessed not.

Emma. Well, Emma was in Los Angeles. Or San Francisco. Or somewhere. There was a picture of her next to J.T.'s, taken when she was maybe fifteen. Fathoming the ways of Providence or not, Cole's parents had blamed themselves for what had happened with her and he had told them no, she made her own life and her own choices and she could live with them. It wasn't anybody else's fault what she was or became. Cole said he would not repeat anything about blessings, but there had been some, he reckoned and he would not say any more on the subject.

When his mother had finished her lunch, Cole sat with her a while. She dozed off. Cole leaned over to kiss her forehead.

He walked out the gate and sat in his truck, still and silent.

The picture outside his mother's room was one that had hung in the hall of their old house, a house his father had built with his own hands when they were both young and life had seemed so full of possibilities. Her eyes were bright blue and her smile beamed from the picture. Cole still remembered when she looked sort of like that, before the cumulative effects of life had worn at her and that wear had begun to show in her eyes. She had never claimed any special grievance or questioned the way the world was made or whether there could have been a better one.

His father would never even have thought to ask such questions. They had no real answers, anyway, and were thus not deemed by him as being anything more than an indulgence and a dangerous one at that. That was his way, and the way of the all the men Cole had known as a boy. Only the pastor occasionally pointed out what he called "a hard teaching" or "a difficult passage" or "the mystery of things." But that was his job, so men like Cole's father did not hold it against him.

Cole started the truck and drove away, avoiding glancing at the building in the rearview mirror.

He headed back to Ely.

*

Cole pulled in and parked at the Market Basket, which was advertising brisket on sale and double coupons.

A skinny boy wearing a feed store cap, his sleeves rolled up a bit, was standing in the parking lot and retying a white apron that said "Market Basket" on the front pocket. He finished, looked at the bottoms of his boots as if he had stepped in something, and pushed some carts back into the store. He nodded at Cole and Cole nodded back.

Cole sat in the truck and took a few deep breaths. He reached into his shirt pocket and looked at the picture one more time.

People change.

Cole put the picture back in his pocket and tried to remember the last time he had seen that particular face, and it was lost to him.

He got out of the pickup and walked in, running into Elroy and Nancy Clover and Cathy Goodwin on their way out. He learned that the high school marching band was holding a car wash this Saturday. Cole was surprised that Cathy was still in town. But she said she was basically a homebody. She'd been to Dallas for a while but came back and he didn't ask why, so as not to pry.

Cole walked into the Market Basket and strolled over to the produce section, which gave him a clear view of the checkout lanes.

She was on lane five. Cole wandered around the vegetables and fruit. She hadn't noticed him.

He picked a package up and walked over to her lane. Two people were ahead of him, one he recognized as the old high school shop teacher, Mr. Haslett. The other was a young girl he didn't know. Cole stayed a step or two back, waiting for his turn. The checker wasn't paying any attention to him. He set the package down on the conveyer belt. The checker finished the young girl's order, then moved the conveyer belt and picked up the package.

"Did you come all the way over here for this?"

Cole glanced at the package and shrugged.

"Sliced mushrooms."

And he said, "Laurie Anne Grace."

"Do you want this?"

"No, I guess not."

Laurie Anne sat it down behind the cash register.

Cole smiled and said, "Got a minute?"

Laurie Anne waved at a tall, strawberry-blonde-haired woman on lane one and said, "Margie, can I take my break now?"

Margie said, "Sure, sugar, we ain't too busy." Margie was eyeing Cole closely, trying to place him. He made a slow, small wave to her and followed Laurie Anne out the door.

Before they got into Cole's pickup, Laurie Anne had looked around her, as if she were scanning the parking lot for witnesses. Then she gave him a hug and said, "I'm awful glad you made it back alright."

She smiled a little smile and got in the truck, saying she couldn't have everbody in town passing by and seeing them. And Cole asked her why not and she said, "I'm married again, Cole, didn't anybody tell you?"

"You don't have a ring on."

She snapped open her pocketbook, reached in and held up a ring on the end of her index finger. Then she put it back in the pocketbook and said, "I don't wear it at work. It gets scratched on the cash register when I ring things up. Anyway, it's a little loose and I need to get it re-sized."

Cole sat there with both hands on the steering wheel.

"Who'd you marry this time?"

"Nick Wainwright."

Cole frowned and looked intently at Laurie Anne.

"Nick?"

"Wainwright. That's correct."

"I thought you couldn't stand him."

She shrugged and said, "Things change."

He tapped his fingers on the steering wheel.

"You still mad at me?"

"No, I'm not mad at you."

"I was in love with you."

"You didn't stay around."

"No, I didn't."

"But you're back now and look what happened."

She didn't look mad. Just a little sad, was all.

"I had one bad marriage. And I was not gonna have another. And you? You wanted to go out and see things for yourself. You were always lookin over the next hill. I couldn't have that."

"Your boy, Joey?"

"He's fine. Got a little sister now."

"What's her name?"

"Amanda."

"That's a pretty name."

They sat there in silence. Cole reached over and squeezed her hand and she squeezed his back and said, "I couldn't wait on you to figure out what you were gonna be when you grew up. Or what everthing was about or whatever else was always eatin at you."

"You're right. We wouldn't a been happy."

Laurie Anne Grace sighed and said, "People can love one another and still not be happy. And who says a person's got a right to be happy, anyhow?"

He looked over at her, noticing the thin lines in her face he hadn't noticed before — or maybe he hadn't wanted to.

"No."

She leaned over and kissed him on the cheek.

"I gotta go back to work."

She opened the door and looked at him one more time and said, "I'm sorry."

"No need to be."

"I couldn't wait on you, darlin."

She tried to shut the door and he scooted over and blocked it open with his right foot and said, "Say it."

"Say what?"

"Call me by my name, Laurie Anne."

"Goodbye, Cole."

She smiled and closed the door and he watched her walk back into the Market Basket.

5

Cole examines the family pictures… A death and a funeral

Cole went through the boxes slowly. He eyed the pictures as if he could enter the past that was portrayed in each photograph and alter it in some way that would change the trajectory of the lives portrayed in them. Some of them had ended prematurely or terribly, having encountered misfortunes unseen and unpredicted that sprang into life from that twilight rim where they wait, ready to pounce on each one of us. Unwary and vulnerable.

How could it be some other way?

If we think of God seeing all and knowing all, the past, the present, and the future, did that mean He had ordained it before we were born? That steps were determined beforehand, destinies assigned? But if God is eternal and made time, then He was outside that time and the notion of his doing something before or after was only a fabrication of our limited minds. There was no *when* to it.

Some preachers said God had a plan for each of us, but it did not seem quite so to Cole. Life was more like an array of possibilities and potentialities that ran parallel to the products of chance and the choices made within and without the subject.

You see the problem.

As a boy, Cole had puzzled over such questions and sometimes voiced his concerns. His mother had been very insistent on avoiding temptations, including the temptation of pride, the pride of smart boys in asking unanswerable questions.

Cole was staring at a picture. On the back was scrawled "1942." His mother was in a white dress, her hair golden and all in curls. She was smiling, looking up at his grandmother and grandfather. They stood in front of a simple white wooden church. He figured it was Easter time.

A young man in uniform was standing next to them. Her brother Nelson was about to go off to fight, never to return, which troubled the life of the family thereafter. He was listed as missing for some time and nobody at the War Department, more honest in its name and about its

66

purpose in those days, had been able to tell the family anything at all until Nelson was declared dead.

The Gold Star banner they gave his grandmother was folded among the photographs.

One was of his grandmother at a ceremony in Houston receiving her son's Purple Heart. She was in black, wearing a hat and looking so distant as a man in uniform lifted the medal from a simple box. She was one among a line of women standing stiffly, waiting their turn, each marking the end of a life and of the terrible waiting and not knowing. But knowing was not easier at that moment in that place, a point of no return.

His sifted through the pictures and stared at one of his father's uncles in uniform. The boys were lined up, looking lean and unhurried, smiling in front of an old truck and a narrow house that stood on blocks on a clear plain with not a tree in sight.

Look back.

A tall man in chaps holding his hat. Uncle Charlie grinning. Another of a stern looking man standing in front of a corral, the woman next to him looking serious, too, in her long dress, the man holding a shotgun, the barrels pointed back away from the woman but looking for all the world as if the man was pointing at someone out there, his eyes cutting away.

Cole's great grandfather, lean and weathered in a high crowned hat, wearing a badge. The holster was hiked up high on his hip, the pistol grips white in the sepia reality of his time. He had a thick mustache, and that serious look that marked a serious man and a serious people. A people of purpose who did not doubt that purpose and found solace there — those who were so inclined, anyway.

Cole's father in a denim jacket, hatless with a toothy grin, sitting on wooden steps, his mother and father in chairs on the narrow porch.

His father and his father's twin brother when they were both small. The twin was killed by a rattlesnake in the Valley.

Emma on a porch swing, making a face when she was maybe ten. J.T. at graduation.

His mother had left him a note written in pencil on a scrap of lined paper: "You might want these," was all it said.

*

Cole was walking toward his mother's room through the common area, eyeing a little bald man banging on something with a toy hammer. The

TV showed a young, skinny, and earnest looking Jimmy Stewart in a tight-looking double-breasted suit. He was talking to Gene Arthur, cheeky and smiling. No one was watching.

Tom introduced himself and Cole gently told him he had to go, which made Tom very sad. He started crying and Cole patted him on the arm and walked toward his mother's room. A middle-aged man in a white coat was standing in the door, looking at him gravely as if Cole might be his next terminal patient.

Cole's mother was lying there in her pajamas, uncovered as if she had lifted the sheets and been ready to rise but could not. Someone had closed her eyes.

Look at her.

She was so frail and withered looking, but if you concentrated you might still see the vague outline of the little girl with the curls and the eyes that looked bright even in the black and white pictures.

This is how the world ends.

*

They called it a Celebration of Life. There were a fair number of people there, mostly old people. They played *In the Garden* and a man in suspenders sang the words. It was her favorite gospel song.

Aunts and uncles and cousins Cole had not seen in years came to pay their respects.

Cole sat in the front row, in a black suit he had bought in Parmer not two days before. He was looking at the pictures by the casket. There was one of the girl with the curls and one of her and his father at their wedding. There was a picture of his mother and all her children.

He sat alone.

Nobody knew where Emma was.

At the cemetery, the wind blew so that the people gathered there seemed to sway as their clothes flapped in the air and their hair danced in the sun. The pastor said some words and people put flowers on the casket and somebody loosed a cage of doves that flew out and disappeared into the wind as if by magic, like spirits briefly making visitation in the material world. The funeral director told Cole there was no extra charge for that.

They lowered the casket into the grave.

The mourners drifted away.

Cole sat for a few minutes in one of the folding chairs at graveside. He experienced an overwhelming sense of acute isolation, as if he were sitting in a chair on the surface of a distant and uninhabited planet.

Afterwards, the mourners gathered in the Parmer Veterans' Hall. The women of his mother's church congregation had made sandwiches and iced tea for everyone. Cole walked among the mourners, thanking them for coming and celebrating his mother's life, which had been a good one, if one marred by so much pain.

"Your momma had a rough time," they said.

"She was a righteous woman."

"She missed your daddy."

"Has anyone heard from Emma?"

"No."

"You came back." (A sense of wonder here. It was almost a question.)

"We hated that they tore that house down."

Laurie Anne and her husband came. Cole dutifully shook hands with them and they said they were real sorry and that his mother was a good woman and would be missed.

Cole shook hands with Charlie Bass and his second wife and with Mr. Longtree. And Sonny Valdez showed up, which was a bit of a surprise. He said his mother had died the year before and Cole said sorry, he didn't know. Sonny said there was practically no way he could have. Sonny told Cole that his father sat in a rocking chair and rocked and didn't say much. Sonny would turn on the TV for him. No reaction. Not even for *The Price is Right*, which was one of the old man's favorites. Sometimes when one person is deceased, said Sonny, more than one person has died. It does seem that way, anyhow.

Later, Cole stood by his pickup and watched the old men gather outside, putting their hats back on and talking about the warmer weather and the prospects for rain, which seemed small leaning to dismal. Then the old women came out and they drifted to their trucks and cars and began leaving. They would drive by him and the men at the steering wheels invariably lifted a couple of fingers on the right hand to wave as they passed and Cole would nod.

Laurie Anne and her husband left without saying goodbye.

He stood there with the truck door open and watched them leave.

The pastor drifted out and stood by the door. Cole looked over at him and the pastor met his glance and nodded.

The door of the hall like the entrance to a sepulcher.

*

Cole kept a calendar. It was on the wall near the kitchen sink. He looked at it every day and he marked those days. He marked the day of his mother's birth and of her passing, and those of other family members, too. And when that calendar was expired, he would mark a new one with the old dates, for how new could a calendar be? A refreshing, but not a replacing, for we cannot replace the years of our lives, nor their substance. His mother had left behind a Bible with a record of births and deaths and he kept that, too, sometimes leafing through the opening pages, reading the lines and remembering.

Cole had established that every act we perform, every action rehearsed and played out by each of us must have significance that echoes beyond the material world for good or ill.

The question is one of purpose.

He wrestled with that question from then on, as it had been gestating in his mind for the eternity of his own life.

6

Cole... The death of Juan Gomez... A meeting with Sheriff Rodriguez (of cousins and soldiers)

[*News item for posting on Channel 12 website/Video for nightly news broadcast version*] Parmer County Sheriff's Department Deputy Cole Landry told investigators that he felt like a "sitting duck." [*Video of investigators at the scene*] Landry had placed his hand into the partially-opened window of a Ford SUV to try and unlock the door to arrest the driver, 32-year-old Juan Gomez, on traffic warrants. According to Landry, Gomez rolled the window up and sped off, with Landry's wrist trapped in the window. [*Cut to video of damaged SUV and officers examining the vehicle; Cut to video of Landry talking to investigators*] Landry reportedly told investigators, "The only thing I could do was jump on the running board and hold on." After Landry freed his hand, he clung to the luggage rack, afraid to jump from the vehicle as it sped down Baylor Drive near old town. [*Cut to video of Department of Public Safety investigator*] "Deputy Landry repeatedly told the driver to stop, but the driver did not respond. The driver was swerving the vehicle back and forth in an attempt to throw the deputy off. This prompted Deputy Landry to draw his weapon and fire repeatedly into the vehicle. Mr. Gomez was fatally wounded as a result. [*Cut to video of reporter surveying the scene of the incident*] The Sheriff's Department is conducting its own internal investigation in cooperation with the DPS. [*Cut to tape of Peter Salinas*] But Peter Salinas of the Council of Latino Citizens says that this is yet another example of law enforcement using excessive force against Latinos. As the incident awaits a grand jury hearing, Mr. Salinas and other civil rights activists are planning to bring up the Parmer shooting at upcoming hearings in the state legislature on recruiting Latino police officers statewide. [*Cut to video of Salinas*] "We thought this problem had been dealt with previously, but our people continue to suffer abuse at the hands of Anglo police officers and other law enforcement officials. Would the situation have been different if the officer stopping Mr. Gomez had been a Latino or at least spoke Spanish?

We think so. There have been too many incidents over the years and, according to our information, Deputy Landry has been involved in at least two previous shootings that led to injuries to our people. Mr. Gomez was naturally afraid." [*Cut to video of reporter*] Tensions are high in Parmer County and its namesake county seat. City and county officials are again looking to County Sheriff Manny Rodriguez to defuse a tense and potentially volatile situation. [*End*]

*

Something like this happens and you can't put all the pieces together. But you better, because they mean to have you. Gomez was a runner. He was protected by the cousins. You knew that. You saw him run a stop sign and pulled up traffic warrants on him. It's a surprise that Rodriguez hadn't done anything about that. But there it is and you have to do something. You walk up to the window and Gomez won't look at you. Is he drunk? Stoned? He won't respond, so you reach in to open the door. Careful. Yeah, I had my hand on my gun. Gomez may be protected by the cousins, but tonight this is a traffic stop and you work for the Sheriff's Department.

He takes off and what happens? You're hanging on. You can't remember the feeling, exactly, just that it's something like a roller coaster ride when you were a kid. Can you jump off? No way. The wind is screaming in your ears and you can't think straight, but your hand goes for the gun. What else is there to do? Your feet are swinging out from under you and you are holding on with one hand and Gomez is screaming like he's leading a charge. If the fall doesn't kill you, then maybe Gomez backs up and finishes you that way. Or maybe he just reaches for his own gun and pops you while you lay there.

You wonder what you are doing there. Why this is happening. You risk your life and for what?

Gomez is swerving all over the road and you start shooting, trying to keep it in the window. You don't reason through all of this while you are about to be flung off a moving vehicle at 50 miles an hour.

And then the car slows and you see shattered glass and blood and a glob of thick, bloody mess blows out the window and into your face. The car keeps rolling. But slower and slower, so that now you see everything like in slow motion.

You know Gomez is dying. He'll be stone cold dead and soon.

I don't know if I killed anybody over there.

*

Cole walked into Rodriguez's office. Calm. No other way to be now.

Rodriguez, glasses perched on the end of his nose, sat behind a large desk framed by flags on each side. The Sheriff of Parmer County was banging away on his computer keyboard like he was slamming out the big finale of a piano piece. He stopped and swivels in his chair, took off his glasses, and said, "Have a seat, *amigo.*"

Cole was quiet, sitting impassively while Rodriguez studied him, as if he were examining a mental patient for signs of illness. Checking his psychic pulse, in a manner of speaking. But Cole was silent. Rodriguez would have to open.

"Cole Landry." Rodriguez squinted, as if thinking hard about a cipher. He nodded and said again, "Cole Landry." He extended the words, savoring them, contemplating them.

He placed his hands palms down on the broad desktop and looked at Cole inquisitively.

On the wall behind him was a picture of Sheriff Rodriguez accepting an award from a former governor. There was a picture of Rodriguez acting as advisor on a movie called *The Shield*, the sheriff and the star, arms cocked on each other's shoulders. Manny Rodriguez, friend of the stars! And more pictures of Rodriguez...

Cole waved his hand at the wall and said, "Very impressive. The Manny Rodriguez Walk of Fame. A shrine to The Man. But there are no pictures of your cousins. That seems ungrateful. No *Pistoleros.* No Mexican Mafia boys. All the homies, Manny. Where are they?"

Rodriguez ignored this and again said, "Cole Landry." He waved his index finger at Cole: "You know, soldier, that's a good name. Strong. I like it. You know..." He waved his finger again and furrowed his brow. Dragging the words out and savoring them. "You know, that name sounds like it could have been a name for, oh, I dunno, maybe a character played by Clint Eastwood. What do you think? No? Maybe more like John Wayne. Yes, that's it! You are John Wayne. Do you remember, Cole Landry? That's more like your time, huh? And closer to mine, too. So, you used to stay up and watch *The Late Show* and they showed John Wayne movies. That's something only us graybeards remember, huh?"

Rodriguez cocked his head to one side.

"And the Duke, he really whacked those bad guys."

Rodriguez was smiling.

"You and Connelly. Connelly the Man Killer. Deputy Sheriff Landry and Deputy Sheriff Connelly have been in some gunfights, no? Maybe Connelly is Clint and you are the Duke. Maybe that's it."

"What does that make you, Pancho or Cisco?"

Rodriguez laughed.

"That's good, soldier. Oh, I'm Cisco all the way, right? Showing our age a little again, no?"

Rodriguez sighed.

"But it's not the wild west any more, eh buddy? At least, it's not *your* wild west. All of you thinking you are John Wayne..."

"What do you want, Manny?"

"John Wayne again. No fooling around. OK, *amigo*."

Rodriguez tapped his finger tips on the desk top.

"Do you know my wife, Cole Landry?"

Cole didn't answer.

"Well, you know that her sister is married to Swordfish. To Connelly. You know that."

"What do you want?"

"Just a minute. Just a minute. You know what it's like dealing with Mexicans, Cole. Indirect. Subtle."

Cole didn't answer.

"Frustrating, no? I feel the same way..."

Rodriguez furrowed his brow again and slowly and clearly said, "The cousins." He tapped his fingertips together and gathered himself. He was about to initiate this man, to reveal a thing thought of as shared only in the craft, but paradoxically as widely known as the simple fact that the sun rises in the East and sets in the West.

Rodriguez smiled and said, "Everybody knows about the cousins. They don't say they know. But they know."

Rodriguez's slightly hooded eyes were meeting Cole's. The sheriff sat back, his elbows resting on the arms of his chair, his fingertips forming an arch representative of the church of which he was the leading local prelate, leaving the impression that once brought in, no man could exist in a prelapsarian state.

"We can speak openly now. The cousins control most things in this county, deputy. We have understandings with the mayors. We receive a consideration for our oversight and protection of businesses large and small. Of ranches and even of schools and churches. We live here, too. And we are publicly minded people."

He was not being ironic. Rodriguez, deft in his sincerity.

Cole folded his hands and waited. Rodriguez liked a dramatic finish, as if to register the event, to do it justice befitting the weight of its import in the affairs of the county and of mankind in general.

"We have a hand in most things. Not all, but most. Do you know, *amigo*, what this power is based on? On ties of blood, yes, but also on ties of friendship. The world is an uncertain place nowadays, as you are no doubt aware. Oh, you can talk to judges and call reporters if you like, but you know that they depend on their relations and friends as all men must, no? And we all share in the same hypocrisy, pretending that things are as they were."

He leaned forward and gave Cole a knowing look.

"The shining city on a hill. Remember that bit, *amigo*? Or maybe, morning in America?"

Rodriguez nodded in affirmation of remembrance or in pity at the hubris in such slogans.

"You Anglos should have had more babies, *amigo*. You couldn't keep up with the cousins, could you? But you couldn't have, anyway, right? Behind every wave was another batch of cousins ready for the trek to *El Norte*. Now things have settled down a bit. And we see the new reality more clearly. So the wise man adjusts to the new reality, no?"

Manny Rodriguez shrugged. He had a gleam in his eye.

"It was the old myth of the Anglo magic that did you in, *amigo*. They didn't become you. You became them. And I," said Rodriguez, "am the result of the...of the *union*."

"And Connelly?"

"Connelly is married to my wife's sister. We have a channel, you might say. A channel to help sort things out and prevent misunderstandings."

"Misunderstandings."

"Exactly."

Rodriguez was looking inquisitive himself, asking questions with his eyes. *Did you not know of the understandings? And of the prevention of misunderstandings?*

"We don't control all. But maybe we don't need to. We cousins have our sphere. And the soldiers theirs. It is only necessary to arrive at a more permanent state of affairs, a balance of interests that is more clearly understood."

"We don't want your money."

"Cole…"

Rodriguez eyed him as he might an older child who still believed in Santa Claus at this late date in the life of the world.

"Where does this money come from? From the devil you say? We are capitalists. You soldiers are more like smallholders. But we all have to function, don't we? We all have to live in this world not of our own making."

Pause.

"And where do we raise this capital? From a terrible and illegal business, you say? Satanic. From corrupting the people. 'The Mexicans are corrupting us,' you say, but we force no one to buy the product, you understand. No one. We give the people what they want for a certain consideration. The market price. And if you condemn us, you must condemn them. For that is the marketplace. If you say we take their souls from them, it is their soul to lose, soldier. They are free agents. Wherein have we done wrong?"

Rodriguez sat forward in his chair in great urgency.

"We are all of a piece in this business, soldier. Production, transport, consumption. That money is plowed back into other businesses. Yes, we own a piece of businesses that are called legitimate by you and yours. So that every time you buy groceries, soldier, you are making a transaction partly with us. Every time you put gas in your truck, soldier, you are sharing with all the owners. All of them. So there is no escaping business and transactions, soldier, and there never has been. To remain pure is an illusion. A fantasy for children. Money is the solvent that breaks down all bonds. And if the Americans complain, the Mexicans can say it is you who have corrupted us. The world is ours and we are of the world. To pretend otherwise is foolish. You may say it is better not to know things. To pretend. But you know."

Rodriguez sat back, looking quite satisfied with himself.

"What's the deal?"

Rodriguez nodded. "The soldier is always direct."

"We cousins are generous, soldier. We can share. We can offer a certain consideration. For a while, at least, there should be no tensions between us. No hostility. We do, after all, have some common enemies."

Rodriguez was rubbing his palms on the desk top, divining for a certain message. Then he softly clasped his hands.

"We shall act against them. Together. We cousins will leave you soldiers undisturbed. Times are hard, soldier. You can use our consideration to keep the army marching, you might say. Your space is old town and the stretch along the old Fort Worth highway. So it will remain."

Cole got up to leave. His back turned, Rodriguez said, "Go tell the soldiers what I have said. You meet on Tuesdays, do you not? Tell them."

Cole reached to open the door.

"And the grand jury? No need to worry, *amigo*."

7

Rodriguez enforces an ordinance.

Rodriguez left his office after dark. He took an unmarked official car and drove through old town, then turned left through the park across from the courthouse and started up the steep ridge to the east of old town, the town square, and the courthouse. Houses were spread out along the hump of the ridge. He parked under a large, looming live oak, turned his lights off, and sat in silence, watching.

He was waiting for someone. A particular someone who did not know that Rodriguez was waiting for him. A someone who had broken an ordinance, violated a code. That someone had pronounced his own sentence, which was always the same in the court that governed them all. Such things demanded the strictest discipline.

Rodriguez watched a car approaching him, moving south along the ridge. It stopped by a mailbox not 100 yards away. The driver rolled the window down and extracted something from the mail box. Then the car, a long, wide, brown Chrysler sedan of a vintage approaching antique, turned around in the adjacent driveway and proceeded back north along the ridge.

Rodriguez started his car and drove without lights. The few streetlights along the ridge were spaced far apart and the driver would likely not notice. Or so Rodriguez had calculated. He never made any such move without calculation and precision of thought. Of what the man he was following would do and how. And where he might go from the drop on the ridge, a drop he had visited three times in the past month.

The Chrysler followed the ridgeback and then the road sloped off the ridge north of town and the car made a southerly turn and headed back for Parmer.

Rodriguez turned left down a gravel road that ran to where he thought the car would end up as it approached town, then the town square. He punched the gas. Gravel was slung from the undercarriage of the unmarked car and Rodriguez had to correct the steering wheel quickly as the backend fishtailed twice on a ride that ended on a paved but severely potholed road behind the Jaguar Club. Only a couple of trucks tricked out in the flashy style of the patrons were parked there. Bright colors, shiny wheels, fringe around the windshields. It was a slow weeknight at the club. Rodriguez backed the car in next to a battered dumpster, thinking that the one he had followed would approach from the other direction and not see him.

Rodriguez reached down and took a pistol and a suppressor from underneath the car seat. He fitted the suppressor on the pistol, which had been altered by a gunsmith to accommodate such a device, checked the weapon, made sure it was armed and ready, and waited. He sat silently, impassive, breathing slowly and deeply.

A Mexican in a straw hat stumbled out the back door of the club, caught himself and walked slowly to one of the pickups. He was oblivious to the unmarked car and to all else that he encountered, as fit his condition. He managed to back out and drive off without incident, the windows down, the truck's sound system emitting the chorus of a Mexican ballad sung with conviction and passion, as all such ballads are.

Headlights swept along the ground behind the Jaguar Club. The Chrysler pulled alongside the remaining pickup. Before the car was off and the lights dimmed, Rodriguez was out of his vehicle, approaching the Chrysler slowly and deliberately, the pistol by his right side. He stood and waited as the driver turned off the lights, then the car, then opened the car door and stepped out, at which time the driver ascertained that a man was standing close by the trunk of the Chrysler. His eyes cut back into the car. He was half standing and half crouched by the brown vehicle. His facial expression showed fear and alarm and Rodriguez said in Spanish for him to stand up straight and still, which he did, for he calculated there were no other options at the moment.

Rodriguez told him to stand still and look at him. "Just look at me," he said. "You will get your chance."

Rodriguez told this man that he had violated an ordinance. "You know which one, don't you?" He told this man that he had been trusted and was not worthy of such trust. "You have stolen our product," he said. "The product we have been entrusted with by our friends. You steal. Just a little, but it is stealing and cannot be tolerated. You understand. Nod if you understand. You don't understand? You do. That's good, for the punishment meted out is of little value if it is not understood by both the person being punished and the punisher. As well as by others who will learn of this, or suspect it, since they will not see you. Watch me now."

Rodriguez noticed that the man's eyes kept cutting back to the car. "Inside, there's something on the seat you left behind. Let's say it is a gun, which you had left, but would have put, say, under the seat, or would have stuck into your belt under your shirt if time had allowed. But it did not. So now," said Rodriguez, "time allows. Go ahead, I give you leave. I will lower my gun again. See, it is by my side. Not pointing at you. But hurry, because someone may come out that back door and I will have to shoot him as well, which I had not planned to do and would make more work for me. Go ahead. I give you a chance. Man to man. It is a small chance, but a chance and every man who is a man should have one. *So go ahead,*" Rodriguez said one more time and the man tried to dive into the car and Rodriguez was pleased at his own reaction time as he brought the pistol to bear on the target and fired, then fired again, into the man's body.

There were only thumping sounds in the dead of night behind the Jaguar Club. The man was quivering, half on the car seat and half on the ground, still trying to reach for something on the seat or just get inside the car. Rodriguez shot him again. He slumped and was breathing with gurgling noises. Rodriguez approached and put one into his brain.

Rodriguez looked in at what was on the car seat. It was a flashlight. Just a flashlight. *What did he think he would do with that?*

Rodriguez sighed and walked back to the unmarked car. He took a large tarp out of the trunk, walked back to the dead man's car, spread out the tarp on the ground and put on some plastic gloves. Then Rodriguez rolled the body up in the tarp. He dragged it back to the unmarked car and strained a bit getting the deadweight inside the trunk. He shut the trunk lid, walked back over to the Chrysler and closed the door, then walked back to his car and drove away. He would come back in a little while and clean up any signs of blood.

Later, a notice that the car had been illegally parked would be stuck on the windshield. Eventually it would be towed away. These small things are important. It was part of the Sheriff's philosophy of law enforcement, as announced to the city council and during his election campaign. Minor violations would be treated seriously. But he never liked the word *minor*, for no violation of an ordinance could be.

8

The soldiers meet... Connelly takes a shot... J.C.'s lament (a picture of Ronald Reagan)... A motion is made

Cole entered the meeting room at the back of the hall. The walls were lined with members' photos. Men in uniform. Veterans on parade. The wall behind one end of the meeting table was festooned with an 1835 Gonzales flag. A star over a cannon barrel. COME AND TAKE IT. A flag with an M-4 carbine in place of the cannon was on the opposite wall. A Gadsen flag faced the door.

The men began to trickle in and take their places at the table. Connelly was last, following behind a hobbling J.C. Bryant (Vietnam). The Chaplain (Afghanistan) offered a prayer and J. C. opened the meeting.

Old business. Charlie Bickford had requested help in guarding a stretch of road on his fence line he thought either some of the cousins or the Gunslingers had been using for a drop point.

"Charlie's old. Hell, he's oldern me. Anyways, he cain't keep a watch by hisself. He needs backup. Or maybe we try approachin the Gunslingers first. We can talk to Will or Sammy Tyrell and see if it's their boys. If not, we either mount a patrol or use Swordfish to talk to the *jefe*. What'll it be?"

The Chaplain said he'd talk to Will or Sammy. They were his cousins. Well, second cousins. J.C. asked if he would turn that into a motion, and he did. The motion carried.

New business. Eddie Hatcher (Grenada) said he couldn't pick up payments this week. Would Swordfish (Iraq) or Fubar Henson (Gulf War) do the honors?

Henson's usual grin disappeared. "Don't call me that. I don't like it no more."

"How's that?"

"This whole country's fucked up beyond all recognition. I ain't. I'm just fucked."

J.C. scratched his chin and said, "Is that a yes or a no, Mr. Henson?"

Henson sighed and said, "It's a fucked up maybe."

Henson skipped a beat and added that he whadn't no character from a fuckin' movie. Henson formerly had the impression that the name had been invented for him personally. Being a mercurial sort, he had decided he hated it.

J. C. tried to get the meeting back on track.

"We've established that as a fact. Maybe we oughta call you effin Henson. Swordfish? OK, two maybes. Looky, we need the operatin funds and the folks on Main Street need us. What say ye? Ya gotta make a motion. Second. Ayes and nays. Motion carries. We keep up collectin payments. Swordfish or Fu … Mr. Henson, excuse me, pick up this week. You all coordinate."

"We got some other new business. Whatta they want, Cole, I mean to deliver the grand jury? That's what this is about, right? This is your meetin. Whatta they want?"

So Cole told them.

"The *jefe* sees it like this. We take a trust cut and lean on the Gunslingers. The crystal meth crowd is a competitor to the cousins. They know about us trying to press Will and Sammy to move their operations. They say they want a compact. They give us a trust cut. We take care of the bikers. They leave us alone on Main Street and the Northeast side. Town and county. The *jefe* says he wants peace. Ease tensions. He's got other problems."

Ricky Hightower (Somalia) said, "Like what?"

"We know what. Espinoza. They hadn't killed him. Yet, anyway. And the red zone is Dallas."

Henson adopted a hostile grimace. "We don't want their damn money. Tell the *jefe* to eat shit and die."

Hightower cut in.

"Hang on a minute. If the Espinoza bunch whacks the *jefe*, we got a small war right here. Think about that." Silence. "If that goes down, we're all in deep shit. This town is. And then what? The taco vendors and that's it. Where do our families go? What happens to them? We got no choice but to make a deal with the *jefe* and hope he stays alive for a while. If he can concentrate on Espinoza and we don't have to worry with the cousins, that's good for us."

Cole squinted and eyed Hightower.

"Look, we know that the *jefe's* cartel has shifted operations west, through Parmer County. The red zone is Dallas. The *jefe* wants to protect his rear and cartel operations. We won't get any help from the feds. Somebody in Dallas is walkin point for the *jefe*. We don't know who or how many. If it winds up with the feds, we don't know how we come off. The cousins have intel from inside and they have friends in the courts."

Henson leaned forward in his chair.

"So you wanna make a deal with those bastards?"

"I don't know what I want. I'm just settin it up, fillin in what the *jefe* was getting at."

"We take their money and we ain't no better than those beaners, Cole."

Bobby Sanchez (Iraq) cut in.

"If we don't make a deal, Cole goes down and they jump on all of us. Maybe Swordfish is next. Maybe I am."

Henson grinned.

"No offense, Bobby. We know you don't like *frijoles*."

J.C. laughed. Bobby lifted the middle finger of his right hand at Henson.

"I ain't no wet. I'm American, you asshole."

Cole nodded at J.C.

"I can leave town and maybe this blows over and you don't have to make any deal with the *jefe*."

Henson looked over at Connelly.

"How come you don't talk, Swordfish?"

Henson didn't have any use for Connelly. Never had.

"Ain't the *jefe* your in-law or somethin?"

The table was silent and still.

"He talks through you, don't he, Swordfish? He wants to make us all his in-laws, ain't that so?"

Connelly rose and turned toward the door.

"What's your trust cut, Man Killer?"

Connelly turned, the Glock in his hand, rising, pointing at Henson like the instrument of fate that it was.

Henson smiled.

"Go ahead, Man Killer, blow my brains out. We know how it is."

The Chaplain rose. J. C. motioned for him to sit down.

Connelly took a step forward, leaned across the table and pressed the barrel against Henson's forehead.

"If you had any brains, you sonofabitch, I'd blow 'em out."

Henson's grin was now a wide smile.

"Sleepin with the enemy, Man Killer."

Connelly was sweating. He pressed the weapon forward on Henson's forehead and screamed like a man walking on the smoldering coals of hell. He jerked the weapon up and fired a shot into the wall.

Then he turned and left the room.

The ears of the men were ringing after the explosion, a sonic boom in the enclosed sanctuary of the meeting room.

Henson started to speak, but J.C. cut him short, pounding his fist on the table.

"Shut the hell up, you dumbass. This meetin is called to order."

J.C. glanced over at the wounded wall. He rose from his chair and walked to the spot of the wound.

"Dammit to hell. Swordfish done shot a hole through my picture."

The picture was J.C. at a Veterans Day celebration in Washington, D.C. Standing next to him was Ronald Reagan, only there was now a large hole separating them. The old veteran gingerly reached out and touched the image with his fingertips, like a pilgrim touching a holy relic. The picture slid down the wall and hit the floor, another casualty of the soldiers' secret war.

J.C. turned and walked back to his chair, disconsolate. He glared at Henson.

"I blame you for this."

Henson shrugged.

"Alright. So what're we doin?"

Henson's blood was up.

"To hell with em, let em come on. I want em to. If we take their money, the feds have got us and the *jefe* can use em to close us down."

Bobby Sanchez answered back.

"If we don't, they can get Cole and then pick us off one at a time. You won't have anybody in the department, dickhead. We don't know which feds are players. Then what?"

Hightower got up and walked to the door.

84

"If they wanna fry their brains with coke and heroin, let em. We have our families to think of."

J.C. sat solemnly, arms crossed.

"What about the country?"

"My country's right here, J.C. There's nothin' we can do for the rest and you know it."

"Then make a motion, Ricky."

9

The Chaplain and Cole… The lost batallion… A meeting at the Texan Café

J.C. closed the meeting and the men drifted out into the hall.

The Chaplain walked over to the coffee pot and poured a cup. He took a long pull on it and waited until Cole strolled by, then followed him.

"Cole."

Cole paused, then kept walking. The Chaplain followed, trailing Cole to his pickup.

"You can't blame yourself for any of this."

Cole opened the door of the pickup and did not turn but said to the Chaplain, "Maybe the *jefe* needs to become a victim of violent crime."

"If you kill Rodriguez, it won't do anything but make this town the red zone."

Cole climbed in the truck and shut the cab door, his arm hanging out the open window.

"Tell me what to do, padre."

"If you want to do right by this town and by us, you have to go along. For now."

Cole put the key in the ignition and started the truck. He revved the motor, then sat back in the seat.

"Shootin Gomez. That's the first time I was really certain I killed anybody. I was on the highway of death and fired my weapon not so much. I was never sure if I hit anybody. But now I know."

"You didn't have any choice."

"No, I guess not, not unless I was ready to depart from this world. I guess I wasn't. What's it like bein dead? I guess that depends, right?"

The Chaplain said, "You've heard it before. The world is corrupt. We live in it. You had no choice and you are not to blame for this particular mess."

Cole leaned forward a bit and eyed the Chaplain before sitting back and saying, "You are startin' to sound just a little bit like Manny

Rodriguez, padre. No, decidedly like the *jefe*. Corrupt world we have to live in and so forth."

Cole gripped the steering wheel with both hands.

"You know, padre, doin what's right ain't hard. It's the knowin that's the hard part. Knowin what's right."

He backed the truck up and pulled away. The Chaplain watched the taillights dim as Cole drove away.

*

Cole circled the patrol car back through town. There were fewer lights on along the town's Main Street at night nowadays. Once outside their fuzzy canopy, the night grew very, very dark, very fast and you were left with a sprinkling of stars, the moon, and the enveloping darkness. But it never matched the utter blackness of the desert on a night when the moon did not glow and you struggled to put one foot in front of the other, as if you had already reached the outer darkness.

Cole drove past the county courthouse, slowing as he eyed the old Confederate monument, one of two war memorials that stood on the courthouse lawn, the other erected in the late 1940s to honor veterans of the two World Wars. Metal thieves had taken a copper sword from the determined-looking rebel years before. There had been talk of a third monument for Vietnam and all the small wars that had followed, but there was an argument about whether there should be separate monuments for each war and that could get expensive. Maybe a monument to all the war veterans would be better. A patriotic park. That was one idea that suited everybody. So every Veterans Day, the soldiers led a parade to the memorial to all war veterans.

Cole was to meet Bobby Sanchez and J. C. at The Texan Café, but a figure clinging close to the walls of the buildings lining Main Street caught his eye and he slowly backed up until he saw a tall, lean man with a beard, wearing a broad brimmed hat and dressed in camo, his tunic braced by a wide belt, a saber in a bare and battered scabbard by his side. An apparition from some distant revolution now materialized on the streets of this settlement. A shade made corporeal. But one confused by its own corporeity. The figure half leaned, half walked, then straightened himself, and walked on as if on parade as Cole's patrol car pulled to the curb.

Cole rolled the passenger side window down and said, "Good evening, Colonel."

The bearded figure assumed the stance of a man at attention. He stood there as if addressing his unseen posterity, but the Colonel spoke not a word one. Then he crisply faced right and Cole watched him march down the cracked sidewalk, an old soldier who would never die, but who would fade away, forgotten among the ranks of the wanderers who haunted the land like waves of ephemeral locusts.

Cole allowed the Colonel a proper distance, then slowly followed.

The Colonel passed boarded-up shops and the pharmacy, almost tripping on a wide crevice in the sidewalk, but maintaining his balance, eyes forward, envisioning the campground ahead.

The Colonel veered right at the old Phillips 66 station, now a barbecue pit run by an old black man with watery eyes everybody called Pops. Up a short grade and over a rise he strode, the rise marked by a pecan tree, its arms stretching into the night, a canopy outlined against a firmament studded with dustings of distant galaxies like frosting on a dark cake. The tall silhouette of the old soldier stood out in relief, not so straight now, but marching with a curious lilting gait.

Cole turned off the patrol car's headlights and slowly veered onto the dirt trail past Pops' barbecue pit and on under the vast pecan, where he halted, straining to make out the cadence of the marching man, his shape skylighted by the glow of a campfire below him, the campfire of his dismal troop, a remnant from an all but forgotten past.

Cole got out of the patrol car, watching as the Colonel entered an open-air barracks marked by a ring of old shopping carts filled with the detritus of the lost battalion. Slumping figures huddled around the campfire. One of the men stood and saluted. Another bowed. The others in this ragtag troop ignored the Colonel, who strode past them, his back straightened again in the proud stance of a soldier who always knows his duty. He marched forward to a makeshift shelter of cardboard and scrap wood, a headquarters for the army of ghosts.

*

When Cole entered the Texan Café, J.C. was eyeing a menu over his readers. Bobby Sanchez waved at him and he headed for their table.

A little Mexican man in a faded cap and yoked shirt sat by the door. His eyes were reddened and weary. He appeared oblivious to the scene before him, as he usually did. He stopped by from time to time and sat, resting. Sometimes he was offered coffee and sometimes something to eat. And sometimes he took it and sometimes he did not, but chose rather to sit and stare at the proceedings, a brown sphinx mounted on a creaky throne. They said his name might be Pablo, but nobody was sure. He had been coming by for going on six months now. Nobody knew where he came from. He apparently had nowhere to go. Cole nodded at Pablo, but the old man was impassive and did not acknowledge Cole's presence.

The faded walls of the Texan Café were adorned with prints of cowboys and longhorns and one depicted a Comanche chief eyeing his domain from a ridgeline. There were sepia-toned photos of oil derricks and wildcatters, men on horseback and women in bonnets in rustic looking frames of dried, gray wood. There was a calendar adorned with a picture of bluebonnets and a faded and cracked ad for Pearl beer. There were only a couple of other customers, solitary old men with straw hats and deeply lined faces who raised two fingers in greeting as Cole went by, patting them on the shoulders.

Mattie the waitress, a skinny girl with reddish hair and an easy smile, dressed in an apron over blue jeans and a T-shirt, came from behind the linoleum-topped counter to pour coffee for J.C. and Bobby. Cole passed on the coffee and sat down, adjusting his belt and gun holster. He said hey to J.C. and Bobby. J.C. put the menu down and eyed his cell phone as if it were an infectious agent, then turned it off.

"I never liked the damned things, anyways. I like it better now they don't work half the time."

Cole asked J.C. what he was having and he said chicken fried steak and Bobby said that was good for him and Cole said why not and they ordered three chicken fried steaks and an iced tea for Cole.

Bobby, his elbows on the table, asked, "What's the word?"

J.C. arched his eyebrows and looked over at Cole.

Cole shrugged. "Swordfish will pass on our answer. No word yet."

Bobby sipped his coffee, eyed the old man at the door, then asked whether Henson or Connelly were making the pickups. J.C. said it was Connelly.

Cole drummed his fingertips on the table top and said, "I just saw the Colonel out on Main Street."

J.C. nodded.

"I hope he was alone this time."

"Alone."

"Didn't wave his sword at nobody, I take it."

"Nope."

Bobby sighed.

"Well, old buddy, I'll let you take care of the Colonel. He's liable to stick me."

J.C. arched his eyebrows in inquiry as he sipped his coffee.

Bobby shrugged.

"He might think I'm Santa Anna."

J.C. pursed his lips and nodded.

10

Connelly makes his rounds… A quinceañera *(Rodriguez holds court)….*
Houston (you had to be there)

Connelly pulled up behind the feed store on Main Street, parked the patrol car, and made his rounds. He stopped by the feed store first, took an envelope from the proprietor and put it in the inside pocket of his jacket, then waved on his way out, a most welcome special postman making a special pickup.

Connelly walked down the street to the Texan Café. He looked over to see if Pablo was present. Not there. Too early for him, probably. It was morning and the place was crowded with patrons drinking their coffee, chatting over bacon and eggs and grits and pancakes. Connelly patted some of the patrons on the shoulder, waved or nodded at others, and shook hands with Billy Bauer, a retired lineman for the power company who had inherited the place from his parents. The two of them stepped back into the kitchen and then over to Billy's office, a cubbyhole with a desk and two chairs on rollers crammed into it. They both went in and Billy closed the door behind them.

Connelly leaned against the door, watching Billy kneel and turn the dial on the safe beside his desk. He absentmindedly surveyed the walls: a portrait of Ronald Reagan; a picture of John Wayne, a massive stars and stripes banner waving behind him, the Duke attired in full *Man Who Shot Liberty Valance* regalia; a feed store calendar; and the 1976 Parmer Rangers in full pads. Coach Ben was holding a pigskin in his massive paws, a whistle dangling from his neck. Billy was on the front row, wearing the number 70, looking very intent and very proud and very young. That was the year Parmer went to the state 3A semi-finals, a time of distant glory fondly remembered, etched in the town's memory as a founding myth is so etched in the collective memory of a people. It was a memory of glory attained and lost, the townspeople dreaming of attaining that glory once more, thereby reestablishing the right order of things.

Billy was squatting, counting bills from the safe. Connelly looked away. A man needs his privacy at certain times.

Satisfied, Billy put the money into an envelope and sealed it shut, rising and handing the packet to Connelly, who slid it inside his jacket.

Connelly turned to leave, then noticed the empty gun rack on the side wall.

"Where you keepin the shotgun, Billy?"

Billy rose and eyed the gun rack.

"Up front."

"I thought you had a handgun for up front."

"I do."

"But you need some more artillery."

"I figure you heard about the *Pistoleros* shootin up Ely a couple of weeks ago."

Connelly nodded affirmatively.

"They rode right through town and shot the place to hell. Lucky nobody got killed. I aim to be ready."

"We got you covered, Billy. They know better than to come here."

Billy Bauer shrugged and said, "All the same."

They walked out through the kitchen toward the front door. The two men shook hands again and Connelly waved on his way out. A tall, lean, young man was entering. Kenny Haywood in a camo cap and a long sleeved, black T-shirt with two old fashioned Colt peacemakers emblazoned on the front. The shirt read "Texas — We don't call 911."

Connelly walked back to his patrol car and drove around to visit the Western Wear and Tack shop, then the washateria and several other businesses within a block of Main Street. He made two stops at the Veterans' Hall to put up money that morning. Connelly didn't like carrying large amounts of cash on him. He was a methodical man by nature, bold when he had to be, but preferring to plan and rehearse his moves mentally. He was not reflective, but not outgoing, either. Connelly, like the men who had preceded him in this country, focused on the practical matter at hand. For Connelly, life was a series of problems to be eyed, studied, and defeated, as nature itself had been for the stern people who had conquered this land.

*

"Your tie's too short, honey."

Natalie looked her husband up and down. Khaki pants. Boots. Leather belt. Silver buckle. Blue shirt. Blue tie. Dark gray, yoked jacket.

She looked at herself in the mirror, adjusted a bang, then said, "I'll help you."

Connelly shrugged and undid the knot to start over for the third time. He eyed himself in the mirror and began. Natalie was smiling, standing behind him. She put her arms around her husband.

"Don't, baby, you're messin with my aim here."

As he fumbled with the alien knot, Natalie laughed and said, "Make the one on the right a little longer, honey."

Connelly shook his head, disconcerted by the ritual. What difference did it make if his tie was a couple of inches longer or shorter either way? It was a mystery his Natalie had the answer to. It was like that with her.

Once his tie passed his wife's inspection, Connelly went outside to start the car, then walked back to the screen door to yell, "Let's go!" one more time. Natalie emerged in her blue dress, looking, as he saw her at that moment and always would, like an angel who for some unknown reason had taken a shine to him. Love was a mystery. It had taken Connelly by surprise when Natalie had seemed to choose him, an unlikely beneficiary of her seemingly unconditional affection for her husband, who could not conceive of himself as lovable in any way. There seemed to be no deserving to love and no explanation for it. He tried to remember the circumstances of his first marriage to Connie and couldn't, as if Natalie's appearance had erased some portion of his past.

He opened the car door for her and she kissed him on the cheek.

Connelly walked to the screen door and yelled again. The boys, looking constricted in their dress clothes, hurried out the front door to the car, a ten-year-old SUV. Will and Jim favored their father. Will, the older of the two at age ten, was fair-haired and blue-eyed. Jim was eight, his facial features reminiscent of his father, but with dark hair and brown eyes like his mother. Connelly locked up and walked to the SUV. The family pulled away in silence and good order, Natalie faintly smiling.

*

Connelly parked on the grass, his SUV surrounded mostly by pickups, many of them tricked out in the flashy manner of the cousins, the owners announcing their status and personal style as much as a middle class Anglo suburbanite might with a subdued, but expensive, sedan. A lowrider version of a Chevy Impala from the 70's was parked next to Connelly's SUV, a matted black bullet with electric looking curb feelers in a sea of bright colors, matched oddly with Connelly's vehicle, which was showing its age. Nearer to St. Jerome's parish were the less garish autos of the leading cousins, including the *jefe*'s silver-gray Mercedes. Older men in ill-fitting dark suits lingered outside, while younger ones in black or in colorful yoked shirts with garish belt buckles and boots with exaggerated pointed tips escorted their wives and girlfriends in their best clothes, fit for the occasion, the *quinceañera* of Jimena Rodriguez, the daughter of one of the *jefe*'s cousins, a celebration of her fifteenth birthday.

The *Quinceañera* wore a white sequined dress for the ceremony. She was crowned with a tiara. This princess of ceremony, a princess truly of God, was accompanied by her parents, beaming as the crowd gathered there and the celebration began. Her godparents, the *jefe* and his wife Karin, as well as a court of seven couples, the *damas* and *chambelanes,* followed. The godparents presented the *Quinceañera* with a pendant depicting the Virgin of Guadalupe.

A celebratory Mass followed. Connelly and his family filed out with the rest to receive Holy Communion, a ceremony Connelly understood as sacramental in this church, which was nominally his as well, though the concept of transubstantiation eluded him, striking his utilitarian and functionally materialist mind as so much magic talk. Yet he did not question its validity, nor the necessity of the infant baptism of his sons, or any other rituals that were far removed from his pragmatic mind and spotty Protestant upbringing. The Crucified Christ of the Catholics, and the crucifix itself, was alien to the foggy memories of his occasional church attendance as a boy, when worshippers gathered in an old wooden church with an empty cross, absent unfathomable ceremonies and elaborate rites, the informality culminating in the altar call. It was all hymns of praise and being born again, salvation via an immediate lightning bolt on a personal road to Damascus, a sudden arrival rather than a lengthy journey.

People Connelly's father derisively described as "Bible thumpers" would come to the door sometimes.

And one day, the boy Connelly had answered their knock.

94

A smiling man and a stern-looking woman asked him if he knew Jesus, confusing the boy a bit. "Know him? You mean believe in Jesus? Yessir. Yes, mam," answered boy Connelly. The man squinted. His brow was furrowed.

"No, boy," he said. "Do you *know* Jesus? Do you have a *personal* relationship with Jesus?"

Boy Connelly searched for an answer he thought might appease them. "Well," he said, "I was baptized. My momma made sure of that. Total immersion."

The answer was not good enough. The man looked a bit flustered. "No, son, he said, do you *walk* with the Lord?"

A perplexed boy Connelly replied that he hadn't laid eyes on him lately, to tell you the truth, sir. "Now son," the man said, "take not the state of your soul lightly nor mock the evangelist."

"Sir," replied boy Connelly, "I don't mock nobody."

That seemed to please him. "Good," he said, nodding his head affirmatively, "then pray with me, boy." And they held hands and prayed right then and there on the front porch, boy Connelly cutting his eyes back and forth. Was anybody watching this? Did anybody see him out here holding hands with two strangers? They finished praying. The stern woman's demeanor changed instantly. She smiled broadly and gave him a pocket-sized New Testament with a red cover and binding. Inside, it had a line for his name and the date when he had come to the Lord, accepting Him as his own personal savior.

*

Following Mass, the sizable crowd filed into the parish hall, spilling out onto the grounds outside. With guests seated or standing pressed against the walls, the *Quinceañera* made her entrance, trailed by her court, the girls in orange-red dresses, the boys in black suits with flaming orange shirts and black ties and vests, the white dress of the *Quinceañera* backgrounding a blaze of color framed against the formal black of the suits, the colors of hope and chastity and vigor and death, a pallet of life that captured the eye and instructed the soul as all such ceremonies are intended.

Rodriguez made the first toast to the *Quinceañera*, followed by her father. Glasses were hastily filled and re-filled and the glasses rose and heads turned up to drink. A band assembled at the far end of the hall and began to play. The *Quinceañera* danced the first dance with her father. Then the *damas* and *chambelanes* joined in. There was clapping and much encouragement from the crowd. The boys were awkward in their attempts at formal dancing, but all beamed as they circled the dance floor of the parish hall, moving jerkily at first, then gaining confidence, assuming correct posture and proper balance.

The crowd cheered as the dance was completed, then grew silent in anticipation. The *Quinceañera* sat down near the band as her father approached. She lifted her long skirt, revealing flat shoes. Her father carried new shoes to her, shoes with heels that would mark another stage in her passage to adulthood and eventually a suitable marriage, her status rising with the elevated stature the shoes symbolically brought to her. He removed her old shoes and placed the new shoes on her feet with a very solemn air. She rose and the crowd cheered once again, her parents gazing at her as if they had seen a vision.

*

Connelly danced with Natalie, the boys watching curiously from a table in a far corner of the hall. They had never seen their parents dance before. The entire celebration struck their unworldly minds as far removed from any life they had known or could know. They observed relatives from their mother's side dancing, arrayed in clothing that seemed to distance them from the boys, who saw their relations with fresh, bewildered eyes in a new setting, as if they had observed a neighbor transformed into an alien life form, exhibiting suitably alien behaviors normally unseen in the boys' Main Street and Northeast-side world. Their common meeting ground was at school, where those same relatives seemed strangely to assume other, less alien forms, changelings who modified their appearance, speech, and clothing in keeping with mysterious transitions comprehensible only to those who held esoteric knowledge of hidden identities.

Will and Jim sat stock still when an older man staggered by, his bolo tie loose on a white shirt stained by some libation, his red eyes assessing them, his lips emitting a stream of Spanish neither could fully understand. He balanced himself with both hands on the table, squinted at them, taking in the blank looks, then shrugged and went on his way, grasping a chain of chair backs to steady his progress through the obstacle course of the parish hall.

*

Watch the *jefe*. See him operate, manipulate, dispense justice, offer advice, or counsel caution while receiving petitioners one at a time, each slyly eyeing the head table, waiting for an opening before sliding into a chair near the *jefe*. He greeted each of the suppliants warmly, as a man of his station should, then cocked his head at a certain angle denoting his superior position in the pecking order of the cousins, all the same whether they asked for a favor or for forgiveness or for something only hinted at that would be concretized at some later juncture. The *jefe*'s countenance displayed his wisdom, his power to forgive or condemn. He reached into his pocket at one point and passed something discreetly under the tablecloth to one petitioner, who gazed at that object as if he had been passed Solomon's seal, then gently placed it into his coat pocket, waiting a decent interval before easing out of the chair and leaving the hall, now protected, his health assured.

The band was taking a break, the crowd beginning to thin out. And still the *jefe* accepted the petitioners, though he was growing weary, for by making such visitations, the pilgrims affirmed him and renewed his powers.

Connelly approached and stood at the table next to the *jefe*, who was sucking on an unlit cigar and looking grand, enjoying the celebration, bathing in the glow of his exalted status. The *jefe*, seeing Connelly, waved off another petitioner, knowing that this man would likely not retaliate for what others would view as an insult. He motioned to Connelly with his cigar and a subtle nod. He got up from the table and Connelly followed him into an office next to the bandstand. The *jefe* pointed to a folding chair and Connelly moved it to sit in front of an old oak desk. The *jefe* closed the door, then slid into an office chair behind the much-needed barrier of the desk, much needed for he and his guest to conduct business in dignity, for what dignity does a man have sitting open and unguarded before another when discussing serious matters? It was a sign of respect calculated by the *jefe* as he calculated all things, being the man that he was.

Connelly turned to glance through a window that looked on the hall. He got up and closed the blinds. He eyed the arrangement and figured that was enough for discretion's sake. Connelly turned and sat down once more.

"So, Swordfish, what do you think, huh? Some celebration, done in the old style, none of the cousins looking like homeboys in some L.A. barrio, right?"

Connelly just nodded.

"Swordfish, you should talk more, you make a man feel lonely. Come on, give it to me in the Texan style, direct, no bullshit. Hell, I'm half a homie to you and the soldiers, too, right?"

"I came to tell you what we'll do."

"Good, good, fuck'n a, we're practically relatives. You and me, we both married up."

The *jefe* was in full Manny Rodriguez campaign mode. He leaned back in the office chair, quite relaxed.

"Me, I'm a lighter skinned *mestizo*, taller than average and sure as hell no *indio*, but my Karin is at least a *castiza,* tall, no flat face or bow legs for my woman, no?"

Rodriguez waved his cigar. "Look, a lot of these motherfuckers would be really happy to get a girl just a shade or two removed from the gorgeous blonde babes they put on those stupid ass Mexican soap operas, right? And they see a guy like you, forgive me for saying so, a redneck, a smart one, a good one, get a girl with some high-class Castilian blood in her, maybe, and your boys, hell, they're white. The envy of all the cousins, what do you think?"

The *jefe* paused. Connelly stared at him, impassive.

"I didn't piss you off, did I, Swordfish? Just kidding around a little, giving you a little Mexican anthropology lesson…You don't have a gun on you, do you?"

Rodriguez sucked on his cigar, eyeing Connelly.

"You see, everything's about shades with the cousins. Very little is straightforward, except a deliberate insult. Everything's so clear to us Americans, right? There's Mexicans and whites and blacks and everything is much more…how to put it? Settled. You don't have to be as sensitive to those grades and scales. Gets frustrating, believe me."

He lifted his hands. What can you do? Life is like that.

"We'll take your deal, Sheriff…"

Rodriguez was holding the cigar, waving it around for effect while he talked. The *jefe* talked with his face and hands.

"Manny, soldier, call me Manny, we been friends for too long. And relatives."

"But we don't want the money."

Rodriguez looked disappointed. Just a little.

"Well, Swordfish, really, that would be a real insult among the cousins, not taking our friendship offering, a little something to build trust."

"We'll take care of the Gunslingers. Manny."

"We could do this together, Swordfish."

"No go. We handle it. They cook their crystal meth here, but they'll have to move the distribution somewhere else. And there's a truce with the cousins. That's what we can pitch to them."

Rodriguez eyed his cigar, then took out a lighter and lit up.

"You talk to Will and Sammy about this?" Puff. "No, let me guess, the Chaplain, he talks to them." Puff. "You know, Swordfish, I might be a little suspicious." Puff. "I mean about you all not going full bore against the bikers." Puff. "Like you might want them to hang around just a little bit in case you want to..."

"Want to what?"

"Oh, I dunnow...have some extra backup if you, heaven forbid, by some accident or misunderstanding, get tangled up with my cousins here." Puff.

"So, what do you want, Manny?"

Rodriguez was looking for something. He spotted an old Dr. Pepper can on a shelf behind the desk. He picked it up, shook it, closed one eye as he looked inside it, then set it down and placed the cigar carefully on top of the can.

"*Amigo*, we want something to bind the agreement. And you might want the consideration to buy off Will and Sammy. Avoid trouble altogether. I don't think my cousins will understand otherwise."

Rodriguez picked up the cigar, took a puff, and put it back on the Dr. Pepper can very carefully, as if he were handling a priceless object of art.

"I want you to do the pickup, Swordfish. I mean, I trust you. And the little bit you get already, that's just to keep everybody safe. We are in-laws, but a little sharing makes you seem alright to the cousins, keeps you and yours safe. You see, my cousins... some of them... don't trust Anglos and they know about the little consideration for you and it makes our relationship seem more aboveboard, you know what I mean?"

"I never wanted your damn money."

"I know, I know, that was for Natalie. And Karin."

Rodriguez looked very sincere, touching his hands to his chest before waving off the argument.

"And me, too, Swordfish. I mean, *amigo*, they see us meeting sometimes outside the station and if you did not get some small consideration at least, they would be thinking there was something fishy about our relationship. Hey, everybody wants to be the king, no? It's not easy keeping the cousins in line, I mean some of them really hate you Anglos. I mean their fathers were lawn boys or something, or did shit jobs for some of the landowners, I mean literally, like cleaning out stables. And their mothers? Cleaning women. And they resent that, never mind it was a strict business proposition and everybody did alright. By their lights, I mean."

Connelly got up to leave. His hand on the door knob, he said, "I'll get back to you."

Manny Rodriguez was all smiles.

"Sure, sure, *amigo*. We'll work it out. Just tell the Chaplain to go see Will and Sammy and we'll start there."

Connelly started to open the door.

"Just one thing, *amigo*."

Connelly closed the door and faced Rodriguez.

"What might that be, Manny?"

"The bikers will want something, man. You'll need the money. And I believe some of you are thinking you might need the bikers sometime. Against the cousins, I mean. That's not a healthy way of thinking about this arrangement. Tell the soldiers I know what they are thinking."

Connelly turned again and reached for the door.

"You know, *amigo,* just what the fuck have you done with the money I've given you? You sure as hell didn't buy a new car. But, what can you say, at least your car doesn't look like one of those fucked up lowrider things my cousins like."

Connelly turned and walked over to the desk.

Rodriguez sat back, eyeing him cautiously.

The soldier reached over and took the cigar from the Dr. Pepper can and dropped it on the floor and ground it with his boot heel.

He turned and opened the door and Manny Rodriguez said, "Just curious, *amigo*."

And Connelly walked out, leaving the door standing open.

*

Rodriguez got home late that night. Karin and the children, Emilio and Juanita, had left the celebration before him as he had business to attend to and Karin always left him to his business. He walked back to his drawing room and opened a safe and set some packets of bills on the desk. He counted and sorted the cash, then placed it in an envelope before putting it back in the safe.

Rodriguez was about to close the safe when he paused, reached in and pulled a package out, then dumped out the contents on the desk. He sorted through the material, transcripts and photographs, until he found the pictures he was looking for. He spread them out on the desk and smiled. He liked being certain about some things in his life.

*

I was in a Humvee that ran over an IED. That's "Improvised Explosive Device" to you folks back in the real world. Funny, I called my ex-wife that, too... Anyway, I got tossed forty feet in the air. It was kinda like bein shot out of a cannon in the circus, only I didn't have a fire suit on like the Human Cannonball used to wear. Yeah, before my time, too.

I was burned over one third of my body, or at least one third of what was there at the time. So, you could say it was one third of my former body. Hey, losing an arm and bein in and out of the hospital for months, I can tell you, that's one effective weight loss program. Better than weight watchers, really. No kiddin.

I guess you had to be there.

My face is messed up on one side, but I try to think of it as a source of one-liners to pick up women. Yeah, that's one tough way to get material, tell me about it. Say I'm in a bar and spot a nice lookin woman kinda starin at me. No lines yet, I just let her stare. I take a sip of a drink, set it down on the bar, and say, deadpan like, "My meth lab blew up." Then they kinda look at you like, "what the hell?" But then you smile and they smile and it works, really.

Say I take her out on a dinner date. The waiter says, "How do like your steak?" to her and I say, "Well done. Like her man friends."

I guess you had to be there.

OK, the truth is maybe she was no prize, either. I'm here to tell ya.

I'm not bitter. No, not bitter at all. I went to fight a war to prevent a mad dictator from using weapons of mass destruction that didn't exist. I killed people who hadn't done me or my country any harm. We went to fight terrorists who didn't show up until after we got there. I saw my friends maimed and killed and found out that the most dangerous weapon of mass destruction was what passed for Dubya's brain. Go ahead, boo, dumbass. Yeah, I'm talkin to you. You think a one-armed man can't fight? Ain't you ever seen The Fugitive? *Yeah, before my time, too.*

Think a minute. Any of you from a small town? Yeah, several out there. There's not much left, is there? I mean, of your hometown. You know what I mean. Think about it. You used to go into the Tastee Freeze or Dairy Queen and see those rows of pictures on the wall. Our heroes. But that town, that Big Dime Box or Little Dime Box or Zephyr or White Oak, that town desperately needed those young people, didn't it? It needed them to do something that takes a kind of everyday courage we don't do enough to celebrate. What ya got to say, boy? Tell me. Nothin. You got nothin. And we are gonna have that. Nothin.

So, I'm not bitter. I just tell people my mother was a fire eater in a circus. Not funny?

You had to be there.

*

"You call that funny, Houston?"

"It's not meant to be falling down funny, Man Killer. It's social commentary wrapped up in some jokes. Bittersweet and all that."

"Sure."

"You never did have elevated tastes."

"And nobody ever knew what the hell you were talkin about."

"To be expected."

Connelly just nodded and grunted.

"I figure some things don't change, right? How did you know I was in Dallas?"

"Paper. It said 'tragedy turned into biting comic commentary' or some such shit. The headline was YOU HAD TO BE THERE."

Connelly made a sweeping motion with his right hand, spanning the banner headline in the air before him.

102

"Well."

"Houston, I believe that's the first time I've ever seen you stumped. Nothin to say."

Pause a few beats.

"I didn't know you had an ex."

"You don't know a lotta things, Man Killer. I just didn't bitch about her. Then. What about yours?"

"I married again."

"Lordy, I never would have figured that."

"It's different this time."

Houston looked surprised. He arched his one — his right — eyebrow.

"Oh. Different this time. Kids?"

"Two boys."

"My God, what came over that woman?"

"Got me. She's too good. Too good for me, I guess."

More surprise from Houston.

"Swordfish. Man Killer. He's talkin reflective like. I didn't know he had it in him."

"Neither did I."

Connelly reached for the beer he hadn't drunk from yet. He took a long swallow, as if he were washing something away.

"How you doin here?"

"I make it. Barely."

"Think about a move?"

Houston arched his eyebrow again.

"And leave the adoring crowds?"

"It's not so far. You can still elevate everbody here and there."

Houston scratched his chin, then took a long pull on his beer.

"What ya got, Swordfish?"

"What I got… What we got, is a little operation that it might be better for somebody outside to manage."

Connelly took another sip of his beer.

"Outside of us. But still one of us."

"I will be damned. Swordfish talkin in riddles. Very puzzling."

"Do you know what the hell is going on in this country? In this state? Do you know?"

Houston leaned forward on his good arm, his brow furrowed.

"Swordfish, what are you tellin me? Yeah, I know what's goin on. What are you into? And why me, whatever that is? What are you up to and who is in it with you?"

Connelly nodded. And he told him.

*

Houston looked out the screen door. It was a clear morning, just now breaking cool. He walked into the kitchen and filled his coffee cup, then went back into the bedroom, where he pulled on a denim jacket, then, straining with one arm, his boots. He walked into the hall, passing a mirror. Houston paused and looked at his face in reflection.

He's half there. The other half, well, it was hard to say. Underneath, he's both the same and changed. The left eyelid sags as if he were about to fall off to sleep. He keeps his hair cut close, as many of the soldiers do, but he does so because the scarred left side of his skull will no longer produce hair. The scalp is burned away. A long, wide, drooping scar cascades from his left eye to his chin like a pale waterfall against the rough and scaly rock formation of the left side of his face. He looks vaguely like some mythic creature, half humanoid and half reptilian, appearing dangerous, as if he is privy to gnostic secrets held in the pale, white fires of the heart.

Houston walked into the kitchen and set the coffee cup down, then reached back into the waistband of his jeans for the Glock. Loaded. Ready. He put it back in place and drank the rest of the coffee.

Houston had been making the pickups throughout the spring and summer and now into the fall. He accounted for the amounts picked up, making deposits in the private office of the president of the Parmer City Bank. For a time, he stayed away from the soldiers. But the cousins knew he was there. He made the drops to the bikers.

He was seen around town. Noticed. But nobody talked about him. Not in public, anyway. He was a soldier, it is plain, brought in for some special plan. But he did not visit the post and he left Parmer several times a week for trips. To Dallas. Fort Worth. Austin. Houston. Oklahoma City. He lived at the old Caldwell place. Nobody knew how that was arranged and nobody asked. They did know that the cousins and the bikers now stayed away from old town. There had been no confrontations on the East side. The historic center of the county seat belonged to the soldiers and to the townspeople and that is all that mattered. Few cared to be initiated into the secret compacts that have secured this arrangement.

But stories about the strange, scarred man were whispered and, in some cases, discussed loudly in private homes. They said the disfigured soldier was wounded on a classified mission in a faraway location. A specialist in such matters, he targeted the Forces of Terror and was terribly wounded after assassinating the secret leader of a terrorist cell. Another story says that he was a deep cover agent for the DEA and was captured and tortured by the drug cartels in Juarez... or was it some other city? And that he had escaped, killing a cartel agent on the American side. Still another says he was involved in an FBI raid on a terrorist mosque in Houston, but the Moslems made such a stink about it that he was shipped away to cover it up. And the scars? Didn't you hear about that mosque burning down in Houston last year? They covered up that it was a raid. And that's why you heard somebody call him "Houston" ...

*

Houston walked out onto the porch. Cottontail rabbits headed for the brush near a barbed wire fence. A big roadrunner raced along the fence line, a lizard dangling from its formidable beak, a predator equipped with dazzling speed, swooping along the dusty surface, an earthbound raptor. In the skies above him, the red-tailed hawks were his counterparts, the turkey buzzards their foul cousins following behind the procession of death like paid mourners, consuming their clients as they went.

Houston climbed into his pickup and circled the house before heading over the cattleguard and out the front gate. He glanced at the white, wooden structure in his rearview mirror.

Houston was silent and reverent in the house. It seemed like a monument to him, a marker of the past in a world with few reference points. The house was not his, but something he had in his possession for safekeeping, as guardian and trustee.

*

Houston told them that he lived in a haunted house. Silence. No kidding. He paced the stage and looked off into the dark recesses of the club. *I live with the ghosts of your grandparents. Okay, not yours, Haji.* Laughter. *Just kidding. Oh, you are from Denton. Picture that, folks, Yusef here and his brethren on the ground in Denton, Texas, of all places, pointed toward Mecca. No offense, really. It just seems odd, is*

105

all. Seems odd to you, too? Yeah? Picture in your mind, say, a Norman Rockwell... OK, look it up on the Internet... Does anybody know who Norman Rockwell was? Yusef knows? Great, so picture Yusef in a barber chair getting a shave in a Norman Rockwell painting... Oops! Sorry, Yusef, yeah, the beard... That's about as big a screw up as serving up pork chops at the Dearborn High cafeteria. Dearborn? In Michigan... Unbelievable. Yusef knew that, though.

Yeah, it's no odder than my face. How'd I get it? My mother was a fire eater in a circus... Hang on, somebody's got to ask what a fire eater in a circus is. Yeah, it happens half the time. No, really, and she thinks she has the right now to bitch to me about acid reflux. Nobody but this guy is laughing.... I guess you had to be there.

11

The Chaplain's story... The patrol... The Easter service... A terrible and wonderful sign (the Chaplain as exorcist)

*

A land of darkness, as darkness itself; and of the shadow of death without any order, and where the light is as the darkness.

*

A decade of war and more than war, the descent of winged death and darkness a shadow on the land. Children grown who have known nothing else but that war and that shadow. I sit in the ashes and wait for the light, patiently, but not without frustration, not without doubt.

I follow the men out on patrol. I am their Chaplain. They cannot think that my life is worth more than theirs. Or think that I think that. I've seen them before, in other patrol camps, in other valleys and amid the fields of wheat and poppy.

I see them and think of the Sabeans that fell upon the children and the servants of the upright man. And I only am escaped to tell thee. I cannot rend my garments, and only can fall upon the ground to worship amid the ashes.

The Lord gave and the Lord hath taken away; blessed be the name of the Lord.

Survey the landscape and the carnage. And you see that the kings and counsellors of the earth have truly built desolate places for themselves. As far as these eyes can see is that desolation. But they cannot see the desolation of the spirit.

I am the minister to that desolation.

I strap on body armor and cinch the strap of my helmet on a cloudy day in that land and I take the Bible and place it in my backpack as I have on many other days. Blessed be the name of the Lord.

Fifteen Marines gather themselves and their gear for the patrol, rifles, machine guns, and mortars, and they glance skyward to see that the clouds have this day covered the white-hot sun. And I tell them that it is their chaplain who has called in the cloud cover for the patrol. It's a special prayer I use. Such is the service I render. And they laugh and one of them pats me on the shoulder. He smiles and I know that he is not a believer, yet he comes to me to speak of the desolation on days after other patrols. And will again.

We file out of Patrol Base Roberts. Roberts was Lance Corporal James Roberts, who was killed on a patrol some weeks back. Only weeks, but like months and years, as if the base has always borne his name. Patrol Base Roberts. As if named for some hero of antiquity. And he is the hero of our antiquity of days and weeks. For we are young and old at the same time. Men of the present antiquity.

And Roberts remains forever young.

The young men lack the tragic sense. But they will learn, though they have no name for it. Part of my job is to give it a name. And to point to hope, which also seems an alien concept to some of them. I give it a name.

We file out over open fields and leap over irrigation canals in this dry and thirsty land. Men with mine detectors sweep the path, scanning the ground for explosives buried in the dirt. I walk, hands at my side, a picture of serenity, or so it seems in this land of shadows.

I think of my task and of my place. Rendering unto Caesar what is his. And unto God what is God's.

These very young men wonder why the Holy Joe doesn't carry a weapon. They assign one of the men to stay close to me for a time, until a Religious Programs Spc. second class, an innocent looking, boyish man named Rich, arrives and bodyguard duty falls to him.

Amid mud walls, the patrol surveys the scene ahead. The men gather behind one of those mud walls and tell stories of miraculous near misses. A man who stepped on an explosive that did not go off. Another shot in the head, the bullet glancing off, just grazing him. Off in the distance, we watch a truck creep down a potholed road. One week ago, another truck had been blown in half on that same road. All eyes are on that truck and we watch and calculate unspoken odds. There is no wind and the sound of the truck carries and we watch.

I know what they are thinking. Is it chance, fate, or something else? I'm here to give that something a name. But I make it clear I do not have answers for all questions. Think of me as an instrument.

I am an instrument for over a thousand like them, spread over outposts and patrol bases. And I walk with them on patrol. They know that another chaplain like me was killed just a year ago. They know I have come here to accept the same risks and burdens. Their risks and burdens. And I sometimes ask the same questions. I'm a man like them, but with a different mission, yet, just the same, a mission, an objective. Objectives, they understand.

I know what it's like out on patrol and that is important. To them. To me. But they need to be reminded that there are people in the world whose objective is not killing. That is easy to forget out here.

They will come to me after patrols. After a friend is killed. After they see something wrenching and terrible. There is no point in trying to make sense of all this. The suffering. The death. The violence. And they will put God on trial, but it is not my job to act as defense counsel for God in a trial that can render no verdict. Part of human experience is suffering. God does not will each explosion, each bullet, each maiming, or every miraculous near miss. I can acknowledge that all questions are ones I have had. They are legitimate. And the mystery of no clear answer, that is legitimate as well. It's no use preaching on men having a will of their own and that being the price of not being automatons.

So I walk as serenely as I can, hands at my side. I've told them that they do not walk alone, so I must conduct myself as though I am certain that I do not walk alone. But certainty is a rare thing. They look at me, puzzled, and I tell them that doubt is a part of faith, for what is faith but believing in things they cannot see or fully explain.

There are plenty of head case specialists they can talk to, but they prefer to talk to me. I am outside the chain of command. Our talks are between us alone. Nobody wants to be seen as a head case.

Talking isn't easy for them. It wasn't always easy for me.

I travel by helicopter or in convoy to outposts in barren lands, outposts with earthen walls and wire and I carry my equipment with me. A stainless steel cross. A chalice. And a bowl. I conduct services and walk on patrol and talk to troubled young men.

At Easter, I drag a ping pong table to the center of a small enclosure at a base camp and mix powdered grape juice, find some crackers and prepare for the service. The light streams through a cloud and through the netting and shines on the altar and I open the book and read the story of the resurrection of Jesus. I ask for prayer requests and we pray for wounded comrades. One man lost both legs. So we pray.

And I remember.

In a medical center at a certain camp they brought in a wounded enemy. He was a young man, as young looking as Rich, but his eyes were reddened and he seemed impassive. I looked at him and his eyes closed, and I placed my hand on his forehead and he died. And I had in that moment felt no compassion for him.

So, at the end of the service on this bright Easter morning, I say a prayer for our enemies. And for ourselves, that we not lose something spiritual, creating a wound more grave than physical wounds ever could be. I think they understand. God, make them understand.

I do a stint at the base camp medical center. I carry a pager. The pager beeps and it says a quad amputee is in the trauma bay. Hurry. I turn and head for the trauma bay and the pager goes off again. Update. Patient died.

An attack helicopter roars overhead.

The pager again.

Gunshot wound to the head.

The trauma bay. A 19-year-old, blood gushing from a head wound. The bullet has passed through his head, one side to the other. They scramble around him and the doctor says he needs more suction. They cram a plastic tube into the boy's mouth and the blood is sucked out, blood from his mouth, from his throat. The heartbeat fades and the doctor begins chest compressions. "I have a pulse," says a nurse. But the brain is swelling, pressing the brain stem and he will stop breathing and his heart will stop again. There is no way to prevent it. No way. The monitor will record the fading life before us as it passes from his body. The doctor pronounces the time of death.

When the doctor is done, I press forward.

"Into your hands, oh Lord, we commend your servant. Receive him by your mercy into the blessed rest of everlasting peace. Of everlasting life. We commend him into God's hands."

I raise my hand in a slow, final salute and turn and walk away. All is silent. All is peaceful.

I sit in the ashes.

*

The Marine leaned back on his weighty backpack, in a field of stone that could be a graveyard or the ruins of an ancient civilization. An obelisk to his right. A pile of stones that could have been the base of a pyramid to his left And ahead? Upright markers like gravestones, their inscriptions long ago eroded and vanished. Mountains ranging around him, he held his rifle in his right hand and pointed with his gloved left hand, eyes invisible behind dark goggles. He looked like an undersea explorer in a fanciful nineteenth century novel. Captain Nemo on the ocean floor.

Silence. The silence of remoteness and high elevations and miles without seeing anyone.

The patrol lasted thirteen hours.

Religious Programs Spc. secondclass Rich lay next to the Chaplain in the field of stone, the silence having been broken by the sound of vehicles in the distance and then only by a barely discernible hum, that hum of spinning planets in the emptiness that turns to a wisp of whistling wind and is gone.

They left the base camp in the dark. The camp perimeter was a postage stamp in the vastness of forbidden ground they have violated, surrounded by sandbags and earthen barriers, a lonely, bare, and unprepossessing Fort Apache deep in Indian country.

The base camp was supplied by helicopter and the occasional convoy, one of which brought the Chaplain back to Patrol Base Roberts. The war has dragged on after the terrorist mastermind has long been dead, hidden, ironically enough, in the heart of the erstwhile ally's military-intelligence-betrayal complex, a seamy web of dubious relations and amoral acts the intrusive guests have grown used to, stubborn in their ignorance, resistant to absurdity, and oblivious to obvious questions.

Like, why are we still here?

The Chaplain, however, *had* noticed, being of inquisitive spirit, armed with a turn of mind that has become subversive. He has tested some answers he shares only with himself, such an inquisition being against regulations, corrosive of the hidden barriers that block unhelpful thoughts, clouding judgment, making waves that nobody among the Washington-connected crowd of pod people in Kabul wished be examined by intellect or un-screened media.

We came in retaliation. Reasonable and just. We remained to spread democracy, which means empowering Afghan women and giving them driving licenses. No one has asked the further, obvious, questions. Like, do these people care? Where will the Afghan women drive to? And the most subversive question of all, *what business is it of ours?*

But there is a two-headed answer that covers all questions requiring explanation. One head is that the pod people imagine themselves as gods. They dispense justice from Olympian heights, deciding life and death and how to spin it all and keep this bankrupt machine running. Tug the bow tie and smile. And the second explanatory head is that this is great fun. Truly, it is. The intrigues of the military-intelligence-betrayal complex. Exotic trips amid exotics. Avoidance of exes and mundane responsibilities. The myriad possibilities for ironic observation. *Now do you understand?*

These thoughts weighed on the soul of our Chaplain. He considered the withering hometowns of the Roberts and the Richs, families unmade in dying map dots, places not unlike the one he came from, and he wondered.

The Chaplain wondered even during the patrol's thirteen hours of boredom and terror, his mind wandering and suddenly focused and then wandering again like a lost soul separated from a desert caravan. And he understood that it was not entirely the fault of the pod people. The Chaplain leaned back on his backpack and looked over at Rich, his rifle held between his knees, Rich's unseen eyes surveying the ground ahead behind dark goggles.

In the fall, the patrol base was almost overrun. The Chaplain was there afterwards, amid the ruins, if ruins are what one could call such a place that was ruinous all along and was built ruinous. Ninety-two dead, bearded men. One dead and one irretrievably maimed from the patrol base. A visiting officer surveying the scene, talking mainly to a reporter decked out in his L.L. Bean foreign correspondent outfit.

And a good time was had by all.

The patrol left camp before dawn. Its mission was to gather intelligence, not to seek a fight. Darkness turned to deep blues and then lighter shades and the depths yielded to a translucent china blue sky. The patrol headed for an Afghan village of ancient mud to search the mud corridors, question the villagers, and find out where the enemy can be found. The Afghan allies conducted the interrogations of the men and boys of the village. The Chaplain wondered how anyone can tell what is really transpiring here, and what information is being exchanged.

Later, they encountered the enemy they sought beneath the shadow of a flat-topped mountain not far from the mud village.

Everybody down.

A convoy passed the field of stone, a convoy of flatbed trucks and pickups transporting men with Kalashnikovs, the convoy proceeding toward a dry riverbed, a wadi.

The patrol was spotted. That much became evident as the men stood up and moved again into a tree line beyond the field of stone and before the wadi. A single gunshot echoed for miles, bouncing off the surrounding hills and mountains. And so the fight began. Kalashnikovs rattling. The patrol answered with machine gun and rifle fire aimed at the wadi. The Chaplain heard the whooshing sound of an RPG, then an explosion. He kept his head down and tried to imagine himself invisible. Rich landed a few yards away, exposed on a dirt path just outside the tree line. Ahead, the Chaplain saw a few others lying in the calf-high grass, firing bursts at the wadi.

A man named Miller pulled a mortar tube from his pack and planted its base in the earth. He ran low and hunched, pulling at the backpacks of those around him until he found a high explosive round and dropped it in the tube, as Toliver called out range and distance. Miller pulled the trigger and a blast drowned out the sounds of the firefight. Another round followed. The enemy broke contact. Silence. The Chaplain never saw anyone to begin with, as if the patrol had been sparring with phantoms, crazed by a mirage in this desolate country. Then came the F-15s and a pair of Apache helicopters. But there was nobody to shoot at.

The enemy had gone.

As they scaled the high ground beyond the wadi, the radio operator groaned and looked at the Chaplain and said, "I hate my job." Then he spat a dry spit and kept walking. He wondered whether they should go back to that damned village and get after them. "They didn't tell us a fuckin thing. Nobody ever knows nothin," he said. "Fuck this place."

The Chaplain just said yeah. Not amen.

*

The men gathered in a hut at the patrol camp the night of the terrible and wonderful sign. Signs and wonders. Those are your fields, Holy Joe, so tell us what it means. Or more crudely put, what the fuck was that? You saw it as plain as us. So, tell us something.

They were eating and talking, telling lies, tales of exes yet untold, and the Chaplain, looking gravely serious, joined them. He sat on a box and lit a pipe, a strange and pleasurable device that the men present did not associate with someone of the Chaplain's age or demeanor. Few of the very young men in the hut had ever witnessed a man smoking a pipe, at least not a tobacco pipe that looked like a relic from an old movie or a rummage through a grandfather's attic. Everybody knew that old meant obsolete, decrepit, and vaguely eccentric. New was better, or at least explicable. That was instinctual to them. There was something creepy about the pipe, several of them admitted at a later juncture, reflecting on the strange event that took place that night.

The Chaplain had grown used to staying inside at the patrol camp unless some pressing business brought him out into the open, thus making him a potential target. But it was quite dark and he needed to walk, so he walked and watched with a sense of wonder and trepidation as clouds yet so black and sinister gathered in a way that made them stand out even against the inky blackness of the distant, forbidding sky above. And they whirled and tangled and gathered, and the Chaplain sensed something terrible was coming. His walking brought him to a particular creaking hut at a specific time in a peculiar place among those very young men, and he sat on the box and smoked and waited.

What would come?

A massive *crack* and then a *boom*, as if a great cannon lodged in the vault of heaven itself had exploded. A mighty, echoing, enveloping wall of deafening sound shook them all and it was but an instant, nay, even a fraction of that, and the bright thing, terrible and frightening, struck, having taken aim at them and only them. A fiery lash of burning light entered the hut through the wall of the enclosure itself. And the fiery, shimmering lash curled up in a glowing ball, a ball of fire come from some holy mountain in the sky. It was so bright their eyes were blinded by it and they turned their heads from the wondrous ball of fiery light as it gathered and concentrated itself and floated in the air among them in the center of the enclosed space of the hut. And then the ball flattened out, floating like a spirit among them as if it were they who were the intruders and not the fiery light, which was exposing them, accusing them. Marshal rose and crashed through the hut's door, and then the light dispersed as the heavy rain began.

When the mysterious light dispersed, it seemed that Evans was dead, but the Chaplain somehow revived him, beating on his chest and breathing into his mouth as Evans took a gasping breath of life. Henceforth, Rich dubbed Evans "Lazarus."

The exploding ball had struck the Chaplain on the left arm and he bore wounds on that arm where the power had passed through him and exited, leaving a scar as a sign. The ball's energy had passed through Evans' body, exiting at his right big toe, which was terribly burned at the point where his boot had exploded. He was covered by dark lines for a time, as if the energy had passed down every nerve ending in his body, transforming Evans into a strange and wondrous chart. Marco, who had sat next to the Chaplain, was burned on his forehead and his left eye was marked by its smaller pupil from then on.

The men had stood in a circle around the Chaplain and Evans, their eyes focused on him and then on the Chaplain, who rose, arm smoldering. The men asked the Chaplain what had happened, and he shook his head in bewilderment.

Henceforth, Rich dubbed the Chaplain "The Exorcist."

Was this an accusation directed against them? Or was Evans' miraculous revival significant of the Chaplain's special powers? Was God angry or was He showing favor to his Holy Joe, as displayed to those who had witnessed the miraculous thing they had all lived through? Maybe it was both.

But to get back to the question that plagued the minds of several of those less convinced of the reality of signs and wonders: *What the fuck was that?*

The Chaplain said he would ponder that question as he was transported to a medical station far from the patrol camp. And he did.

He spoke with some of the more widely educated denizens of the medical facility and one of them, a doctor, proposed ball lightning as an answer. The doctor in question, one Jankowsky, claimed that this phenomenon was a source of controversy among scientists, some of whom claimed it was an illusion, while others thought it some strange and unexplained force that could pass through walls and windows, a force that could not be duplicated in a laboratory. Jankowsky said that the glowing balls of light were frequently seen in old-world churches. Mystics associated it with miraculous events, like the burning bush.

In the meantime, Evans, a.k.a. "Lazarus," had returned home. And Rich? He told the story of patrol camp Lazarus and The Exorcist time and again. Some of the rednecks seemed to take the story seriously, while the skeptics were troublesome to Rich. They thought Lazarus was the name of a death metal band, maybe, and he explained to them that Lazarus was in the Bible, which they seemed wholly unaware of. As for The Exorcist — "…it's a movie, stupid," Rich said, many times. "You guys are culturally illiterate."

12

*Tommy Mock and the fate of Jimmy G (the Gunslingers and Parmer)...
Will and Sammy go to town... Charlie Bass delivers a pizza... The
evening news*

The big man rose from the couch and walked to the linoleum table at
the center of the kitchen. He had on jeans and heavy boots and a denim
shirt with the sleeves rolled up, revealing intricate patterns of tattoos on
both of his thick arms. One tat on his right forearm was of two Colt
Peacemakers crossed and smoking. He had long, stringy hair, blond
going gray, a square face and deep blue eyes. He opened a box on the
table and in it were two guns, one an Army .45, the other an S&W .40
caliber. There were extra magazines for both. He picked up the .45, a
favorite of his, and weighed it in his hand. Then he set it down in the
foam of the gun box and picked up the S&W. He held it in his right hand
and lifted it up quickly as if he were preparing to shoot, then he lowered
it and shoved it in his belt and pulled it out again.

The big man set the gun down and walked to the refrigerator. He took
out a can of beer, tore the tab off, and took a long drink. He picked up a
cell phone from the table and put it in his shirt pocket. A large leather
wallet was stuck in the back pocket of his jeans, held in place by a
dangling chain. He reached to shove it deeper into the pocket and walked
back to the bedroom. Jen was asleep, the butt of a joint in the ash tray on
the nightstand. The big man put on his vest and walked back into the
kitchen and picked up the S&W, then reached down into a gym bag by
the table and pulled out a leather holster he fitted on his belt. He put the
gun in the holster, picked up the extra magazine and put it in his pants
pocket. The big man tilted back the beer, drained the can, and crushed it.
He walked out of the front door of the cabin and down the steps past his
bike and over to Sammy's double wide. He tossed the can into a battered
trash bin as he walked down the steps of the porch.

The sunset was orange and red and purple and blue on the Western
horizon.

There was a patch sewn onto the front of the big man's vest that read "President." The back of the black leather vest showed two Colt Peacemakers of the classic variety, caliber .45, crossed at the barrels. Across the shoulders of the vest, framing the picture, was "Gunslingers" and beneath, "Texas."

An aluminum building, his shop, stood to the big man's left A row of cars sat out front, and the shop sported a flag pole. Two flags stirred in the light breeze, one a Lone Star state flag, the other a black POW/MIA banner. A sign on the front of the shop identified the enterprise as TYRELL BROTHERS AUTO AND MOTORCYCLE REPAIRS in tall red lettering.

Will Tyrell walked up the steps to Sammy's place and banged on the door before walking in. Sammy was slouched on a divan watching his satellite TV. It was a hunting show, mule deer in the brush country of South Texas. Sammy glanced up and over at his big brother just as the hunter took his shot. And damn if he didn't miss.

Sammy was as tall as Will, but darker and leaner. He had a chin beard and hazel eyes and was wearing a camo cap and a black Harley Davidson T-shirt with long sleeves. He looked up at Will and said, "What?"

Will picked up the remote off the coffee table and turned the sound down on the TV.

"We gotta talk, brother."

Sammy pushed himself up a bit and looked over at Will. "Whatta we gotta talk about?"

"Those damn *Pistoleros*. Ely. Two of our bikes shot up. The *jefe* pushing on us. That's what we gotta talk about, Sammy."

Sammy frowned and said, "We need to talk to the veterans about that. Maybe the old soldiers will give us some backup, then we can move... Maybe Swordfish can..."

"I don't give a shit what they say about this."

Will's voice was a husky, low hiss, as if he were a gigantic coiled rattler. Sammy took notice. That was the tone that meant Will might be hard to handle. But somebody had to. Handle him, that is. Jen sure as hell couldn't and his boy Ty could be as wild as his daddy. Being Will Tyrell's brother could be a pain in the ass. It *was* a pain in the ass.

Will paused, then the gravelly hiss continued: "This is our fight and if they wanna back us up against that fuckin *jefe*, well dammit, they can move their ass and do it. This is our town and they can get with it and help us kick those damn wetbacks back into their own shithole country. But you gotta remember somethin, brother."

Sammy looked away.

"What I gotta remember?"

Will was pointing a thick index finger at him. Will's meaty fist was otherwise balled up and a death's head ring showed, gleaming and evil in look and intent. This, also, was not a good sign, but let him holler a little and sometimes he would calm down.

Will squinted hard and emphasized every word with the thick index finger hammering the point home. "The soldiers want us out of Parmer, too. *That's* what you gotta remember."

Sammy spoke slowly, pressing on each word. "We don't deal in Parmer, Will. That's kept em off us...*after* Tommy Mock."

Let that sink in.

Now go on. "All of us wanna keep the cousins under control."

Will looked a little shaken up. Good, let him chew on that.

Will again, softer this time, his eyes cutting from one side to the other, the fist and accusing index finger lowered. "Tommy was a dumbass."

"Yeah," said Sammy, "a 16-year-old dumbass who was a relative of one of the soldiers. So, who was bein dumb that time?"

Will brushed the hair back out of his face again and kicked the coffee table. He shoved his hands into the pockets of his jeans and looked away from his brother.

"We took care of the boy's momma and got rid of Jimmy G."

Will turned back, rubbing his forehead, buying some time to think.

The Tommy Mock thing slowed him up some, throwing the heated rhythm of his anger off. The Gunslingers always took care of their hometown, right? Except for that dumb kid. Will had killed Jimmy G himself and dumped the body in the middle of town near the Veterans monument, like a ritual sacrifice. Jimmy took a load of double aught over by the shop. You could still see the damage on the aluminum walls near bay one. Had to be done. Jimmy — and that meant the club — had broken faith with Parmer, and Parmer had to know that the breach of faith had been made good.

The hiss from Will's voice was gone. Maybe that little reminder took some of the steam out of him. Sammy cocked his left eyebrow and waited. What was next? There was something else.

"The soldiers are making some kinda deal with the *jefe*."

Sammy sat up and tugged at the bill of his cap.

"Who says?"

The hands were back in Will's pockets. He tried to rebound after being hit hard by the Tommy Mock and Jimmy G thing.

Will leaned forward, eyeing his brother, and continued, "Sonny Valdez *says*. He was talking to Cam Bowden about it. Sonny was on the West side and caught wind of some kinda meetin' between Landry and the *jefe*, then the *jefe* and Connelly. Somethin's goin down."

Sammy spoke slowly and clearly to his brother: "Will, Sonny Valdez is a friend of Cole's, but he *ain't* a veteran. Sonny's drunk half the time…"

But Will didn't let him finish. Sammy knew that drill, too. He was reminding little brother which one of them was the club president.

"Drunk or not drunk, we gotta take care of business ourselves, Sammy."

Will was restless. He walked into the living room and pounded his fist on the wall.

Sammy sighed.

"Will…Look, *Mr*. President, we gotta talk to the MC about this. This is gotta be voted on by all of us."

Sammy scratched his chin and tugged on his beard.

"Have you talked to the Chaplain?"

Will crossed his arms and leaned against the wall.

Sammy arched his eyebrows. Will hadn't talked to him. He hadn't talked to anybody before he got his ass up in the air and started coming up with some halfcocked plan. So Sammy asked him again. *Keep it slow*, "Have you talked to our cousin, Will? He'd know."

"He wants to come out here and see us."

"Who wants to come out here and see us?"

"The Chaplain. Our cousin."

"Well, there ya go."

Will leaned over, hands on his knees. He looked his brother in the eye, pressing and peering.

"They're comin tonight."

There he goes again. Sammy knew he had to take the initiative back from big brother.

"Who's comin tonight? Dammit, talk some fuckin sense, Will…"

"A couple of the *Pistoleros*."

"Where are they comin to?"

"The Jaguar Club. They're comin to make a buy. Some M-4s."

Sammy was thinking fast now. *OK, you slowed him down a little. Make him explain and let him know he's moving too fast. Make him understand he can't go blowing away some Pistoleros on his own, without thinking this through. Go.*

"The Jaguar club is on their side of town, Will. If they don't cross Main, there's no sense in fuckin with em. Anyway, who told ya that? Sonny? He don't know jack, Will."

Will started for the door, reached for the door knob, then turned to Sammy. Sammy could tell he was slowed down some and that was good, but he could just as soon go off again.

"We can find out who is makin the sale, brother. We can see what they're pickin up. How many. We'll need to know what they might be packin when we go after em. At least we can do that. Dammit to hell, Sammy, we gotta do somethin besides sittin on our ass and waitin for em to come after us. We can tell the MC, talk to our cousin, see what's up. But you, Sammy Tyrell, are the club VP and the two leaders of the fuckin club need to know what the fuck is going on in our own damn town."

Sammy sighed again. He felt weary, like the teacher of a difficult and unpredictable child who no longer wanted the job. But, all the same, his brother's keeper.

Sammy stood up from the divan and said, "Alright, Will. We go take a look. But we gotta be careful. We need to go in a car they don't know and keep outta sight."

Will started to open the door and Sammy said, "One more thing."

Will turned and nodded.

"Don't wear your colors in Beaner town, OK?"

Will cut his eyes as if he could see over his shoulder and check the colors himself.

"OK."

The two tall men walked over to the shop with night falling. Silent lightning lit up the sky in the distance, leaving a glowing aftershock in their eyes.

Sammy, who believed in signs, didn't like it.

Will didn't pay it any mind.

*

Charlie Bass gunned the motor of the old Chevy, then pulled himself out of the open window to check whether the sign on top of the old clunker was lit up. The sign on top read EL RANCHO TACOS AND PIZZA: WE DELIVER!, but the light in the WE DELIVER! part was cutting out. Charlie reached up and thumped it hard with the flat of his hand. The sign lit up. Good. If he didn't hit any potholes or run over anything he might keep the damn sign lit up like it was supposed to be.

Expansion from his base in Ely had worked out so far. Since offering deliveries to the neighboring county seat, his backup driver, a Mexican boy name of Jimenez, or Jimmy when he was on the East side, had handled orders to Parmer on certain nights of the week, especially on the cousins' side of town. Drove an old Ford pickup that had a shimmy in the front end. Charlie had cautiously stayed out of Cousinville himself, but would take the extra money if he could get it. Then Jimmy didn't show up for work and the calls were coming in. Charlie didn't speak Spanish and didn't care to take a knife or a bullet from a surly cousin if somebody didn't like his looks. But times were hard, so Charlie Bass decided to take the orders — all they had to do was give a number. If the caller didn't speak English, Charlie could understand the Spanish for the numbers. He had been practicing.

Charlie thought he was gettin too old for this shit, but if he wanted to stay in business, he had to go. No choice, really. He had a hammerless .38 snub nose clipped to his belt and that would have to do the trick. Hell, the cousins were liable to have machine guns, but the pistol would have to do it.

Ray Don had up and cut out for Dallas when his first ex-wife had called and invited him to move in, so Charlie didn't have any other helpers. Charlie didn't have much faith in Ray Don and his trash ex-wife amounting to anything. No good could come of that, but there it was. Charlie's wife and her friend Nelda Baker cooked the pizza and made the tacos. He had tried barbecue, too, but it amounted to too much work.

He had managed so far, but Charlie Bass was beginning to wonder whether he had more luck than sense. And when his luck ran out, no amount of sense would do any good.

*

Charlie crossed Main in Parmer and made for an address dead center in the middle of Cousinville. The order was three extra-large meat lover's pizzas. He wasn't a block off of Main with the sun setting and clouds gathering, but in the fading light of dusk, the last brightness wearing shallow and tinny, he couldn't help but notice the immediate change. The lowrider cars, the pickups painted bright colors, the kids riding low slung bikes, looking at the white man with blank stares, some of the houses with cinder block walls around them. An old man pushing a taco cart — his competition, Charlie guessed — down the street, the paving cracking and giving way, just like the town itself. The old man had dead eyes and didn't look up when Charlie Bass passed him.

Charlie glanced in the rearview mirror at a kid on a bike. He had heard that in Mexico, they were kidnapping boys like that to work as mules for the narcos. No shit. He wondered whether that had happened in Parmer yet. Or if it had, whether anybody gave a shit any more.

Charlie felt his blood getting up, but he steeled himself and drove on. His own grandparents had once lived in one of these old houses and when he passed it, it pissed him off to see cur dogs out front and a young Mexican in baggy pants and a shirt two sizes too big drinking a beer on the steps of their front porch. The Mexican eyed the Chevy suspiciously as it sputtered by, squinting in the gathering darkness with the porch light glaring behind him. *Just drive, Charlie. Don't look. Probly got a machine gun stuck up under his shirt. You never can tell. The sumbitch probly has tattoos on his face or somethin. Maybe he thinks me sellin tacos is funny. Is the damn sign still on?*

Charlie hung a left and went past some new houses, all with the cinder block walls around them, some with barbed wire on top of the walls. The big houses were painted purple, bright green, and one was a sick pink, built by the narco bosses as the *jefe's* influence grew and the big trucks and vans started pulling through warehouses in Parmer. One of them had a video surveillance camera at the front gate. *Smile for the camera, Charlie.* He decided not to flip the camera off.

Charlie Bass noted that weather was coming on, streaks of lightning tearing through black, dense clouds that were closing in on Parmer.

He took a right turn onto a street of boarded up brick buildings, some of them covered in graffiti. One of the buildings wasn't boarded up. It was a store that sold Mexican movies and CDs. Charlie eyed a Spanish-language billboard advertising Budweiser beer on the wall of the movie store. The billboard sported a picture of a light skinned, half-dressed girl holding a Bud, eyeing you with a little pout like all it took was a cold *cerveza*. In your dreams, cousins.

A building to Charlie's left was decorated by a mural painting of a Mexican holy man hero, emanating an aura signifying his blessed state, gold teeth shining from a toothy grin (there had to be some gold in there). The sumbitch was making gang signs with his hands, as if he were mocking Charlie Bass. Some punk motherfucker rode by on a kid's low-slung bike. He sneered at Charlie Bass and said something in Spanish.

And that's when Charlie Bass ran out of luck and sense.

*

At the same moment Charlie Bass was looking at the punk on the bike, Will and Sammy Tyrell got in a black GMC pickup truck and headed into Parmer. Sammy had armed himself with a Walther 9MM pistol. They would take Main, then cut down side streets to approach the Jaguar club from behind. Sammy began to wonder whether the *Pistoleros* would show with the weather coming on.

*

You ask me, "Charlie, what in the hell were you thinkin'?" Well, how long you lived around here? Most a your life. And in most a your life, was there a pack of wets shippin dope from your town? No. Was there purple and green and pink houses with big fences around here? I didn't think so. And did ya feel like a man had to wear a gun just to deliver a damn pizza? You wouldn't have. Neither would I. And Ely ain't no better off. I had enough. Enough. You know the Pistoleros *shot up Ely not long ago. You know that. Ain't nobody else did that. And the law ain't gonna do shit. Cousins. Hell, what's the difference?* Pistoleros. Aztecs. *They're all cousins. Don't go blank on me. You all know better'n me. Hell, there's heads stuck on poles showin up in Dallas. In Dallas, dammit! You think Americans did that?*

This punk looked over at me. Said somethin in Mex and sneered, like he owned the damn place. Well, he don't own it. He owns a broke leg, what I hear. And that ain't all of it. I don't know what'd happened if the Tyrells hadn't showed up. Like out of the blue and there they was. You ever kilt a man? Yeah, I forgot. That Mex in the SUV, what was his name? So you know. Now they want my ass. The jefe ain't gonna fix anything for me. No sir. I didn't ask for this to happen. Wish't it hadn't. If only Jimmy'd showed up. But he didn't and all this happened because of that one little thing. How you make sense of that? How you make sense of anything any more? It just happens.

My wife. I gotta think a her. And Ray Don. He's in Dallas now. They could go after my son. No account. But my son. What am I gonna do?

*

Charlie Bass swerved the Chevy at the little mother just enough to scare him. The dipshit turned, cussing in Mex again. He wasn't looking, hit a big pothole in the road, and took a leap over his handle bars. Charlie hit the brakes. He looked in his rearview mirror, squinting to see what had happened. He noticed a pickup — this damn wet had a brand new truck, no shit — had stopped and a couple of cousins had hopped out. And down the street, he saw more of them pour out of the movie store. It was coming on to dark. Charlie Bass pulled the .38 out and held it in his lap. A mob of wets coming for him on a street with a gold toothed Mexican holy man drug lord grinning at him and making gang signs. In America. Ain't that some shit? Charlie wondered what the hell he had got himself into.

*

Will asked, "What's goin' on down there?" At first, all Sammy could see was the WE DELIVER! sign. A crowd of cousins were around the car. Then a tall, thin figure, had to be Charlie Bass, was standing by the car door and waving with his hand, telling the cousins to back off. Sammy said "Turn here, Will, that's…Charlie Bass. Yeah, Charlie Bass. What the hell does he think he's doin over here? The damn fool. Will, that motherfucker has a gun! Will!"

Will hit the gas and took a sharp left.

One of the cousins had pushed through the crowd and pulled a Glock out of his pants. He was standing just behind and to the left of Charlie Bass. Will gunned the truck and laid on the horn. Charlie Bass turned

125

and saw the grinning face and the gun and it was Charlie Bass who fired first, hitting Paco Escobar in the chest. The crowd collectively ducked and started to turn as Will pulled up and damn near hit one of them. The guy jumped up on the hood of the truck and rolled off. Will and Sammy turned out of the truck fast and raised their weapons. All this time the *pendejo* with the bike was laying there and groaning and nobody paid any attention to him at all.

*

They scattered when me and Will pulled up and jumped out. The Mex Charlie shot was staggerin around, lookin real surprised. Charlie ducked back into his car and the wet with the gun turned and looked at us and raised his arm, and then Charlie shot him again in the back. Funny, he kept walkin toward us. No, his gun arm was down. That's about when the shots from across the street hit the truck. No, Charlie ain't nothin to me. But this is our town, too. We don't care for the cousins gangin up on our people. So, Charlie did somethin stupid. He didn't kill that kid or mean to really hurt him. He's had enough, that's what he says. And that's what I say. You can tell the jefe *that. He's your fuckin in-law, ain't he.*

*

Paco Escobar fell to his knees just as the shots hit Will and Sammy's truck windshield. The shots were from an SUV that had approached the scene and turned sideways to deliver fire. Two shooters fired from the SUV's windows. 9mm rounds. Will and Sammy returned fire and hit the SUV. Two of the three men inside were wounded. No names. Nobody wants to tell us who they were. The cousins have their own doctor for that shit. The SUV, a ten-year-old Ford, cut over to get behind a live oak where the streets met. Corner of Eighth and Parmer Park road.

*

We yelled at Charlie and he run over to us. Will and me jacked some rounds at the SUV. Charlie come over and Will said "Let's get the fuck outta here," and we did.

*

By the time the storm came that night, Charlie Bass's car was smoldering after a mob came and smashed it to pieces with bricks and hammers and lengths of pipe and baseball bats and they shot it all to hell, too, then dumped gasoline on it and set it afire. The old Chevy lit up like a Roman candle and exploded. People had taken to the streets on both the East and West sides by then and watched the hunks of flaming metal fly in the air. It lit up the town. And they all stood there in the rain and watched it and wondered what comes next.

*

[*News item for posting on Channel 12 website/Video for nightly news broadcast version*] This week's shooting of a Parmer man has reopened old wounds in a town that has seen tensions between Latinos and Anglos flare up a number of times over the past several years. Parmer County Sheriff Manuel "Manny" Rodriguez, who has played a key role in mediating such disputes in the past, is working with Mayor Michael Carranza, veteran City Councilman Darrin Doolittle, son of past long time Mayor Benjamin J. "Buddy" Doolittle, and officers of the Texas Department of Public Safety to ease tensions and see that justice is done. [*Cut to video of Sheriff Rodriguez*] Paco Escobar was shot after a traffic incident at the corner of 8th Street and Parmer Park Road last Thursday night. According to eyewitnesses, a delivery vehicle probably driven by Charles Bass of Ely, the registered owner of the vehicle, was involved in an incident in which a local boy was injured. A crowd gathered and a man fitting the description of Mr. Bass became agitated and fired shots at the crowd with a .38 caliber revolver. Mr. Escobar was hit twice and died at the scene. A truck with two Anglo men approached and almost hit the crowd. The shooter left the scene with the two men. Some of the neighborhood people were angered by the events and set fire to the car. Sheriff's Department officers have been on full alert since the shooting and we have doubled patrols in Parmer. We are discussing with the DPS the possibility of bringing in Texas Rangers to assist in the investigation and in maintaining order. The mayor, the city council, and I have been meeting with civic groups in the county to ask their assistance in keeping the situation under control. So far, we have not located Mr. Bass and the identities of the two other men are unknown. With Veterans Day approaching, heightened security measures will remain in place [*Cut to video of Mayor Carranza, speaking at a session of the city council*] Veterans Day has become a major celebration in this state, in our county, and in our town. As it stands, the city and county are still planning the annual Veterans Day parade and celebration. It is our duty to honor our veterans, many of whom have made great sacrifices to spread democracy around the globe and to protect our freedoms. We plan to do our duty this year. [*Cut to file video of the car wreckage in Parmer*] Since the incident last week, there have been several altercations, including a shooting, involving Latino and Anglo residents of Parmer County. Though no one has been seriously injured, tensions remain high as county and city leaders look for answers. [*End*]

13

Rodriguez and the soldiers ponder a deal... The fate of Charlie Bass...
An ultimatum

"We have a problem. Yes, we do. And we may not be able to smooth things over this time."

It's Rodriguez, adopting his official look, nodding, looking serious. Then he transitioned to his role as *jefe,* palms flat on the table, eyeing the soldiers.

"I have used my influence to keep the peace in our town." A cocked left eyebrow was always a punctuation mark with the *jefe.* "Landry kills a man. The cousins are not happy about that, but I use my... *weight* to not only calm the cousins, but to..." He snapped his fingers, the magician's prestidigitation. "*Deal* with the legal problems that ensued." Rodriguez nodded affirmatively. *You agree, don't you?*

"We made a trade. Not quite completed, but a trade. I help Landry. Our friends Will and Sammy..."

Rodriguez wrinkled his brow in deep concentration, then looked agitated, perhaps disappointed, as a father might be disappointed in a spoiled child's behavior. "What did Will and Sammy think they were doing?" Rodriguez appeared earnest, sober, serious. "Why did they get themselves into this mess? For Charlie Bass? But he's not one of them. Charlie Bass? Why, Charlie's not anything to anybody. No?" Raised eyebrows for effect.

Rodriguez sighed deeply.

"Well, the deal was that the bikers were to be pushed out of Parmer. They can cook, but they distribute with their regulars outside the county and, frankly, they do not get in my way. Or, excuse me, the way of my cousins. And, of course I meant 'our' way. They don't get in our way. No other business here, either. No moving guns, nothing."

Rodriguez was, at first, angry looking, but he followed up with a short smile. *Keep them off guard.*

"Excuse me, Chaplain, I know you are here as the contact with Will and Sammy. But I would have preferred that we, together, push them out.

Permanently. It can be done, you know, and I can make sure there is no… I'm looking for another word. Ah, yes. *Blowback*."

Now that's a good word. Rodriguez adopted a superior, satisfied look.

"But here we are."

Rodriguez glanced reflectively around the table.

Cole, deadpan, eyed Rodriguez.

"So what do you want? What's on your wish list, *jefe*?"

Cole noted that Rodriguez had adjusted the lights in the conference room, with a bright circle around himself, the rest of the table under dimmer lights, fading to darkness by table's end. The *jefe* was not a man, but an unfolding drama.

The *jefe* rubbed his chin. He was thinking, rolling around various solutions like marbles on a tray.

"Charlie Bass."

Connelly started to speak, but Cole touched his arm.

"Go on."

Rodriguez leaned back in his chair, light encircling his radiant, pockmarked face. He stroked his moustache.

"We do the deal. On Will and Sammy. I'm not greedy, soldier. I'll let it ride for now and we can think about a final solution of the biker problem at some later date."

Cole tapped his right index finger on the table. Hard.

"Charlie gets a trial in a different county. We'll talk about the judge. And we want the jury to know Escobar pulled a gun first."

The *jefe* looked surprised. He leaned forward, grinning.

"Cole. I want him dead."

No response.

"I want Charlie Bass dead."

"We won't give him to you."

The *jefe* nodded and sat back in his seat.

"Alright, do it yourselves."

The *jefe* paused, eyeing Cole, a quizzical look on his face.

"I seem to remember Will and Sammy handling a certain issue themselves. What was the issue's name?"

No answer.

So Rodriguez answered his own question. You can't hide anything from the *jefe*.

"Oh, yes, I remember. Jimmy G. Following the untimely death of one Tommy Mock."

Rodriguez nodded affirmatively.

"And the Sheriff's Department did not interfere. You see, soldier, I have obligations to my cousins, as all of us do to those who depend on us, to our partners, friends, relations. Charlie Bass dies. If he dies, then perhaps I can save his family."

The *jefe* moved on.

"The late Mr. Escobar. His uncle lives in that big purple house over on the West side. You know the place. It is the friends and relations of the late Mr. Escobar who have been making trouble. And I cannot guarantee that the relatives of those who suffered otherwise will not seek vengeance against the bikers, but that's their problem, yes?"

Connelly lifted his head. He did not speak directly to the *jefe*.

"If you use that story to cover a hit on the Tyrells, we might not honor our agreement."

"Swordfish. After all the time we have known one another."

The *jefe* was looking disappointed again. "Will and Sammy have Sonny Valdez to pass on rumors to them from Beaner town, right? Look, if some people's relatives get hot-headed, I think Will and Sammy can handle them. If it's me, you'd know, because they would both die. Them and their biker friends. You see, I would not stop short. So, if I did that, you'd know. I need the peace. We — all of us — have other pressing matters to take care of. And," the *jefe*'s voice was suddenly gravelly and growling, "don't forget our financial arrangements. Maybe the Rangers would get curious about that."

"You don't own them," Cole replied.

Rodriguez was smiling broadly.

"The Rangers? No, but I could throw some things out there they could not ignore. And you forget — I have other important friends. So, who is it I own, soldier?"

Rodriguez rubbed his eyes.

"Look, be reasonable *amigo*. Look at Charlie as... collateral damage."

Another clever look followed from The Man. Rodriguez stood up. There were no games now. Just the word.

"Charlie Bass's body at the corner of Eighth Street and Parmer Park Road. It's Sunday night. You soldiers meet on Tuesday and talk it over.

But his body at that corner. I first thought of giving you only until Thursday morning of next week. But I'll give you plenty of time to arrange this and figure out a cover story. I'm not an unreasonable man. Let's say by start of business on Veterans Day. Eight o'clock on November eleventh. If he shows up sooner, then all the better."

Rodriguez walked to the door and spoke once more, without turning around.

"Or you can give him to me. But if you do, I doubt he will die quickly."

14

The preacher's witness… The death of Paco Escobar… A bonfire in Parmer… An observation and a sermon

The night Charlie Bass shot Paco Escobar, an itinerant preacher who had lost his name, forgotten his place of birth, and had taken to the road to preach repentance, stood on a hill in Parmer Park and watched the violent drama below. He had seen the boy fly over the handlebars of the bike and watched with foreboding as the crowd gathered. He stood stock still and watched, absorbing the scene: his mind was focused with the heat of a hundred suns on the approaching disaster below.

There was killing in the air. The scent of violence. He had smelled it before. The preacher knew death was present even before the guns were drawn.

The preacher found a thick live oak and sat leaning against its trunk as he watched the pyre below, light from the flames reflected in the pupils of his gray eyes, flashing across the deep crevices lining his face.

He sat in the glow of the flames, a gargoyle molded by hands unseen and placed on the cathedral pillars of the earth.

Near dusk, the preacher had walked down Main Street. He did not plan where he was going or what he would do. He was called to preach repentance and would do so as the need and opportunity arose.

He had once had a name and a job. He vaguely remembered a family that was lost somewhere, he could not remember when or how, only that the loss itself was part of a terrible judgment the people had called upon themselves. He knew he must walk the four corners of the earth seeking the repentance of the few who would listen.

The preacher had walked down Main Street and turned to the West. People stood in the yards of the decrepit houses and children rode by on bikes silently, little waifs, dark eyed and sullen and no one, no one speaking to him, just following him with their eyes. He spotted the hill above and made for it. He walked by a liquor store. A shop marked with signs reading XXX, a man with bloodshot eyes and a scar on his face opening its door. A slouching old man with a food cart, blindly pushing his wares on a street that was caving in. Only the old man with the cart, a fellow wanderer between the winds, seemed not to notice the preacher as the itinerant followed the path to the high place.

Here, in this town, he would again preach the Word as he had in other places. The preacher would spread his arms wide and shout: "Babylon the great has fallen!" And one man might look at him and say he was crazy, and another would clap and perhaps a woman would hurry past him, having become suddenly aware of a missed appointment. Maybe a policeman would approach, yawning as he listened. Some would smile and say, "You tell em, preacher!" And some others would complain of fanatics and what good did this ever do anybody? "You have to hunt for the great truths, brother," the preacher would say.

The preacher turned up a gravel road toward the hill, passing a small white building. A wooden cross stood in front. There was a hand painted sign in Spanish. He couldn't make it all out, but the sign ended with the words *El Pastor.*

He reached the high place at dusk, turning to survey the land below. And he beheld the killing and the bonfire and rain that followed. Despite the rain, the bonfire glowed deeply, flame red and orange, into the night and on into the following day, mixing with the glow of the sunrise, the sun easing the cool moon away, stars glowing in the firmament that framed the whole of the world the preacher knew.

15

The sicario... *The creation of* El Brazo... El Brazo *and the warlock...* El Brazo *and* Santa Muerte... *Calvera searches for* El Brazo *(Espinoza's order)*

The *sicario*'s first job had not been directly for the cartel. It was for a father, a small man who worked as a small official in the more obscure halls of officialdom. He, like the others, took the payoffs, the *sobre*, and was very important in his way, providing the proper paperwork for transactions involving the cartel as it insinuated its tentacles into all manner of businesses, so that it became nearly impossible to distinguish the body of the octopus from the tentacles.

This is the story of how a particular man became a celebrated *sicario*, a legendary figure in the nether world, an assassin of the highest ranking, an archangel of the fallen ones.

It began with the abduction of a young girl.

It was a case of the old custom of *rapto*.

A soldier who had deserted the army and transferred his services to the cartel had long desired the daughter of the small official. It remains unclear when and where he first set eyes on the girl. Maybe he saw her walking to school. But he became captivated by her.

Being an uneducated sort, not mindful of formality, he abducted this girl, who was, what, 13 at the time? The details of the many versions of the tale vary, but this part of the story is the same: this soldier abducted the girl and raped her.

If he had followed the finer parts of the custom, the cartel soldier might have married the girl and at least not dishonored her so blatantly. Perhaps the father would not have been so outraged. Upset, of course, but willing to overlook the kidnapping and rape, since the kidnapper was, after all, a soldier in the army of the cartel the small man unofficially worked for.

But this was not to be.

The cartel soldier found the girl unsatisfying. You see, he enjoyed the prospect of her innocence in the abstract, but concretely, he had expected more.

It was the wages of his own corruption.

He had been with too many whores. Too many women of sluttish tendencies. The glow of the innocent girl was attractive to him in theory, but her wailing and resistance, her terror at the prospect of losing her virginity to the rather salacious cartel soldier was not something he thought so much of.

You understand.

So, he took her back.

Well, not exactly. He dumped the poor child, crying, in a daze, beaten and bloodied, on a street not far from her home. And she and her family felt great shame.

Now, you may say that the girl was, under the circumstances, quite lucky.

She had not been gang raped, after all.

And she was alive. Present. Not disappeared.

But the shame was there. And it haunted the small official.

He had not been able to protect his own daughter.

There are several different versions of this story. Not all of them agree. We cannot be certain how the father found out the identity of the cartel soldier who had shamed his daughter. But there is one interesting version of the tale that makes sense in the way that things make sense in the depraved world we live in. They say there was a priest who took the confessions of the cartel soldiers. This priest was corrupt himself, a man who had lost his faith, turning his calling into a business. Think of him as another version of the small official himself.

This priest — disgraceful as it was — sold the information on the rape of the daughter to her father.

So, the father now knew what he had half dreaded knowing: The identity of the beast who had shamed his daughter, had beaten her and treated her like the lowest whore.

Knowing this, and trembling even as he paid the priest and heard the story, the father had no choice. He had to avenge the wrong done to his daughter and to his family.

This is where the celebrated *sicario*, who was not celebrated then, entered the story.

His background was like that of many others. He was from a poor family, but not so poor that he did not eat. His father and mother worked constantly to support their children. He was baptized, took his first communion, and as a schoolboy worked making deliveries for the police. Those deliveries, were, of course, of narcotics that he drove across the border. He did not know, exactly, what he delivered and did not care. The money was good, and he and his friends got cocaine and women.

Life was good for him in this way.

But it could have been better.

He joined the state police. The pay was good, and the drugs and women were good, too. He was trained by American specialists, eventually becoming a commander at a very young age.

He commanded a unit that specialized in kidnapping. The young commander acquired a taste for the good life of cocaine and women, of kidnapping ransoms and partying with his comrades.

He had been, by his lights, very fortunate.

Yet the cocaine cost him, as did extravagant spending on parties. It was expected of him, as a leader, to spend lots of money and show his men that he was a generous and important man worthy of respect. The men were loyal to him. But to confirm his status and show that he was not slipping, he must keep up the spending and the parties.

That was not easy.

Soon, he was short of cash.

He would stay up for days on end, managing his crew, collecting ransoms, running drugs across the border, partying. It was like a treadmill that our young commander could not get off of. There was no way to get off. Not and stay alive. If he did not maintain a certain cash flow, then he would not remain among the living.

You see the problem.

It was during this period that he killed for the first time.

His crew was divided into a kidnapping section and one that disappeared people. Sometimes, the kidnappers held the victims, and sometimes the victims were turned over to the disappearers. They were supposed to keep the victims captive until the ransom was paid, but this proved inconvenient, so they often simply killed them.

Thus, the kidnapped became the disappeared as well.

There was a subtle distinction — those who were designated as disappeared were tortured first. After all, there was a reason for their disappearance and the crew had standards. No, the inconvenient kidnapped were merely killed, dispatched rather quickly with a shot to the head, often, mercifully, to the back of the head. It was a job. Or better, a chore. There was no professional standing at stake, as in an ordered disappearance or a carefully planned assassination.

So, the young commander, who had been awake for three days at the time and was feeling invincible from the cocaine, brought one who had been kidnapped to the disappearers. And he decided to kill this one himself.

It was easy.

And he even found that he enjoyed it a bit.

He had had power before. Even over life and death. But he had never entered the temple himself, though he was viewed as a high priest. It was appropriate that he take this step. He could not have his men finding out that he had not been formally initiated. That would have ruined his standing.

Or so went his reasoning at the time.

He was very nonchalant about it. He simply walked up behind this man, whose hands were bound, and fired a round into the back of his skull. Then he walked away, not showing any emotion whatever.

Thus, he killed for the first time. He had moved from narcotics trafficking to kidnapping, to overseeing the disappearing, and now he was on the verge of his real glory.

He was on his way, but his first professional job was for the small official on behalf of that official's daughter. We have no record of how they made contact or why the budding *sicario* decided to do the job himself and not simply have the soldier disappeared by his crew. It may have had something to do with the complex system of arrangements between the state police and the city's cartel — after all, the soldier had not caused his employers any trouble. Nevertheless, the small official contacted his superior in the hidden chain of command about this matter. And permission was given to kill the cartel soldier. This permission was not given lightly — after all, the cartel had to maintain the loyalty of its troops. It came down from on high. How high? The top man, they say.

This one was different.

There would be no simple shooting.

The young commander, who prided himself on his physical strength, used his strong right arm and strangled the cartel soldier to death after his crew had seized him on a busy central avenue, the same one where the soldier had kidnapped the official's daughter. The young commander's crew watched. They had been professional killers for some time, but they were impressed by their commander's display of prowess. He was very brave and supremely confident, even unbinding the cartel soldier and removing his blindfold. "Go for it," he said, "I'm here. Make a fight for your life. I'll tell my crew not to interfere. There, I told them. So what now, brave one?" The soldier tried to kick the young commander and run past him, but the young commander locked his strong arm around the soldier's neck and twisted the man's left arm behind his back as he squeezed the life out of him.

His strong arm was a bit sore for a few days, but it subsequently got plenty of exercise. And he became more and more skilled at using it. The young commander became known as *El Brazo*. The Arm. His men would laugh and feel the strong right arm that did the work. He seemed to grow lopsided, listing a bit, favoring the powerful arm.

The strong right arm became a part of his image and, finally, his *El Brazo* persona seemed to possess him and he nearly forgot all that had gone before, as if he had no family, no father, no mother, nothing that linked him to any kind of normal life. It was as if he had never been born, but had fallen from some distant, hostile planet or, better, had emerged fully grown from hell itself. *El Brazo* was all that he was and would be, a myth, not a man.

That gave him added power.

El Brazo made tens of thousands of dollars for each skilled assassination. His style and variety of methods, the knife, the gun, the rope, but especially the use of his strong right arm, appealed to the romanticism in his clients, who were often celebrated, practically supernatural, figures themselves.

They said *El Brazo* was a handsome man once and at first glance remained so. But his eyes grew as cold and distant as a dying star. His voice became flat in tone, lacking expressiveness at times, as the killer persona replaced his former self. There was even a legend that he has killed a number of men who knew him before, so as not to have them reveal anything of his former life.

Should we believe this?

They also say that he sometimes even eats the hearts of his victims.

But maybe this is part of the myth of *El Brazo*.

It was especially the killing of the warlock Torres that helped create that myth. *El Brazo* made sure that the story of the death of the warlock was told far and wide.

The warlock Torres was renowned for his powers. Many people had come to him for potions and spells to ward off sickness or perhaps to bewitch a woman or a man with a love spell. But the violence of the cartels increased the warlock's standing as well.

Torres, you see, had gained a reputation as a warlock who could protect the people. The story was that none who had visited him had, in fact, been kidnapped or disappeared. So, the people came to his modest home and left refreshed and unafraid. He was a practical man who told his clients that his magic had practical applications.

And being made present, not disappeared, was a matter of pressing importance.

Torres would rub egg white over the body of the client and chant his ancient chants. His father and grandfather were warlocks. His hometown was known as a center of wizardry from times long before the Spanish came, bringing the black-robed priests to assault the power of the old religion.

Some came back again and again, any time they experienced an evil premonition about themselves or about their children.

They would ask Torres if he had any fear, even as a warlock with mysterious powers, that he himself could be disappeared. Were the cartels afraid of him? He would smile and say that he knew the hour and time of his own death. He had foreseen it. And it was years and years away in the future. He was prepared for that and had no fear himself of being disappeared.

You see the problem for the disappearers.

A large part of their power, too, lay in the mystery that surrounded them. They seemed like omnipresent phantoms. In the flash of an eye, the phantoms could emerge from the ether and disappear someone.

But the warlock had made them less mysterious, by increasing the reach of his own powers. It appeared that he had rendered the disappearers impotent. Some claimed that policemen and soldiers of the cartels themselves had gone to the warlock for protection. Thus did the reputation of Torres the warlock grow and grow.

Torres again rose in stature when a story circulated through the bars, cafés, and markets of the town about his receiving a phone call from a trafficker's father. The trafficker, so went the tale, had been jailed in Texas, and the father asked for a ceremony to secure his release. The father cried tears of great joy when the son was let out of a Texas jail — six months later, it was true, but the release, he was sure, had been secured by the powers of the warlock. They even said that Torres had used his powers of clairvoyance to lead the police to a mass grave. But he failed to secure a contract to determine the identities of the unfortunates, since he would not yield to police entreaties to set a group rate for the task.

Torres enjoyed his notoriety. He began to dress the part, affecting a look of importance, gravitas, and mystery: the drawn, emaciated warlock dressed in black and wore dark glasses about town. The warlock even adopted a style of walking in which he stood straight, took on a smooth, short, stride, and did not glance about him, seeming to glide through the streets. Some even claimed that they saw him literally gliding past, his feet not moving, but there is another opinion that the witnesses were drunk, so the story has remained unconfirmed.

One day, the warlock was gliding through the plaza and noticed a strange man nearby. He felt an impulse, an electricity of primal forces about him, and he glanced over at a strange, powerfully-built man, also in dark glasses, who stood and watched him and smiled.

For the first time in years, the warlock felt a certain sensation, a tingling in his scalp and a certain inchoate deadness in his bones that denoted fear. And the strange man turned, listing like a grounded battleship a bit to his strong side as he walked away and vanished in the crowd.

The warlock tried to dismiss the malevolent vision. He replayed the premonition of his own death, set in the future, at a time distant enough to relieve the mind, body, and spirit. But he had clearly experienced a disturbance. An energy as yet undefined.

The energy defined itself when the warlock entered his modest home and saw the listing stranger in the waiting room.

The stranger took off his dark glasses and placed them in his shirt pocket and stared at the warlock with vacant eyes and he said Torres, the warlock. And Torres stiffened and told the stranger that he was, in fact,

Torres the warlock, and the stranger nodded and approached and enveloped the warlock in a massive bear hug and squeezed the emaciated magician and stared into his eyes and said that this warlock wouldn't disappear, don't worry.

Prospective clients found the warlock's broken dark glasses in the waiting room.

The warlock's body was not found that day or the next or the next. It appeared thereafter, bug eyed and naked, the body folded like a thin blanket on the plaza, a sign around his neck that read THE WARLOCK'S POWER IS BROKEN BY *El Brazo*.

We cannot say how all of this is known, but it is, and is faithfully rendered here.

*

They say that *El Brazo* has a special relationship with *Santa Muerte*. Let us pray that we never know the full truth of this, but there is this story.

One of the *sicario's* crew even defected ineffectually to the police. His act of defection was, of course, futile, as the police promptly killed him, but he did make the effort. He told the police of a strange scene that had shaken even him, prompting him to seek refuge, running in panic to ironically meet his fate.

The story is of an altar in the house where *El Brazo* was staying at the time, an altar to the saint of death, *Santa Muerte*. You may have seen the image yourself and remained ignorant of what you had seen: a skeletal grim reaper with scythe in hand, a grinning death's head. Some of the crews have this image in their cars and trucks. At an altar of the *sicarios,* the figure may have an M-4 or Kalashnikov propped alongside it.

The man of *El Brazo*'s crew saw the *sicario* bow to the image, while all around him were ten human heads, as if *El Brazo* were making a ritual sacrifice. And the man swore *El Brazo* drank the blood of his victims from a cup kept at the altar. *El Brazo* is a member of the death cult and it grows among the people as well. There are other stories of *El Brazo* and the cult and what bizarre practices they engage in with young girls and sometimes boys, but that is not something that will be told here.

Let us pray for the soul of the dead man, the man of *El Brazo*'s crew. He did not wish to be initiated into the further mysteries of the *sicario's* ritual. And that is well for him, no matter what else he may have done in this life.

*

Espinoza had called in his chief of staff, Calvera, and told him to find *El Brazo* and summon him for a special task that only he was suited for. Calvera had delivered such a summons before, but it was not a task he looked on with relish. His men would avoid *El Brazo* as they would a plague or the angel of death.

So Calvera sought out the *sicario* himself.

He made discreet inquiries at certain houses *El Brazo* was known to visit, places where he visited the girls, some of whom fled afterwards. They say one girl went mad and killed herself. So the proprietors had to go to extraordinary lengths to get the girls to stay. It wasn't easy. They told them that *El Brazo* would find them, anyway. It was best to let him visit them there. If *El Brazo* had to search for a particular girl — and he usually knew which he wanted on each occasion — it would be worse for that girl. The proprietors told them that maybe there was a connection between the hundreds of women found killed in the city, and the wrath of *El Brazo*. And they would nod and shudder.

So Calvera discreetly made his rounds, seeking the *sicario* with the painstaking caution and professionalism for which he was vaunted in his circles.

The many stories of the *sicario*'s whereabouts were diffuse and varied, dissipating in the wind like smoke from a fire unseen: *El Brazo* had murdered an entire family here in *Ciudad Juarez*, not sparing the family pet, a dog in some versions, a cat in others, whose body was used in a mysterious ceremony; *El Brazo* was in the capital, receiving a special medal from members of the death cult in the army; *El Brazo* was in Sinaloa. For what? Why would any sane man want to know?

Calvera knew that no sane man would. But he had his orders. He made his careful, half whispering, discreet inquiries, knowing that *El Brazo* would hear of them, as he always did. Calvera was not a coward, but was no fool, either. He understood that when he met *El Brazo*, he was encountering something unique and horrible, like a terrible beast thought to be extinct.

Why, if *El Brazo* was so feared and so uncontrolled, did they not kill him? He was but one man, if a strange, deadly, and mysterious one.

143

They say this is a story. A fairy tale. But many believe it. Perhaps it was spread by *El Brazo*'s romantically-inclined customers, who wished to share in the power the *sicario* brought to them through the fulfilment of his tasks. The story is that if someone did manage to kill *El Brazo*, he would return from the dead to exact his vengeance on the killer and the killer's family. It was a powerful deterrent, restraining many who would otherwise have tried to balance the scales.

So Calvera made his rounds and waited.

One evening, while he was making his way to one of the houses *El Brazo* was known to frequent, Calvera felt a strange sensation, a tingling in his neck he had experienced before. He was walking down a sidewalk, cracked and barren, but growing more crowded as night fell and the men came to the houses, pickup trucks blaring the *narcocorridos* as they passed by, the music strangely the same, as if the trucks and their passengers were part of an interminable carousel.

Calvera stopped momentarily. His bodyguards were a few steps ahead and behind him. He turned and faced the street and then turned to continue walking. He did not see anything unusual. Calvera entered the lobby of the next house, nodded at the doormen, and instructed his bodyguards to wait in the lobby. He proceeded to the bar and ordered a beer and waited.

Calvera did not try to stay alert or to spot the *sicario*'s entry. It was better to simply wait. That was difficult, since the pulsed sensations of fear made manifest in his neck and spine continued coming in waves, subsiding, then washing over him again. He sat in a booth and drank his beer, then had another. And as he lifted his second glass to drink the last swallow, the sensation of pricking needles overtook him, for over the brim of his glass he saw *El Brazo* in a black shirt and dark glasses standing at the entrance to the bar. Calvera set the beer glass down and briefly glanced at the figure of *El Brazo*, slightly leaning to his right, impassively surveying the bar.

Calvera's eyes involuntarily cut away from the listing figure approaching his table.

16

Cole pays a debt.

Cole parked the car one block over from the house and lifted the packet in his lap, a zippered plastic bag. He opened it and counted some money, slid the cash into his pants pocket, put the plastic bag under the seat, and waited.

It was full dark and only a few of the street lights on the block worked. There was nobody out.

He slid his gun from its holster and held it in his lap, from time to time glancing in the rearview mirror. The house to his right had been empty for some time.

Cole saw the boy coming his way, turning the corner at the stop sign and approaching the car. He checked his mirrors again. Nobody else was around. He would do the transfer quickly and get going.

The boy approached the passenger side door and Cole motioned him to get in. He opened the door gingerly and slid into the car, partly closing the door to keep the dome light off.

"You talked to Sonny?"

The boy nodded.

Cole took the money from his pocket, along with a small plastic storage bag, and put the money in the bag and sealed it. He slid it across the car seat to the boy.

The boy picked up the bag and started to open the door. Cole told him to put the money in his pocket and he did. The boy opened the door and got out and Cole said, "I'll be watching." Cole knew the boy understood English, but he pointed at his eyes with the first two fingers of his right hand, then at the street. And the boy nodded his head and went on his way.

Cole waited until the boy had turned left at the stop sign, then he started the car and slowly eased up to the stop. He watched the boy turn down the next street. Cole turned left and stopped the car at the intersection. He swiveled his head to watch the boy mount the steps of the house and open the screen door.

17

Charlie Bass ponders his story... Cole discusses the power of memory... The Chaplain and the soldiers look ahead to Veterans Day... Cole and Connelly hold a meeting

*

They've had their meetin's and they have talked it all over and then again. They think Charlie Bass don't know, but I do. And they think I don't know what they're talkin about, but I do.

I lived in this country my whole life and if you think some terrible story like this one is new, well, you're wrong.

The old folks used to tell us stories told to them by their old folks. I remember one about a whole family being massacred by Comanches, all but a infant boy and a little girl and I'm here to tell you that this mess we're in ain't more bloody or messier than that. The story goes that the infant boy was killed right away — I won't tell ya how, it's not somethin I care to repeat — but the girl was carried off. And that girl's uncle, who had nothin and nobody left but his niece, spent years lookin for her. Somehow that man survived travelin deep into Comanche country.

He caught wind of a story about a white girl raised by Comanches, now one of the wives of a chief. I always wondered what that man was thinkin. When he heard that story, I mean. The girl was his blood. And she was motherin little Comanche babies in a band that had wiped out her own family. Think about that a minute or two if ya care to. And think about what them bodies looked like when the Comanches got done with em.

I don't know what this man was thinkin. I guess nobody does. But he led a company of Rangers into the Comanche camp in the Texas panhandle. And the only reason they got that girl back was they run off the band's pony herd. And they kilt the chief. They brought the girl and a half-Comanche baby back with em.

Now this uncle, he set out to try and raise that girl, who whatdn't but say 16 or 17 by then, and provide for her and this half-breed pup. What he was thinkin I don't know. But they say that takin in a Indian was like tryin to tame a wild animal. It couldn't be caged up in the white man's world or somethin, like a wild tiger ya throw into a zoo, and the tiger just withers and dies. Well, this baby boy withered away and died. The uncle, ya understand, had done all he could. But the boy up and died and that's the truth.

Good intentions don't make a damn.

The girl was in a torment a grief, as the story goes. And the uncle kept findin her wanderin off, like she thought she was gonna walk back to Comanche country, or maybe just disappear into the plains. He'd bring her back and she'd up and take off again. He took to lockin her in, but he couldn't abide by it. She'd wander out to that baby's grave — it was given a Christin burial — and she would sit by that grave and pine for her baby.

And one day, she up an kilt herself. They say that girl climbed a tree, tied a rope to her neck and a tree limb and hopped offa that tree limb and hung herself. And that the uncle walked up on it.

What become of the uncle, you might ask. Years later, long after the girl done hung herself and that baby had long been in the ground, that man put a gun to his temple and blew his brains out.

Just like that.

What was that man thinkin? I'm here to tell you I don't know.

*

Cole stared at the story and read it one more time.

No adequate explanation could be found, not one that was readily apparent, anyhow.

Cole set the newspaper down and gently pushed it across the table with his finger tips to Bobby Sanchez.

Bobby looked startled when the paper bumped into his arm. He was busy eating some fried eggs and bacon.

He gave Cole a quizzical look and said, "What?"

"Read it."

"Read what?"

"Just read it."

Bobby picked up the paper, squinted, and began reading.

He twice looked up from the page and gave Cole quizzical looks, turning to bewilderment, as if he were deciphering hieroglyphics from an ancient sarcophagus, struggling to connect symbols to words and words to meanings.

Bobby sat the paper down on the table and crossed himself.

Cole squinted and said, "I thought you was a protestant these days, Bobby."

Bobby shrugged.

"It seemed like the thing to do."

"And I guess that seemed like the thing to do for them."

"Why would they do that? It don't make no sense."

"No note."

"No note, nobody knows any reason for it."

"They were old, Bobby."

"What's that got to do with it?"

Bobby lowered his head as if in prayer.

"They just walked out on the tracks, hugged each other, and waited."

Cole sighed.

"The older son and daughter have been dead a long time. The other one killed in a bullshit war. They outlived their friends, they outlived their own children. They got no grandchildren. And this town? They were both born and raised here."

"Yeah, but that? Why?"

Bobby looked profoundly shocked, as if the most fundamental things taken as a given had suddenly proved false. As if he had come face to face with something grand or terrible or both. Something he had doubted existed. An angel or a demon.

Bobby sat back in his chair, seeming to sink into it a little.

Cole picked up the paper and slapped it on the table.

"We ain't givin anybody up, Bobby."

*

The Chaplain addressed the meeting.

He told those assembled that he had been asked to do a service for the two of them. Mr. McRae had been a soldier once and I'm a chaplain, he said, and they asked me to do some kind of service for them, but I don't know how to perform such a service.

J.C. wondered whether the Chaplain couldn't just make something up. Mr. McRae was a member of this organization. Maybe the Chaplain could just read the twenty-third Psalm. Play taps.

148

Connelly stood by the door, holding a shotgun dangling from his right arm. Henson eyed him suspiciously.

Bobby Sanchez enjoyed Henson's nervousness.

Connelly insisted that they bury Mr. McRae on Veterans Day, right before the parade. Him and the missus.

And then?

Connelly said they should just be ready.

Hightower looked over his shoulder at Connelly.

"There has got to be some other way. My family. I got to figure out what to do with them, where to send them."

Connelly nodded his head negatively.

"There's no other way."

J. C. scratched his head and said Eddie Hatcher claimed they could get Charlie out of the county, out of the state.

Cole, arms folded over his chest, said, "And then what?"

Henson asked about the money.

"I hear tell Cole has been soothin his conscience by givin a cut to the family of that fella he greased. Why bother?"

Cole did not reply.

Connelly patted the shotgun against his leg and again said to just be ready.

"I'll let Rodriguez know the arrangement's over with."

Hightower again: "What the hell do we think we're doing? What about the town? What about our families? Nobody is going to back us up."

Connelly took off his sunglasses, tapped the shotgun on his leg, and approached the table.

"Who do you think all this is for? If we give up Charlie... if we give in, we give up."

Henson was grinning again. He laughed out loud and slapped the table.

Hightower said, "That's crazy."

And Henson reached across the table and grabbed him by the arm.

"Just whose side are you on, Hightower?"

Hightower looked surprised, as though he had been ambushed.

"You took the same oath we did, dammit. Are you in or out? Which is it?"

Hightower sighed.

"There's nobody, nobody who'll back us up."

Bobby Sanchez scratched his chin and said, "There's Will and Sammy Tyrell."

Hightower, incredulous: "Will and Sammy? *Will and Sammy?*"

Bobby crossed his arms.

"That's what I said."

Hightower got up to leave, but Connelly barred the door with the shotgun.

"Are you in or out?"

Hightower sighed and looked around the room and the men in it, at the flags and the pictures and all the regalia of the soldiers and he sighed another deep, regretful sigh and said, "I guess I'm in."

Connelly lowered the shotgun and Hightower left.

Henson grinned at the Chaplain.

"Well, padre, I think it's time for an amen."

*

Connelly and Cole had set up a special meeting with the *jefe*'s dispenser of the *sobre*. They would meet at a neutral site, Rosa's Café in Ely.

Rosa's Café was a long hall with a bar on one side and a kitchen on the other. In the back was a private room for parties and receptions.

Cole and Connelly waited there.

Connelly sat with a Glock in his right hand and the shotgun in a tote bag at his feet. The bag was unzipped so he could reach for it if needed. He would use the Glock first, then go for the shotgun if he had to. Cole held his service Beretta in his lap.

The cousins would know something was up — why else the special meeting? And they, too, would be ready. You could count on it. Henson and Bobby Sanchez had the back door, keeping watch in Bobby's patrol car.

Their table faced double doors that opened into the hall of the café. They could see all the way to the front door and out onto the sidewalk in front of Rosa's.

Cole and Connelly both sat up when they saw the black pickup park in front of the café.

Enrique, the *jefe*'s money man, stepped out of the passenger's side. The driver got out and accompanied him inside.

Connelly recognized the driver as one of the *Pistoleros*, a man named Rivera. As the two of them entered the café, another man, seated and eating a meal, stood up and walked behind them. Connelly had already spotted him as one of the cousins.

Enrique was a short, round man with a goatee and an ironic half smile that never seemed to leave his face. The three men entered the room and stopped a few feet from the table where Cole and Connelly sat.

Enrique was carrying a satchel. He held it front of him with both hands. He was wearing a jacket and Connelly and Cole both noted he was wearing body armor underneath.

Connelly eyed them and deadpanned, "You don't trust us, Enrique?"

Enrique raised his eyebrows and said, "And you do not rise to greet us, Swordfish." He paused, and smiled widely. "It pays to be careful. These are dangerous times we live in, yes?"

Enrique shrugged and said, "May I come forward?"

Connelly nodded affirmatively.

Enrique approached them and gingerly placed the satchel down on the table before stepping back.

Connelly picked up the satchel by its handle and tossed it on the floor in front of Enrique.

Enrique sighed and nodded his head negatively, as if he were facing a recalcitrant child, thinking of a rebuke for that child's careless or malicious action.

He reached down and picked up the bag and took a few steps back.

Enrique was back to a half grin, ambushed by this foolishness or masking some other emotion. Fear or anger, it was hard to tell. He had practiced and refined this facial expression so as to keep people guessing. It gave him a certain edge and reflected Enrique's ironic view of the human condition, which was ever present in his manner. He really was the *jefe*'s cousin and it showed in his sense of style and flair for drama.

"I always liked you, Swordfish, why you doin this foolish thing?"

Cole spoke for the first time.

"Tell the *jefe* there's no deal."

Enrique, still grinning, bobbed his head back and forth as if considering the meaning of the words.

"No *this* deal or no *all* deals?"

Cole said, "Tell the *jefe* there are no deals, then."

151

Enrique shook his head, astonished by the ridiculous answer: "That's not good, man."

Cole said, "That's the way it is."

"Do you soldiers realize what this means? Have you considered all consequences of not keeping our agreements and not accepting..." he held up the satchel "...our friendship?"

Cole repeated, "That's the way it is."

Enrique nodded.

"As you wish. I respect your decision to protect one of your people, however poor and unworthy."

As he was turning, Enrique paused and asked them a question, "And my friends, you do not intend to shoot a poor messenger in the back, no?" He paused and smiled broadly and said, "No, that it is not your style."

And Enrique turned and motioned for them to leave and walked out past his bodyguards, who backed up a few steps before turning and hurriedly making their exit, the bearers of bad tidings to the *jefe*.

18

The history of the third son and the disappearers (the parallel lives of El Pastor *and the* sicario)*... The informer's story revisited...* El Pastor *meets the* jefe *(the* jefe *issues a warning)*

The story of *El Pastor* runs parallel in many ways to that of the *sicario*, *El Brazo*, but at a certain time and place the man who was much like the *sicario* became a different man, and he, too, in his humble way, became a legend in the city of the dead. And it was providential, yes, providential that both men turned up in the same place at a certain time. The whole story has come back to us from *El Norte*.

First, this man who became *El Pastor* was older than the *sicario*, though not so old as he appeared. As he became *El Pastor*, his hair turned white and his once open and not unhandsome face became wrinkled and worn in appearance, as if the transgressions of the sinners he protected had burdened him in body as well as in spirit. He was nonetheless a kindly man and his eyes still showed that the kindness in him was genuine.

He was born in the city, the third son in a family that was genuinely poor. His father died when he was young, and his older brothers left, gone to *El Norte*, though they sent money back to the family, which was a help. They even offered to bring the mother to them, but she sternly refused, saying that she could not leave her country, and would be frightened by a strange place.

The third son's mother worked tirelessly. He pledged that she would not live in poverty, broken by the burden of caring for her family, the remaining third son and three daughters.

One of the daughters disappeared. Another became a whore, causing her mother such torment that the third son hated the sister. As for the third daughter, she eventually left for *El Norte*, the gateway a border crossing dividing the twin cities of the plain.

The third son went his own way. He met a man who paid him to drive cars to El Paso. There was nothing in the cars, but the idea was to distract the Americans, while the shipments were made by other means. The third son was held many times on the American side, but always released. He had done nothing illegal and collected good money. He met the police who aided the real shipments and began to do jobs for them, too, for they had their own business. He delivered the *sobre*, for instance, to local officials and journalists. But this was all in the long years before his city became the city of death. The killings were not so many then, so that people had less difficulty pretending they lived in a normal time.

But the third son was different. He was burdened with the ability to see. Not just eyesight, of course. We are talking of something else, of the sight that penetrates through the veil and sees things others ignore or pretend they do not see. In their blindness, they were quite content, for we must face the truth that most men are blind and in need of the opening of their eyes, but few really desire this as it would be a burden too terrible to contemplate. They did not wish to see, they had no need of truth, preferring that others take on such burdens.

The third son understood this and it embittered him. He was embittered first because he saw himself for what he really was and this dealt him a large blow, since he had been aware of his special sight for all his days and had thought it would make him a better and happier person, and it had not.

And second, he grew to feel contempt for the blind ones. If he tried to explain reality to them in plain terms, they would walk away, turning their backs on him.

As for the third son's knowledge of what he really was... He had made a small inner place where he kept that to himself. In this inner place, he held the knowledge that he was not pure in heart, that though he had partly convinced himself he had done nothing so terrible as to warrant damnation, in fact he, too, was a part of the evil that enslaved his captive city. He buried this terrible truth, while outwardly displaying arrogance and contempt for the blind ones.

In his dreams, he sometimes saw himself as an enabler of evil. He saw himself urging the Christ to accept the terms of the tempter, for if He did, then the third son had no need to justify himself. The dreams tormented him, and the torment made him resent the burdens God had placed on Man and on his wretched city.

154

And the third son began to drink, a habit he had avoided out of contempt for the blind ones, who he saw as representing the sum of the wretchedness of his own people.

He fell into a desperate state and, in his despair, he committed the greatest crime of his life.

It was he who delivered up to the disappearers a cartel soldier who had turned informer.

It happened following one of his trips across the border. He had delivered news of a coming shipment and was picking up a stolen SUV for a car theft ring in his city. As he approached the SUV, he saw a policeman he had dealt with stepping out of what was clearly, to his now trained eyes, an unmarked car used by the American authorities.

He hid in the shadows while the policeman stepped away from the Americans, walking swiftly, distancing himself from the evidence of his informing.

The third son became *El Pastor* in the years after his betrayal of the policeman.

The change in the third son began with the appearance of the beheaded corpse of the policeman on a certain street corner in his city. The head, as if a decoration, was set on the hood of the policeman's car. And a sign on the car read WATCH AND LEARN.

The third son later followed the funeral procession to the policeman's open grave, watching as the family wailed and cried, tormented as if suffering the tortures of the damned.

Now a drunkard himself, he lost all connection with his family. His mother was ashamed of him. His sister prayed for him. And his eyes that could see noted that she prayed at a church rebuilt with the money of the cartel. The priest was happy with his blood money. The third son despaired and drank himself into the oblivion of the lost.

He wandered the streets of the city. He lived in squalor, another man in filthy rags with bloodshot eyes and an empty, lined face, reflecting a damaged soul.

And then this lost man heard stories of the blessed Informer, a man who had repented of his sins and delivered himself to the executioners, a man unafraid and willing to take on the sins of the whole city of the dead.

There was a shrine at the spot where the blessed Informer's tortured body was found, his Golgotha. His blessedness was in not only telling the truth of the cartel's depraved destruction of his own wretched people, but in recognizing that he was the chief of sinners, that he, too, bore responsibility. And he confessed all and prayed for the redemption of the people, of the killers, and of the cartel bosses. Deliver them!

The people of the city heard tales of drug addicts purged of their demons after praying at the shrine to the blessed Informer.

One day, the drunkard third son wandered by the shrine and at that moment, in the half light of dusk in the city of the damned, the box he had kept within burst open and he fell to his knees and confessed that he was the wretched one, that he had eyes and had blinded himself, making him worse than all those he had cursed for so long. He asked for God's forgiveness and rejected the tempter, calling for Christ as he wandered away, a crowd gathering around him, some laughing, some looking terribly frightened, some crossing themselves and following him, some fleeing as if they had seen Christ Himself coming in a cloud to exact judgment on all.

And the third son began his preaching, calling for confession and repentance.

It was as if the Baptist were walking through hell itself, preaching his message of the coming of the Great One.

He occupied an abandoned warehouse and the people of the streets came there and asked him to absolve them, and they prayed together.

The family of a courageous newspaper publisher murdered by the cartel gave him money and he bought the warehouse and the street preacher became *El Pastor*. His disciples opened more homes for the wretched, for the addicts, for the whores, for the blind ones, all with one aim: lift the scales from their eyes!

The story does not end there, but takes *El Pastor* to the north. Hear me now and listen, those who have ears. See, those who have eyes…

*

The police car pulled around the small, white building, marked by a cross in the yard and a sign in Spanish calling for the people to repent, pledging aid to drug addicts, alcoholics, and others who were suffering. Underneath this call were the words *El Pastor*.

The driver paused by the sign before parking behind the building.

Rodriguez stepped out of the car and approached the back entrance. There was a window in the door looking into the hall and beyond to the pews. He pressed his face close to the window and squinted, but saw no one there.

It was late evening, the sun dipping below the horizon.

Rodriguez knew the preacher here, Santos, but had heard that *El Pastor* himself was about.

He walked to the front entrance and paused by the open door, looking down the hall into the pale line of diminishing sunlight that marked the path between the pews to the pulpit and the cross.

*

The naked and disfigured body of the informer was hung upside down on a memorial to fallen police officers. A sign was draped on the monument that read NOW DO YOU UNDERSTAND?

Rodriguez had gazed on the body in passing. He was across the square, watching the crowd that had gathered by the memorial. His breathing was heavy and labored and he forced himself to gaze on the body of the man. He prevented himself from blinking, just as he had when the informer had been tortured.

Yes, he said aloud, I understand.

*

"I know you."

"We have never met."

"But I know you, *jefe*, all the same."

"How can you know me?"

"We once served the same master."

"Maybe you serve that same master now."

"That is what you tell yourself."

"And what do you tell yourself?"

"That we do not."

Rodriguez stood outside the open door, looking in on *El Pastor*, a man with white hair and sparkling eyes wearing a plain white shirt and pants, looking for all the world like a Hollywood version of a peasant from the poor neighbor to the south. Was this affected? It pleased Rodriguez to think so.

"It has been a long time coming, *jefe*."

Rodriguez gazed impassively at the white-haired man.

"Our meeting."

"Yes, a long time."

El Pastor turned and walked in his stooped fashion toward the cross, passing the first pews, stopping momentarily, then going on, halting before the cross and turning to face Rodriguez so the sun shone with his shadow blocking a space in the aisle of the simple building, the cross looming behind him. He motioned with his right hand for Rodriguez to enter.

Rodriguez walked slowly inside, pausing to glance at a picture of the memorial to the blessed Informer before continuing.

He halted midway down the aisle and sat in one of the simple wooden pews.

Rodriguez stared at *El Pastor*.

"Why did you come here?"

The white-haired man folded his hands before him, as if he were about to pray.

"The cartels know very well that their own people begin using narcotics. The beast begins to consume itself."

Rodriguez watched him, showing no expression, revealing nothing.

"There are lost souls here, too, *jefe*."

"What do you want?"

"Let me tell you a story, *jefe*."

"Tell it."

"There once was a man blessed with perfect eyesight. It was like that of an eagle. He could see far, seeing things that others could not. His admonishing of the mob, the crowd that could not see or did not wish to even look, caused great anger among them. So, they dragged the far-sighted man to their temple and they blinded him, using hot irons to destroy his eyes."

"Did he live?"

"Yes, *jefe*, he lived. And also, his sight became better."

"How so? He was blinded."

"It was only in his physical blindness that his spirit began to see even more clearly. He saw things both inside himself and without, more clearly than he had ever seen them physically."

"Is this the only story?"

"There is another version, *jefe,* that says the man even blinded himself, so that he might see."

"You speak in riddles."

"It is clear. To you as well."

"You preachers. You blessed ones. You blind men who see. You are all the same. And all of you end as all of us will. You may see clearly, and if so, you see that the only victor is death. He is the one who stands at the end of every road, old man. He stands at the end of this very aisle. He is standing beside you now. He is behind you. He is everywhere you go. He is omnipresent. But you are a simple, uneducated man. Perhaps I ask too much of you."

"I understand you, *jefe.* You, like the mob who blinded the far-sighted man, do not really wish for your own freedom."

"I have rejected your ideas on what is freedom, old man, long ago. And the truth is that not even your wretched flock wants this freedom. No one does."

"You, too, can be free and have eternal life."

"Even if I believed you, what would I want of that? In my way, I make my own life. And I will die, as all men die, but as a man who made his own truth, who created his own mystery and did not go begging for it. And that is my reality."

"There is only one reality and one truth, *jefe.*"

"There are many, old man."

"I saw you that day."

"What did you see?"

"I saw a man struggling with himself. You were there, watching the crowd around the body of the blessed Informer. I was watching. And I saw you. I have known you for a long time."

"And what have you known?"

"That you are just a man, *jefe,* nothing more. You cannot create a world, even for yourself alone in your mind, a world you keep in a special place for yourself. It is an illusion, *jefe,* I know this."

"I could kill you."

"Yes, and of what benefit would that be?"

"Old man, I'd be creating a reality of my own making. For that one instant, I am omnipotent — all powerful, simple man, you understand? Not your God, not even death, but me creating this new reality."

"It is an illusion of power, *jefe*, like the boys with their guns, the disappearers who themselves disappear, untraced, unknown. It is an act of futility, not of creation. That is beyond you and your guns. Now do you understand?"

"You speak to me ironically, old man. I extend my compliments."

"With your permission, *jefe*, I speak to you truthfully."

Rodriguez stood up, adjusted his gun belt and patted his side arm. His eyes locked on the figure of *El Pastor*.

"Today, I let you live, old man. But do not get in my way."

He turned and started out.

"Your way is the way of your own destruction and that of others, *jefe*. It is not too late, it is never too late."

Rodriguez paused and without turning to face the old man said, "You are wrong, holy man. It is always too late."

And he walked out of the building and left.

El Pastor stood at the cross, his hands folded, looking after the *jefe*.

19

*Cole seeks advice from an old ranger… Captain Wallace reminisces…
A white bean*

The old ranger was sitting on the front porch of his cabin when Cole
drove up and parked his pickup beneath a wide-canopied live oak. He did
not move or even adjust the expression of resigned dignity on his
weathered face. The stump of a cigar was held in his left hand like a
prop. It wasn't lit. The clawed hand moved and the cigar stub was like an
extra finger, as if it was surgically fused to the hand. One of his long
legs, the left one, stretched out far from the rocking chair he sat in, the
long, once lean body now stooped, the black boots weathered as the
man's face. But the bright blue orbs in his puffy, long countenance still
glowed with the vital energy of the man, the old ranger inseparable from
the limestone ridges and the flora and fauna of this harsh, haunted place,
like a rock formation worn over eons from the land itself. His hair was
swept straight back from his brow, where the tan line from his hat — a
weathered broad-brimmed Stetson that hung by a peg at the door to the
cabin — was most evident. His hair was steel gray atop, surrounded by
white, as if snow had melted and slid from the plateau of a high place.

Cole stepped out of the cab of his truck and turned toward the porch
and the old ranger. He noticed the saggy figure of an ancient hound
crouched near the rocking chair, the dog as unmoved by his presence as
the old ranger himself, but as Cole approached the porch, the dog's brow
shifted on one side of the gathered jowls as the animal growled lowly.
The old ranger did not react.

The cabin itself was limestone, roofed with aluminum, built in dog run
fashion. Cole could see no sign of a vehicle nearby or any horse or other
means of transport, ancient or modern.

As Cole grew nearer, the eyes of the old ranger focused in a long
squint and his right hand, wrapped around an old-fashioned Peacemaker
revolver, rose up from the man's lap. He rested the revolver on the arm
of the rocker.

"That's far enough," said the old ranger. The dog growled again and the ranger told him to hush and the dog hushed, shifted its weight, sighed, and was at rest — only with the eyes wide open now, honing in on the stranger.

"Oh, hell, a little closer. Take a coupla steps. My eyes ain't what they used to be."

So Cole took a couple of steps. He held his hands out to his sides, palms facing the old ranger.

"No need for that. I can see now. Cole..." he pressed hard inwardly with his brows and forced out the rest of the memory: "...Cole... It's a Landry, I believe. A Cole Landry."

"That'd be me."

"Step forward and state your business."

The old ranger put the hand gripping the Peacemaker back in his lap.

"Your dog..."

"Ol' Jack won't bother ya. He can tell I ain't bothered, just come on up. You're a friendly."

Cole walked deliberately up the steps and onto the porch. The old ranger stiffly pushed himself up from his chair, stuck the Peacemaker in a leather holster hanging from the back of the rocker, and held out a leathery, thick fingered mitt of a hand. They shook and the ranger nodded toward a row of plain wooden chairs near the door and said, "Pull up a chair and sit down. Tell me what's on your mind, Mr. Cole Landry."

Cole brought one of the chairs close to the rocker and sat down facing the old ranger, whose name was Roy Wallace, slapping his hands on his knees and leaning forward to speak.

"Captain Wallace..."

"You can call me Roy..."

"Yessir... Well, ah, Roy... I come for a little information and some advice."

"If I got any to give, you are welcome to it."

Roy Wallace leaned back in his rocker, his eyes focused on the horizon.

Cole nodded affirmatively and the two men talked...

*

One thing the Comanche didn't count on, or have the foggiest understandin of, was that the Americans was not like the Spanish or Mexicans. The Americans was armed and determined, and would not give up, which was puzzlin to the Comanche. And they had a bravery that was borderin on crazy. Think about that. Takin your family to the Texas frontier, home of the meanest, most savage tribe ever to scourge men, red, white, or brown. And this enemy, the Comanche, was mobile, as well as hostile. The greatest riders who ever took to the back of a horse. Now at first, the Texians, so called in them days, tried to fight the Comanche like they had fought Eastern Indians on the other side of the Mississippi. I mean on foot — and that was not gonna work.

Bear with me, there's a point to all this.

The earliest pursuers of the Comanche raiders took to callin themselves rangin companies, all volunteers. They got that part right—you had to pursue the Comanche to his sanctuary and hit em there. They whatdn't expectin that.

But the Texians had a tactical problem and a firepower problem. First, they would dismount and come up on the Comanche camp afoot. Your Comanche would mount up, run off your horse herd and close in to wipe ya out, so now you are on the defensive. Then there's the firepower problem — muzzle loaders worked fine from a defensive position firin at an approachin' enemy. But the Comanche would not keep comin to take a secured position. Wouldn't do er. And a Comanche with a quiver of arrows could out gun ya, so to speak. I mean rate a fire.

So, along comes Colonel Colt. Your brace of revolvers can outgun the Comanche. You stay on horseback, close with the enemy, and don't let up. Follow me? One more thing. You are gonna need scouts that can follow sign. Tonks might do it. They hated the Comanche, who had driven em near to extinction. Not many white men could follow Indian sign like them. A few could, like Captain Ben McCulloch, but there weren't many of em like that.

Then you need a man as hard as the land these people were tryin to take. A man like Jack Hays. He learned how to fight his enemy first hand at the Battle of Plum Creek, when the Texians charged the Comanche band and they broke. Hays learned how to track like a Comanche and fight like one. He followed the vultures attracted to the bloody refuse the raiders left behind. He pressed home and it was war to the knife. Hays

163

learned to keep a couple of men behind the main body to see if he was bein followed — and if he was, he was liable to turn around and mount a charge right into em. And Jack Hays didn't fall for no tricks, like some Comanche showin theirselves and then turnin and runnin to lead the Texians into a trap.

Jack Hays fought Mexicans the same way.

Fight smart, use your organization, use the right weapon. Learn how your opponent thinks and how he fights.

I'm a descendant of Bigfoot Wallace. A lot of people don't believe me and young people don't even know who he was, but if you lose that memory, you forget to read the sign or learn from em. Follow me? Good.

You know the story of Bigfoot and the white bean.

Now Bigfoot liked to stretch the blanket, they say, and I cain't vouch for ever story told by him or about him, but I do know that he came to Texas for one of the oldest reasons men have for doin anything at all. He came to avenge the deaths of his brother and cousin, who was with Fannin at Goliad. He spent his life trackin bandits and Indians and was with em when they stormed the Bishop's palace in Monterrey in eighteen and forty-eight. But the most famous story of Bigfoot — and one everbody swears is true — is the story of the Mier expedition and the white bean.

It was after a Mexican raid in eighteen and forty-two. They was a punitive expedition mounted to pay back the Mexicans. And Bigfoot was in it. He was with a group that was captured near the town of Mier, south of the Rio Grande. After some of em tried to escape, Santa Anna ordered executions as punishment. They was 176 Texians that had survived the forced march to the *Hacienda Salado*.

It was decided the Texians be punished by lottery. One hundred fifty-nine white beans and 17 black beans was poured in a pot. Anybody drawin a black bean would face the firin squad. Bigfoot shoved his hand in the pot and grasped two beans — one large and one small. Believin that the white beans was smaller, he dropped the bigger one and kept the small one.

He was right. It was a white bean.

When the drawin was done, Bigfoot saw that four of the other Rangers had drew black beans, along with 13 others. "Boys," says Bigfoot, "I never did cotton to white beans. I'll trade ya a white one for a black one," but none of the condemned men took him up on his offer. And them boys was shot along with the rest.

The ranger tradition was made that very day. Any ranger has to be ready to offer his life for his comrades. And never, never surrender. You understand?

*

When Cole stood, the dog got up, too, eyeing him, staying close to his master. Roy Wallace raised himself up from his rocker and shook Cole's hand.

"I think y'all know what to do," he said.

Cole walked to his truck and got in. He started it up and began to turn around to make his departure. And there on the porch stood Ranger Wallace, now looking tall and straight and sturdy, his dog by his side. Cole put the truck in gear and began to pull away and the old man raised his right hand from the elbow.

20

Sammy and Charlie Bass... Charlie Bass whistles a tune... El Brazo's
*nighttime drive ... The preacher takes a stroll and wonders at the fate of
Man... The day of the dead...* El Brazo *leaves a warning... The story of
the* jefe, *the blessed one, and Luis Rojas...* Santa Muerte... El Pastor
defies the evil one

"They bound to know where I'm at."

Charlie Bass sat under the wide canopy of a live oak near Will and
Sammy's place. No paved roads. A well. And a small cabin where the
exiled man lived, hidden from sight, but not out of mind of Ely or Parmer
or the whole county, and surely not of the *jefe.*

Sammy leaned back on the seat of a chopper near the edge of the
canopy, which provided shade from the startling sunlight, accenting the
smoky shadows of what passed for an encroaching fall in this dry and
sunlit land.

Sammy said, "We won't let em have ya."

Charlie Bass scratched his pointed chin, now covered in brushy stubble
and said, "What about my family?"

Sammy turned his head to spit.

"They are bein took care of, Charlie."

"Where?"

"Not here. It's best if not too many know, not even you."

Charlie Bass reached in his back pocket for a dip, inserted the pungent
tobacco in his lip, slid the circular can back in his pocket and asked,
"Why are you doin this?"

No answer.

The words hung there in the air, then drifted away on a small breeze in
a way that made the speaker of the lost words wonder if he had ever
actually uttered them.

Charlie Bass spit a stream of brown fluid on the ground and said, "I'm
nothin to you."

Sammy stared straight ahead, addressing the man behind him or others
dead and gone, memory dominant over foresight, action over reflection.

"You became somethin that night."

Charlie leaned his head back against the tree trunk and said, "I didn't ask fer this."

"Nobody ever does, Charlie."

*

On the wings of a snow-white dove, He sends his pure, sweet love
A sign from above
On the wings of a dove

The words drifted in and out of Charlie's mind and he whistled the tune, a favorite of his grandmother's, as he walked too close to the fence line. Sammy had warned him to keep out of sight of the state highway below.

He heard it at a distance, rumbling down the highway, headed northeast toward Fort Worth and Dallas and points beyond. Charlie Bass eyed the curve in the state highway at the base of the hill, flinching at the 18-wheeler's roar when it barreled into sight. He studied the scene carefully. The big rig made the curve at the base of the hill below, blowing smoke, roaring like a great mechanical beast. He stared at the highway as the roar of the big rig faded away, out of sight, disappearing to that place everything goes when you can no longer see it.

Veterans Day was right around the corner, looming like a threat or a hard-kept promise.

*

The car tended to drift right, as the driver favored his strong side. He had to concentrate as he sped through the night on the two-lane state road, twisting and turning through the rocky crags as he approached the town. He could have easily drifted off the shoulder, slamming into the rocks, or overcorrected, meeting a truck careening through the night head on.

Such was the experience of driving for The Arm.

He drove in silence, one window cracked open, the wind whistling through the car making a sound like a lost soul seeking its way out of Perdition. The lonely whistling sound was fitting for the utter darkness of an overcast night, *El Brazo* enclosed in a capsule careening through the ether, utterly and completely alone in space.

The man himself was tranquil. Silent. Silent and accepting of his damnation. Accepting of his mission both current and metaphysical. He had no past and thought little of the future, living in a sort of limbo marked by brief spurts of frantic activity, *El Brazo* emerging from the astral plane, seeking silence in utter annihilation chosen, asserted, and dominated by his being.

*

El Brazo slowed down and took in the scene before him. A simple white building. A cross. A floodlight out front, its light projecting onto the cross, forming a shadow on the white background.

El Brazo turned off the car's headlights and approached the building. He turned the car and drifted ever so slowly around its perimeter.

He soaked in the scene, savoring it, focusing on it, foreseeing his moves. The old man at the altar, kneeling perhaps, the look on his face suggesting certainty of salvation, but worn by the years and the burdens of others' sins.

El Brazo would enter the unfolding drama as the annihilator.

The old one rises from his prayers without sensing the large figure behind him. He backs away from the altar and meets the resistance of a solid body and he starts to turn his head, but the thick appendage coils around his neck like an anaconda and the old man never sees what has struck him.

But he knows.

November eleventh was approaching. And so was *El Brazo*.

El Brazo backed the car into the darkness and turned off the engine.

As a boy, before he was *El Brazo* and so lived another life that was now all but erased from the minds of men, he had watched as an eagle swept down to attack a snake, a thick and deadly rattler. This memory had stayed with him, even as he erased so many others.

The Spanish had been wrong. The serpent in the lore of the sun people was not the equivalent of the serpent in the garden of Christian scripture. Truly, the eagle represented the god *Huitzilopochtli*, while the serpent was representative of wisdom and was connected to the god *Quetzalcoatl*. The Spanish priests had turned the symbols of the sun people into Christian allegory.

But the boy had watched an eagle attack a serpent. And he had watched the serpent escape, the eagle perching on a tree, battling gods free to carry on ancient struggles. The eagle bore deadly nobility. The serpent was wise and stealthy. The boy would remember this, wishing to take both unto himself. And he grew to understand that the struggle was its own end. The creatures themselves were as gods in creating their own being, determining their own terms of annihilation.

The boy thought of himself as belonging to *Tenochtitlan*. A priest of the highest order in an earlier incarnation, he had removed the living hearts of human sacrifices and burned them. And as he cut into their chests and removed the still beating hearts, first one at a time, then hundreds, then mass sacrifices of thousands so that his arms grew numb with the work and thick with coagulating blood to the elbows, he began to see that the sun people should have embraced the serpent, not seeking the appeasement of helpless gods who fell to the Spanish sword, but embracing defiance and death itself. Yet they did assert one truth: The supernatural powers that be had no mercy. They were no shepherds, but thirsted for the fuel of violence. Their cruelty was their power.

*

The preacher turned his gaze skyward in an attempt to penetrate the clouds and see the stars, but he could only dream of it. It was so dark he stumbled to put one foot in front of the other and move through the pitch blackness.

Something had drawn him out, awakening him from a dreamless sleep, telling him to walk.

He crested a hill parallel to the church of *El Pastor* and saw a strange sight: a car, its headlights turned off, slowly circling the building in the deep darkness, like a predator circling its prey just beyond the sight of its victim.

The preacher squatted and observed this ritual in a vain attempt to ascertain its origins and intentions.

As the car circled, he caught glimpses of a large figure at the wheel briefly outlined against the backdrop of the church building.

*

The people visited graves and built small shrines, placing there pictures of the deceased, often including food and beverages favored by the departed ones. In the coming days there would be more prayers and remembrances of children and infants and the adults who had gone on. Sometimes they told stories of the departed and laughed a lot. And sometimes, especially concerning the soul of an infant, they prayed harder and had no stories anyone wished to tell. Some brought flowers to the grave or shrine or held a picnic and ate traditional foods such as *pan de muerto*. They wished to attract the souls of the dead to them, so that the departed might hear the prayers and the stories. The figure of *La catrina*, a skeleton dressed in elegant female attire, was much in evidence, as were foods often shaped as skulls. The death mask was seen most often during the procession of the *Día de los Muertos*...

La catrina danced by on stilts, a tall skeleton figure in a top hat dancing behind her. A float followed, with mounds of food stacked around a pig's head accompanied by more skeletons, a group of them playing various musical instruments. A mock funeral procession consisted of skeleton men carrying a coffin in which the corpse sat up and waved at the crowd. A dog skeleton amused the crowd greatly, especially when he relieved himself at the feet of a man who appeared to be quite drunk and completely unaware of the supernatural occurrence.

As dusk came on and night began to fall, the proceedings took on the air of carnival, with much music, both of the traditional kind and the blaring sounds emitted from the pickups lining the streets of the West side. The skull masks were lifted so that the celebrants could drink deeply, the skeletons dancing and carrying bottles of various kinds of liquor as drums rattled and smoke drifted from the pickup cabs. A fat woman wearing a blond wig, her face painted as the mask of death, lifted her top and shook her breasts at the crowd and another woman fell and cut herself as her beer bottle broke on the crumbling sidewalk. A group of men gathered around the fat woman and squeezed her breasts, laughing and blowing marijuana smoke at her face. Sometime in the night, there were gunshots as a fight broke out between adherents of *Los Pistoleros* and some Mexican Mafia celebrants visiting from Dallas. The dispute was sparked by an argument over dueling music and the question of preference: *narcocorridos* or rap?

A bulky, listing, death masked figure dressed all in black walked through the crowd. Underneath his mask, he smiled quite broadly.

A man bearing the identifying tattoos of *Los Pistoleros* ignited a Roman candle as the bulky figure walked by, the flaming balls landing at his feet, his gaze unaverted.

*

At the church of *El Pastor*, the people brought candles to burn for their dead. *El Pastor* railed against the corruption of the traditional observance, meant to be one of remembrance, a celebration of prayer for the departed souls, now descending into violence and debauchery, as if the people had never known Christ.

Outside, the little ones, costumed as skeletons or as heroes from popular films, carried baskets and grocery bags with them on their quest for such treats as the adults wished to give them.

*

Near Connelly's home on the East side, Will and Jim, both costumed as Rangers, followed a troop of friends trick or treating. For several blocks around, neighbors had planned a trick or treat route, excepting those few remaining who objected to the ghoulish practice in principle as encouraging the works of the evil one. In time, there were fewer dissidents as the practice took on an air of nostalgia, a remembrance of things past, rather than an artifact of the dark arts. Many parents enjoyed the ritual more than the children themselves, who could not remember even the faded, fuzzy-edged memory of memories that their parents' ideal was based on, a print faded and time worn, not even the original, which hung in the cluttered attics of old peoples' minds like a misplaced portrait.

Connelly followed behind at a safe distance. Beside him walked Houston, the stump of his left arm crossed over his torso as if he were walking in some solemn ceremonial procession, a maimed dignitary or perhaps a ghoul himself in a procession of lost souls.

The sounds of music and revelry drifted from the West side, fireworks bursting like dying stars in the night air.

"I'd fit right in over there with the cousins," said Houston, craning his neck to squint and watch the bursts with his good eye.

Connelly, eyes forward, resisting even acknowledging the carnival of the cousins, answered, "How's that?"

"I get up every morning wearing a death mask."

Connelly didn't reply.

"Yessir, every day is the day of the dead."

"You tryin out new material?"

"You bet, buddy. Everything is grist for the one-armed man's mill. Some days I'm Captain Ahab..." he looked over at the impassive Connelly. "That's a character from literature, Man Killer."

"I know. Chasin a whale. One that took off his leg."

Houston stopped in his tracks, turned his good eye at Connelly and said, "I'll be — I'd a never guessed Man Killer was turnin literate on us."

Connelly paused, then took a step and replied, "Saw the movie."

Houston nodded his head negatively, lamenting the loss of cultural literacy.

"Famous last words."

The two started walking again, then paused as the group of trick or treaters approached a house.

Connelly eyed the proceedings as if he were witnessing a secret ceremony. Houston noted that it was the Swordfish way to impart the utmost gravity and seriousness to everything he did. Must be tiring, he thought.

"How's that?"

"How's what?"

"You said, 'famous last words.'"

"Of a declining culture."

"Oh."

The children were already moving ahead, so Connelly and Houston/Ahab followed in due course.

Across the street, a stream of parents and children were on the reverse course, treats duly collected from the opposite side. One house did not offer treats, but small passages of scripture rolled up and tied with ribbon, a cross lit in flood lights, the cross covered with small, radiant white lights marking the distribution point. An elderly couple, each armed with a basket of scrolls, distributed the passages with smiles and invitations to visit their church.

Houston had stopped, eyeing the distribution across the street.

"Didn't Opie used to call you 'reverend?'"

Houston was holding his stump crossed over his good right arm, watching the proceedings, a distribution of the sacred framed by drifting wafts of Westside background noise and sudden bursts of exploding bottle rockets.

He glanced back at Connelly, then back at the glowing white cross.

"Yeah."

"I don't think he liked you much."

"Who?"

"Opie."

172

"Opie didn't know what to make of me is all."

"Neither did anybody else...reverend." Connelly turned and followed the stream of children, led by two Rangers, a pack of ghosts and super heroes questing into the night.

*

The boys and Natalie were asleep.

Connelly sat in the dark living room, his right hand holding a handgun. He had heard a distant burst of gunfire, then another.

No call, no sirens. And there would be no police report, no mention in the papers or the TV news.

What was happening? And what was the *jefe*'s plan?

*

El Brazo, a bulky form with the face of a skeleton and the dead eyes of one unburied and unmourned, had witnessed the shooting from a rise near the center of the carnival. Two had fallen, one from each side of the struggle. They were borne away in vehicles from their respective sides as the crowd dispersed. He watched as a Sheriff's Department car approached. The man who stepped out of the car was the local *jefe* and ultimate object of Espinoza's manipulations. Two SUVs arrived shortly thereafter, men armed with M-4s conducting a reconnaissance of the combat zone under the direction of the *jefe*. On the streets around this scene, small groups of hardy revelers remained, questioned by the brigade of gunmen while the *jefe* smoked a cigar and observed.

One half hour later, the masked figure stood near the church of *El Pastor*. He hefted the body of a boy of no more than fifteen and set it at the foot of the cross adorning the approach to this place of worship. The boy's head hung limp, eyes wide open, glaring into space with a look of wonder or surprise. The bulky skeleton placed a hand-written sign on the body reading in Spanish HE COMES FOR YOU.

*

While wandering that night on his solitary track, the preacher saw the body at the church of *El Pastor*. He squinted in a vain attempt to read the sign, as if his squinting would provide translation. But he knew the very night he had seen the strange car near the church that a day of reckoning was quickly approaching. He stood in the night air by the floodlight and wondered at the fate of Man.

*

173

El Pastor saw the body as he walked from the church entrance near dawn. He felt no great shock or bolt of fear, only a weary sadness accompanied by a sense of steely and resigned determination. He bent down to read the sign: HE COMES FOR YOU. And he knelt there, his knees aching, his spirit heavy, and prayed for the boy.

*

The West side fracas did not make the papers or the TV news in Dallas or Fort Worth, but the killing of the boy, one Eduardo "Eddie" Gomez, did. He was fourteen, the son of a mother who had lost her husband somewhere, sometime during their travels in *El Norte*. He had five brothers and sisters and was not known to have been involved in what was called "gang activity" by law enforcement officials. The killing seemed to be aimed at the man known as *El Pastor*, one Luis Rojas of Juarez, lately of Parmer, a man loved and admired by many and, perhaps, feared by the cartels. The depositing of the body at the church of *El Pastor* was portrayed by news media as a warning. Perhaps *they* saw Rojas as a troublemaker, an irritant, a blot on their perfect record of cleaning all slates, removing all blemishes, his fiery preaching tarnishing the Robin Hood image of the cartel bosses. *El Pastor* had reportedly refused cartel money and had turned away drug runners, pimps, and pornographers, refusing to grant them his blessing without their repentance, an exchange they seemed not to understand. So, a warning had been made, a position stated.

But another story began to circulate on the West side, a story told by Sonny Valdez.

Sonny had first heard the tale from some of his relatives who had returned from business in Mexico, then heard a version of the same story being told in the Jaguar Club by one of the Escobars. And the story went like this: There was once a holy man in Juarez, one they called the blessed Informer, a man who, according to popular belief, had sacrificed himself for the souls of the lost people. And after the body of the Informer turned up, a certain small cog in the cartel's machine, a certain man who had not previously been worthy of notice, was turned, they said, was remade, they claimed, was blessed and redeemed they declared, and this man called Luis Rojas became *El Pastor*. As *El Pastor*, Luis Rojas set out to do work inspired by the life and gruesome death of the blessed Informer.

But that was not the whole of the story, for there was another part, and that part concerned a police official from the north who had come to the city of the dead as part of a mutual arrangement between governments and police forces north and south. That man was *noticed*. The man was, in fact, a betrayer who had given up the blessed Informer to the disappearers and had witnessed the crowd gathered by the body of the blessed one. He had taken the cartel's money and returned to *El Norte* as an agent in the cartel's network. That man was none other than Rodriguez. And he was known by *El Pastor*, who had also taken notice of him.

In this way, *El Pastor* was a disturbance to the cartel, a walking violation of all ordinances. He was an incomplete, unfinished, undone part of the *jefe*'s life, left there on that day on the spot where the body of the man Rodriguez had given up was discovered.

But the story was incomplete. What did the warning mean? HE COMES FOR YOU. Who was coming? The manner of the boy's death suggested an answer. He was not shot. He had not been knifed. Nor were his hands bound in the customary manner. And there were no signs of the usual hideous tortures. There was no tape over the victim's mouth. He had been laid there in a state of quiet deathliness as peaceful as if he were in a state of dreamless sleep. His neck was broken. Smoothly, utterly, cleanly.

HE COMES FOR YOU.

The identity of the killer became a source of much speculation on the West side. And gradually, slowly, imperceptibly, the mysterious killer began to take form. And that form was of a strange, listing figure, a lopsided hulk seen on the night of the recent festival in a death mask. No one spoke his name. But wafting in the airy spaces between their words were dreadful hints that *he* was here. And the people began to glance with wary, fearful, and worshipful eyes at the figure of *Santa Muerte*.

*

El Pastor eyed the congregants and finished his sermon.

"So, I have been told, brothers and sisters. *He* comes for *me*. But he, the evil one, comes for all of us. He awaits our moment of weakness. He waits to pounce like the panther. He takes many forms. The pimp. The drug dealer. The pornographer. The *sicario*. The disappearers. He smiles and invites us to our death. With our permission, he beckons us to the flames of eternal damnation. Let him come, brothers and sisters. I am not afraid. *We* must not be afraid. Not of the death cult worshippers nor of the worshippers of the flesh nor of the worshippers of money. For there is another 'He' who will come for us. He will return. He has defeated death, defied the evil one. We are not afraid."

*

The people filed out of the church and *El Pastor* stood at the door and blessed them, every one. Some of them were misty-eyed as they looked at him, hinting at a pain that was not openly declared, but held closely about them like a cloak in the winter. And some of them embraced him and held him as a precious object. They asked for prayers and one man, an old one with reddish and clouded eyes, bowed to him and asked his blessing and then, before he departed, offered his prayers for *El Pastor*, who, he was sure, would need them.

21

Early November in Parmer... The fate of Miguel Conteras... The jefe *questions Connelly and Cole... The Chaplain and Charlie Bass discuss the meaning of life (dry lightning)... Espinoza ponders his plans... Houston and the Preacher*

It was early November and the weather, as is normal in that part of the state, turned finally, mercifully cooler following Halloween and the festival of the dead. With only a modicum of recent rainfall, the leaves would turn very quickly, go brown and die, falling like the drying scales of some mighty serpent to blow in the cool November winds.

It became a time of dread on the West side, for another body was discovered by a boy exploring the bed of the creek that ran through the town park. It was the body of an old man named Miguel Conteras, who passed his time selling food from his cart on the West side, then customarily spent his money as quickly as possible, for who knows what life will bring? So said Miguel Conteras, encapsulating his philosophy and that of his people, truth be told.

A crowd had gathered as the Sheriff's Department cars arrived and the deputies marked off the scene of the dreadful crime. The *jefe* himself showed up, climbing down into the creek bed to view the body at first hand. He pondered the corpse of Miguel Conteras from various angles, a deeply contemplative expression on his face. He said little to the men around him, as there was a perplexed air about all of them.

Miguel Conteras had died with his neck broken. And it was clear that his body had not naturally assumed its present position at the bottom of the creek bed in the park above the West side of the county seat in the cool November air, a place that would not have been among the old alcoholic's usual haunts. He was laid across a bed of rocks in sacrificial repose, his arms extended on either side, his eyes closed, his feet crossed in an arrangement of symbolic crucifixion that lent the crime scene the air of both solemnity and a terrible sense of blasphemy. And the object end of the symbolic placement was evidently to convey to those who viewed the scene a sense of impending and intent, purposeful destruction.

Rodriguez felt eyes on his back and he turned his head to see Cole and Connelly at the edge of the creek bed, looking down on the scene below. Pictures of the victim were being taken. Media vans would arrive soon and Rodriguez would be forced into making some kind of statement in two languages.

Rodriguez turned and raised his right hand, then just the index finger as if to say, "Just a minute" to the two soldiers. He climbed out of the creek bed, motioning them to come and get in his car. Cole sat in the front seat, while Connelly assumed a seat in the back on the passenger's side. Rodriguez got in the car and closed the door, motioning them to do the same, then arranged the rearview mirror so he could easily glance at Connelly as he spoke.

Rodriguez nodded and placed both his hands on the steering wheel, as if he were about to drive off.

He spoke first to Connelly, eyeing him in the rearview mirror.

"*Amigo*, can you tell me anything about this?"

No reaction. Connelly stared back at the *jefe's* eyes and said nothing.

Rodriguez shifted his gaze to Cole.

"Deputy Sheriff Landry?"

Cole shifted in his seat, turning a bit to address Rodriguez.

"Why would we know anything about this?"

Rodriguez scratched his chin, pondering the question and formulating a reply. He sighed and turned his gaze to the November morning.

"Veterans Day is coming fast, soldier, and you boys don't want to play the game according to the rules. Is this some kind of thumb in old Manny's eye? A way to make trouble for the sheriff of Parmer County?"

Rodriguez glanced in the mirror at Connelly, then turned his gaze back to Cole before continuing.

"But this weird little ritual, this is not the soldiers' style. No, the soldiers come out guns blazing. A showdown at the OK Corral, a gunfight at high noon. That's the soldier way."

Silence.

A few beats passed and Connelly said, "We didn't do this. We wouldn't kill that old man. There's no reason."

Rodriguez nodded his head affirmatively.

"You know, *amigo*, I believe you."

Rodriguez began tapping on the steering wheel with his fingers, rapping out a coded message known only to himself.

"This has the subtle touch of a mind far more crafty and less direct than that of the soldier. It is an act by a member of my tribe, not yours. One thing, though. I begin to wonder whether maybe you soldiers — and the Tyrells, too — may be thinking you can cut a better deal, get better terms, from one of my competitors. Somebody who would approach this problem from an entirely different, indirect angle, meaning to throw me off, to sew confusion and undermine old Manny on his home turf. The only thing I can't figure is what comes next."

Rodriguez looked at Connelly, then at Cole and said, "You see the problem."

Rodriguez scratched his chin again and went on.

"I can see a benefit for certain parties if this kind of thing continues on the West side — say, some of the cousins begin to get stirred up against Manny, thinking that his medicine has gone bad, that the *jefe* has lost favor with the spirit world. Don't laugh at that, the cousins are very superstitious."

Rodriguez was nodding again, this time in a negative fashion.

"So, I'm thinking that the soldiers may not be the hand that broke that old man's neck, but maybe they shook that hand sometime, say, recently, to head off a reckoning on Veterans Day, setting the stage for — for what? How are you going to get rid of me? Something else is brewing, no?"

The *jefe* raised his eyebrows and again looked back at Connelly, then over at Cole.

Cole spoke up first.

"If you think you can try and blame us for this, forget it. Nobody'd believe it. That's one."

He paused and Rodriguez, eyebrows lifted again said, "And two?"

"That's for you to find out. Maybe you should call off your little game of chicken, *jefe*, with the bad medicine around and all."

Cole opened the door and stepped out of the car. Connelly followed suit. They both walked away from the sheriff's car, leaving the doors open.

Rodriguez shook his head, bewildered by such behavior.

"Such disrespect for your superior."

As they walked away from Rodriguez's car, Connelly asked in passing, "What's number two?"

Cole shrugged. "I don't know. Just screwin with the *jefe*. All I know is that we got to be ready. Will and Sammy got to get ready. We can mobilize the East side. The citizens' committee is with us."

Cole nodded back at Rodriguez's car.

"He's behind this somehow."

Connelly picked up the pace and said, "Maybe we hit them first. Why wait? Whatever he's up to, we can't just wait on him to play this out. We need to get Sonny poking around again."

Cole caught up with Connelly and touched his arm in a gesture meant to restrain Man Killer's aggression.

"We gotta make this look right. Let him make the first move, then we make our strike at the cousins. We have a contact with the Rangers. We can bring them in, maybe the *jefe* goes... Maybe he kills the Mex preacher and we can bring it down on him..."

"Then what?"

"Then... I don't know."

"I always like it when we have such clear plans."

"Look, Man Killer, there's a way to play this back at the *jefe*. We'll see."

The two soldiers split up, one to the right, one to the left. They got in their patrol cars and drove away.

*

Charlie Bass sat outside his little house and took a dip.

He pushed against the rusty metal back of his lawn chair, a type of chair seen mostly in faded photographs, wondering if the chair would break through at its rusty wounds and he would die in the strangest accident yet seen in a place that had known many strange accidents. Charlie Bass impaled by the broken metal arm of a rusty lawn chair. There would be cameras and police cars and a pretty female reporter interviewing the sobbing widow denying her husband was a killer, insisting that he did not deserve such a fate. If she broke down and couldn't speak, all the better. The audience loved tears.

But that scene, as bad as it would be, was still better than being found naked and burned, cut to pieces, with a sign of warning tied around his limp neck.

Either way, the news vultures would get their story. And the Charlie Bass problem would be solved.

Charlie Bass heard the crackling sound of tires on gravel long before the pickup made it up the winding drive that rose from the gate. The cabin's location gave you enough time to prepare to fight or to run or to say a quick prayer and get ready to die.

There was just time enough for any one of those.

At first, Charlie Bass felt the strange sensation of anticipation and fear you get when you aren't really sure what unseen thing is coming, but it passed quickly.

He recognized the truck.

It was the Chaplain, probably coming here to tell me something, thought Charlie Bass, something he and the soldiers and Will and Sammy have worked out. Maybe a solution to the Charlie Bass problem.

Charlie Bass spat a stream of tobacco juice at a line of ants marching in a steady column near the tip of his right boot and waited as the Chaplain parked, got out of the truck, and paused to stare at a darkening sky that was filling up with clouds forming a semi-circle over the ground he was about to walk. He squinted and gazed at the approaching clouds, which seemed strangely to have adopted an almost imperceptible rolling motion.

A rumble of thunder.

Charlie Bass and the Chaplain simultaneously jerked their heads around to stare at the approaching banks of clouds, the thunder an omen of things to come. *Everybody is looking for signs and omens*, thought Charlie Bass. *It's what you do when you feel helpless.*

The Chaplain approached and they shook hands. Then he backed away a few steps, ostensibly to gaze at the wondrous storm. He was gathering his thoughts, as Charlie Bass saw it. Preparing to make a pronouncement or issue a decree.

"So," said Charlie as he rubbed his hands together and spat tobacco juice at the ants again, "what's it to be, Chaplain? Me and the *jefe* facin off at high noon in Parmer? Or is it me handed over to the Escobars? Maybe they passed the job on to you."

The Chaplain shook his head negatively.

"What job, Charlie?"

Charlie Bass spat again, then looped his right index finger in his lower lip and tossed the dip into the grass.

"To terminate one Charlie Bass and save everbody a lot of trouble, includin my family."

"Do you think we would do that?"

Charlie took off his cap and scratched his thinning scalp.

"Naw, I don't believe ya would. Just get gloomy up here by myself, is all."

He paused and went on, getting to the point.

"But they was that Mock boy and Jimmy G. If Will and Sammy got to thinkin this was all my fault, that I done wrong and was causin big trouble for everbody… well, it does set ya to thinkin."

"I think they've told you otherwise, haven't they?"

Charlie had his hands in pockets as he drew a small circle in the dirt with the tip of this right boot.

"Yeah, they have."

"You believe them."

"Yeah, I guess I do."

Charlie finished drawing the circle and they both turned their heads once more in reaction to distant thunder. They witnessed bony fingers of stark white light flash across a rainless sky. The clouds, accompanied by a sharply cooler breeze, were blotting out the November sun.

Charlie Bass said, "When we used to see it rainin on a sunny day, my momma would say the devil was beatin his wife. What do they say when it's ligthnin and no rain, Chaplain?"

The wind kicked up and Charlie lifted his right hand to hold on to the bill of his camo cap. The Chaplain wondered if he had ever seen Charlie Bass without it.

"They call that dry lightning. I thought it was already too cool for that. I hear it happens mostly up north in warmer weather."

"That's what they say, is it? A strange sight, Chaplain, a strange sight. But I guess the dry kind can kill ya just as soon as in a rain storm."

Thick cloud mountains, dark and majestic, had formed over their heads.

The Chaplain told Charlie Bass that dry lightning was more apt to start a grass fire.

The Chaplain wondered if he somehow attracted strange bouts of natural electricity. Was he a lightning rod of sorts, perhaps of a metaphysical nature? But the metaphysical realm kept that secret from him, so he was left only to wonder.

"Charlie... I came to tell you we are thinking of moving you further away from here. There have been some strange things going on in Parmer, stranger than any of us can explain."

"Should I know about em, Chaplain?"

The cooler air had raised goose pimples on Charlie Bass's thin arms. The Chaplain rubbed his jaw and said, "Only if you want to know, Charlie. But none of us can figure out any connection between..."

His voice drifted off, the wind carrying his words away.

Charlie asked who was dead and the Chaplain said he wouldn't know them. Two of them. With their necks broken.

A huge chasm seemed to open before Charlie Bass and he stepped back from it and asked the Chaplain some questions.

He started by asking him if he ever wondered what he was here for. And the Chaplain asked if he meant here like on earth here, and Charlie said yes, I do. And the Chaplain said yes, he did wonder, sometimes, but maybe the best answer he had came when he was in the service. "How's that," asked Charlie, so the Chaplain told him some of his stories, which he had not shared with many. Charlie and he stood there in the cool wind with Charlie Bass nodding his head and telling the Chaplain that he was way ahead of him, yessir, way ahead.

Charlie asked him if leavin here might be a reason for bein here, in a manner of speakin and the Chaplain looked puzzled and asked what Charlie meant by that.

But Charlie didn't answer. He just said let him know about goin somewhere else and the Chaplain said they were thinking over a couple of locations and they might move him by Veterans Day, just two days off now, depending. Charlie just nodded and waved and walked in the house and shut the door behind him.

The Chaplain stood there in the wind and then turned and walked back and got in his truck and drove away, wondering what Charlie Bass had meant.

*

Espinoza sat in his usual place in the bar and made swirls of damp condensation on the table top with his beer glass.

He was waiting for the tall man, Posey.

His DEA contact would have questions for him. Many questions.

Posey had an arrangement with Rodriguez and must be persuaded to make new arrangements. And it must not appear as if he, Posey, was betraying Rodriguez. Trust was important in this business. And Posey had a reputation as a man who abided by the stipulations of all his arrangements. So, if something happened to Rodriguez, Posey must not be held responsible. True, the arrangement between them had always been subject to modification if circumstances changed. Rodriguez would understand that.

Posey's questions would have to be answered convincingly.

And he, Espinoza, had many questions himself regarding the present situation.

He had engaged the services of the feared and mysterious *El Brazo*. That was one. Two: this strange and deadly *sicario* was to kill *El Pastor*. *El Pastor*'s death would accomplish two goals — first, removing the troublesome preacher and settling accounts; and second, opening the door to identifying Rodriguez as the responsible party. The DEA would shut down the local *jefe*'s operations for a time, allowing Posey to claim credit for a major victory against the drug runners, improving his chances for further promotion. Removing Rodriguez would help the Escobars, unhappy with the *jefe*'s dealings with the soldiers, to eventually step in and bring the operation back, using product that would be supplied by the Espinoza organization.

There were a few details yet to be worked out — seeing to it that a reliable replacement for Rodriguez was found, for one, and seeking some accommodation with, or the destruction of, the soldiers, for another.

Espinoza had to admit it was a plan of remarkable subtlety. He had always prided himself on being brighter, more sophisticated than the others, an artist of this business, something that set him apart from the usual run of crude operators.

But something was not right.

The operation had begun to go awry as *El Brazo* went on a killing spree, while *El Pastor* remained alive and well.

184

Espinoza, a wise and long-lived man, a visionary in this business — he had to recognize this himself — had to explain to Posey what was going on. It seemed that this most expert, feared, and mysterious *sicario* had reached some point of transmutation, perhaps believing in his own myth, and was now simply an angel — or devil — of death.

Others in the *sicario* business had reached a point where they had burned out and had to be eliminated for the good of all concerned. Some killed themselves. It was a hazard of the profession.

Espinoza, who had been a student at some of the best universities in both his own country and in the north, did not believe in the superstitions of the common people. He did not believe that *El Brazo* was supernatural in substance and lineage, yet this episode had caused him much distress. The celebrated *sicario* had brought too much drama to the present game and was endangering the Espinoza plan, as well as the Espinoza reputation for omnipotence in all business matters.

Espinoza tapped his glass and rehearsed his talk with Posey. You see the problem, my friend? Yes?

Perhaps *El Brazo* had reached some end that could not be reversed. And that might require someone else to set things right.

He might try and hint at this to Posey, but the Anglo mind was not subtle or even aware of mystery and of the importance of ritual. At times, thought Espinoza, the Anglo mind seemed even unaware of itself. Of its separate existence and place. So, he would have to approach this problem in one way with Posey and in quite another with his own people.

*

The preacher watched the people on Main Street from his vantage point atop a hill in the city park. And some strange, nearly gravitational force drew him down the hill and towards Main Street, as if he himself was not propelling his own body.

The preacher reached Main Street, standing arms lifted to the November skies.

And he began to speak.

Before him stood an old man in overalls, squinting, hands in his back pockets. A little Mexican girl clutched at a doll and backed away. A man in a sweat-stained Stetson scratched his chin in puzzled witness. And a thin woman in sunglasses announced, "That's that crazy preacher."

The *jefe*, who had business on Main Street that day, had noticed the preacher and cocked his head to watch him. Hands in his jacket pockets, head still cocked, Rodriguez approached him and stood by the people gathered there, squinting and listening attentively to everything the strange itinerant had to say…

*

"What did he mean?"

The question was from Connelly. He sat with Cole and Houston, sipping coffee in the Texan café.

Connelly again.

"What was that about the trees?"

Connelly set his coffee cup down and adjusted his sunglasses.

"Answer my question, reverend, or forever hold your peace. He pointed to you. The scarred man with the arm, like walking death. Now what did he mean by all that?"

"By all what?"

"The arm. Walking death."

Houston got up and walked behind Cole, drawing the stump of his left arm under Cole's chin.

Cole, looking slightly alarmed, said, "What the hell do you think you're doin?"

Houston grinned at Connelly, then told Cole, "Sit still while I show you what that preacher man meant."

Houston clinched the left stump with his right hand and squeezed just a little.

"OK, I get it, let go a me, dammit."

Houston relaxed his grip and waved at Floyd Price, who was scratching his chin, eyeing the scarred soldier curiously.

"Just making a little demonstration, Floyd."

Floyd nodded his head affirmatively and resumed eating his breakfast.

Houston sat down again and said, "Maybe I should go find that preacher. Maybe he knows or has seen this man with the arm. The arm that can break a neck like it was a reed."

Connelly shook his head.

Cole finished his coffee and tapped the cup on the table top.

"Why the hell are we arguin over what some crazy street preacher said, anyway?"

Connelly stirred his coffee.

He eyed Houston once more.

"You never did answer me about the trees, reverend."

Houston pushed his chair back and stood up before bending toward Connelly and asking whether Man Killer had ever been to Sunday school.

Connelly shrugged.

Houston cocked his remaining eyebrow at the Man Killer.

"Tree of knowledge. Tree of life. You can't keep partaking of the fruit of the one and expect to benefit from the fruit of the other. Understand? No?"

"You talk in riddles, reverend."

Houston sighed and walked out of the café.

Connelly turned to Cole.

"We better get to the mobilization plan for tomorrow. And we need to talk to the Chaplain about the funeral."

Cole stood up and started counting out some bills he threw on the table.

"I hope it ain't ours."

*

Houston had crossed the street as the preacher, his expression wild and distraught, his hands gesticulating, expounded on diverse threads of seemingly random thoughts, the people gathered there backing up as if escaping the heat of the burning bush itself.

The eyes of the preacher focused on the scarred, one armed man before him. And the preacher began to speak of the Plain of Shinar and the confounding of Nimrod's people and of Nimrod the hunter and builder of cities calling to storm heaven itself... And he spoke of the whited sepulcher... Of a man with a strong arm who was walking death... Of the Tree of Knowledge, of the Tree of Life...

The preacher gasped as if his lungs had failed him, or as if the air he breathed had been fouled by poisonous fumes... He raised his right hand and pointed at Houston and said, "You. You know."

As Houston walked away, Rodriguez slowly pivoted on his heel, watching him, then gazed over his shoulder at the preacher man who saw visions.

22

The soldiers meet… El Brazo's premonition… Houston has a hunch…
Connelly and family… Charlie Bass solves a problem… El Brazo *(The*
sicario*'s approach; Houston; El Pastor; the Preacher)*

That evening, the soldiers met at the Veterans' hall. J. C. called the
meeting to order. The question before them, posed by Cole, was this:
should they press the mayor to call off the parade and the ceremony at
the war memorial set for tomorrow? And what about the McRae funeral?

J.C. leaned back in his chair and scratched his chin and said, "Well I
don't know. Have Will and Sammy moved Charlie Bass?"

And the Chaplain supplied the answer of "…not yet they haven't.
Tonight." He couldn't say where they intended to move him to.

J. C. turned to Connelly next and wanted to know about the *jefe*. What
was he thinkin?

"He's not," said Connelly.

J.C. had a comical look on his face. It was a look that asked those
present what in the world had he done to deserve this mess? He leaned
back in his chair and sighed.

"Not what, Swordfish?"

"Thinkin."

"Not thinkin. Then just what in the Sam Hill is he doin?"

Connelly was chewing gum, leaning back in his chair, arms crossed.
He stopped chewing the gum, took it out, wrapped it in a bit of tissue
paper he pulled from his pocket and set it in an ash tray on the table.
Connelly slid his sunglasses up on his forehead.

"He don't have to think, J. C. He told us what he wanted and gave us a
deadline. The cousins know damn well he did."

"And that means what, exactly?"

"It means he's got to do somethin tomorrow. He'll have to make a
point. The murders, the broken necks. He thinks we're tryin to draw him
in."

"Draw him into what, if ya don't mind me askin."

Connelly paused and leaned forward, elbows on the table. He didn't mind.

"Into some kinda trap. He thinks we have a line to Espinoza. We draw him into a trap, get him arrested, send him up. He's thinkin somebody in the cousins' organization has sold him out to the Ezpinoza cartel. Probably the Escobars. The broken necks, they show the *jefe* has lost his medicine. The Escobars have already stirred up talk that the *jefe* hasn't taken vengeance for their boy's death. And he's my brother-in-law… He can't pin it all down, but that's what he's got on his mind. And he'll have to do somethin tomorrow or the cousins will see him backed down. Big talk. No action. So, he can't let his deadline go. *Sabe?*"

J.C. grunted and said he *sabe*d plenty.

Cole banged the table with his fist and rubbed his brow, exasperated.

"And if we call everything off, what will the town see? That it's us who arc backin down. That the soldiers can't deliver. There's been lots of talk, J.C. You've all heard it. Some of the hotheads want a war."

Henson pushed his chair back from the table. He crossed his arms, adopting a sardonic expression.

"Then let's have it, dammit."

Cole looked over at Henson, then at Connelly. He glanced around the table at the men seated there, noting that Hightower was looking especially grim.

"We have to keep this organized. Somebody has got to be in charge and that somebody is us. We got the citizens' committee. They'll be out tomorrow and they will take orders from us, like we agreed."

Henson grinned and thumped a can of dip he pulled out of his back pocket. He twisted the lid and opened it, took a pinch and grinned some more.

"So what's the plan, general?"

*

El Brazo had experienced a premonition.

It came in the form of a dream.

El Brazo was staying in a house not far from Parmer, one prepared for him by his contact with the Escobars.

He had locked all the doors and windows of the little house and placed a kitchen chair so that it braced the front door. He laid down fully clothed on top of the bed sheets. *El Brazo* folded his arms over his chest,

189

his right hand holding a Glock .40 caliber, and closed his eyes. And he fell into the nether world of half sleep. A door in his mind opened as it always did and he saw the things that entered via that door, images he would attempt to interpret.

And what did he see?

The thing that he saw was a vehicle of indeterminate color and shape, but bright, even glowing. Was it a train? A moving vehicle, in any case. And out of that vehicle stepped a young boy, in appearance much like himself as a boy.

The boy began walking through a desolate land. He approached a large mesquite tree in this land of desolation and he halted there, his eyes fixed on a huge rattlesnake that slithered from under the mesquite, baring its fangs at him. And then the great rattlesnake was struck by the swift assault of an eagle that had hovered on wing high above the serpent.

The boy squatted in the dust and watched the eagle kill the serpent. The eagle seemed oblivious to the attempts of the rattler to strike, as if it were immune to the serpent's venom.

When the battle was done, the boy rose, only this time taller, bearing the look of a grown man, striding boldly back in the direction whence he came. And he met a smiling, finely dressed older man and they walked away together.

The next day, *El Brazo* drove past the church of *El Pastor*.

He often liked to be close to his victim. He thought of himself as a predator circling his prey, like a shark circling a helpless swimmer in a warm ocean, the swimmer unsuspecting, the shark a machine that moved closer and closer, hardly making a wake in the still waters until it struck.

This was an image that often came to him when he made his reconnaissance drives.

It was then that he noticed that he was being followed. The driver held back and was quite good at appearing not to be following, but it was so, all the same.

The driver was a young man of a type he had often seen in Juarez. *El Brazo* pretended to be adjusting his rear-view mirror, while he looked at the face, fleetingly, but the image was clear enough. The truck the young man drove was of a reddish orange tone.

And then *El Brazo* knew the correct interpretation of his dream.

*

190

Houston left his house on the evening of the tenth of November and drove out of town toward Ely. He parked outside the Market Basket, back away from the store front, avoiding the lights in the parking lot, and waited until it closed. The employees slowly began to filter out.

When a tall, strawberry-blonde-headed woman everybody called Margie was walking to her car, lighting a cigarette on the way, Houston rolled his window down and said "Hey." And she stopped and squinted to see who was talking to her and she said "Hey yourself," and laughed.

A half hour later, she stood facing the hallway mirror in the old house Houston stayed in. Houston stroked her hair and asked her whether he was ugly and she looked back at him in the mirror's image and mouthed no silently.

Later that night, Houston dropped Margie off at her car and headed for Parmer, seeking Sonny Valdez. She hadn't thought it strange that he told her he had to leave and she hadn't said a word as he dropped her off. She walked away silently.

*

Houston squatted in the branches of a scrub cedar and watched.

A floodlight illuminated the churchyard below him, the church appearing hopeful, defiant of the fates.

Houston had found Sonny Valdez, learning more of the mysteries of the West side and of the story of a man named Rojas.

He did not know whether to expect anyone tonight or not. But it was the eve of Veterans Day. And he had a hunch that the game with the man called *El Pastor* might play out this very night.

Houston patiently watched the churchyard. He heard a car approaching and squinted in the darkness, trying to make it out. He saw it moving slowly, off road, behind a row of brush and mesquite.

*

The tears streamed down Natalie's cheeks. She said, "I'll go but I want you to come with me."

And Connelly said "No, I can't."

Natalie said, "This does not have to happen. He's my sister's husband."

Connelly got up from sitting on the bed and said, "I don't know what will happen, but it could be bad. Go to Fort Worth. Leave now. You and the boys."

191

Natalie wiped her eyes with a tissue and said, "She's my sister. He's her husband. You can't let this go too far, baby."

And Connelly sighed and said "It's already gone that far. And Manny may not be able to protect you if it gets real bad. He might not be the *jefe* for much longer, sweetheart. Go now and take the boys."

Connelly helped her pack and he hugged the boys and watched them drive away. He had given her a gun. She knew how to use it. He told her to stay on the freeway as much as she could. It's safer.

Connelly walked back into the house and collected his gear. He was wondering when they would come for him.

*

On the evening of the tenth of November, Charlie Bass was sitting in his lawn chair outside his hideaway place. He was waiting. Waiting on Will and Sammy to come and take him someplace else to hide. The soldiers and the bikers were worried, he could tell, though nobody said anything about being worried at all.

Tomorrow was Veterans Day.

Charlie Bass got up. It was right at full dark. They wouldn't be here for a while. They'd move him late tonight most likely.

He put on his denim jacket, as there was a chill in the air. He leaned over and took his dip out and tossed it into the grass and lifted his cap and scratched his head and put it back on and started walking.

Charlie Bass was a problem, so Charlie Bass had to figure his own way out.

He walked down the hill, braced himself on a fence post and pushed down on the rusty barbed wire to step through the fence line, stumbling in the dark as it was a steep incline.

Charlie Bass made his way down to the base of the hill and stood next to a tall cedar where the state highway made its sharp turn, heading northeast for Fort Worth and Dallas.

He had been watching the highway from above.

Not a lot of traffic. Much of it trucks heading toward the metropolitan areas of North Texas.

As he stood and waited, in his mind's eye Charlie Bass replayed a scene from one of his favorite movies. Tom Doniphon was talking to the wounded Ransom Stoddard, who had pledged to see Liberty Valance thrown in jail. Doniphon lifted the .45 in his hand, then slipped it back in its holster, slapped the holster on his hip and said that out here a man solves his own problems.

Charlie Bass heard the big rig rounding the corner, gaining speed.

*

El Brazo had given the *sicario* plenty of room, plenty of time to catch up. The young *sicario* was a good watcher. He had held back, headlights off, then moved in closer, close enough to see where *El Brazo* was headed.

El Brazo had been careful. He had looked over his car, checking for explosives before getting in and turning the key.

The car was clear. That was good. *El Brazo* wanted the time and place to be of his own choosing. This game would play out and end on his terms.

El Brazo had set the metal gasoline canister on the floorboard on the passenger's side of the front seat. He had his Glock on the seat next to him as he started the car and pulled away. *El Brazo* had called his contact and had the church of *El Pastor* watched all afternoon and into the evening. He knew that Rojas was there now.

He waited for the *sicario* to catch up, watching but being careful not to be seen watching as the red-orange truck pulled up closer.

*

Houston squatted on his haunches, pistol in hand. The car was pulling out of the brush and slowly heading up a slight incline toward the church of *El Pastor*.

Houston slowly made his way out of the brush, positioning himself to run down the hill and intercept the car if need be. If the car stopped and the large figure inside got out, he would wait and see what the assassin's next move would be before making his own countermove.

It was at that moment that Houston noticed another vehicle moving through the brush. He squinted in the dark and made out the cab of a pickup truck.

Then Houston heard movement behind him and he turned and beheld the itinerant preacher, glassy eyed and as wild in appearance as John the Baptist in the wilderness, eating locusts and honey.

*

El Pastor knelt before the altar, reciting his nightly prayers. The rows of pews were cloaked in darkness. A small light illuminated the altar. *El Pastor* preferred the tranquility and stillness of the relative darkness, enveloping the self symbolically as the inevitable passing away of all flesh, a light pointing the way to the cross.

El Pastor finished his prayers. He rose, turned and walked toward the vestibule where his room was. He noticed movement in the churchyard, beyond the church's floodlight. *El Pastor* continued walking and watching. He could just make out a car approaching the church.

*

The *sicario* stopped the truck. He cradled an M-4 in his lap, quickly taking in the scene before him and formulating his plan. If *El Brazo* killed Rojas, then one thing. If not, another. But The Arm would be dead and the credit for his and *El Pastor*'s deaths would be attributed to the young *sicario* and no other.

A new legend would be made this night.

The *sicario* opened the truck door, slinging the M-4 by its strap over his left shoulder. He reached for a metal toolbox straddling the bed of the pickup, lifted the toolbox's lid, and carefully extracted a grenade launcher.

*

El Brazo began laughing, his laugh resonating through the night air. The young *sicario*, startled, puzzled over the laughter. Houston turned from the preacher and started down the hill, while *El Pastor* began backing away from the vestibule as *El Brazo* gunned his car's motor and mashed down hard on the accelerator, laughing. The car slammed into the front of the church just as *El Brazo* opened fire. The gas canister exploded and the fire spread as *El Brazo's* body lurched over the steering wheel. The *sicario* fired the grenade launcher at *El Brazo*'s car. A fireball climbed to the sky. *El Pastor* was running headlong toward the altar when the explosion shook the church and he left his feet. Houston hit the ground, rolling to his right, opening fire on the *sicario*'s pickup. The preacher stood in the churchyard gazing at the fire, flinching at the report of Houston's pistol, shouting "Dear God, God Almighty, great God…"

*

194

The flames consuming the church of *El Pastor* climbed high into the night until the darkness engulfed them, the spirit of the blaze disappearing into the heavens.

The *sicario* wondered what he would call himself. What would *they* call him? He planned a ceremony for *Santa Muerte* to commemorate this night as he walked toward the burning church, ready to return fire with his M-4 should the one-armed man offer more resistance.

But the one-armed man was gone.

The *sicario* eyed the car encasing the flaming carcass of *El Brazo*. Strange how the body stiffened, the arms raised, as *El Brazo* burned with a flame that seemed like a flare, his flesh consumed by multi-colored bursts of fire.

And then he saw it.

The flames had whipped up a wind, a wall of air that blew the object away from the car, so that as the *sicario* halted his approach to the flames, the fragile object floated until it landed at his feet. The *sicario* bent over and felt the hot material and the object burned his fingers and he let it go. He stood looking down at a face that stared at him from the ashes and the dust, perhaps the ashes of the flesh and bones of *El Brazo* himself, and the death mask grinned up at him.

*

As the pyre enveloped the church, its wind was sucked into a vacuum created as the building began to fall inward on itself, a black hole beckoning all to enter its consuming center. The *sicario* heard sirens in the distance, but did not turn to observe the red and blue lights creating frantic patterns in the darkness.

He stood in the flame brightened darkness, a death mask as his face.

He turned and went to his truck and drove away, avoiding the sirens and the lights, disappearing into the darkness.

23

*Veterans Day… Posey surveys the landscape… * El Brazo*'s fate… The legend of* El Pastor

Connelly had told him long ago that when you've done it once, it gets easier. That's what he said and Cole believed him.

Cole checked his weapon, placed it firmly in the holster on his right hip and walked out of the Veterans' hall into the cool breeze of the November eleventh morning.

And this is what he saw: old men in caps with the organization's insignia, standing at the ready. Some wore rows of medals on their chests. Cole tried to imagine them as they were when they had been young and faced the fire. The tall, stooped one had been straight and sturdy, his white hair maybe brown. The short thick one had walked without the bow in his legs. The heavy one had been thin, perhaps, and without glasses. A lean man with a long neck and another, shoulders hunched, but still sturdy, held the flags that waved and flapped in the wind, one the Stars and Stripes, the other the Lone Star banner. The men formed two columns abreast behind the flag bearers. They were armed with handguns and rifles and shotguns. One of them carried a wreath for the ceremony at the Veterans Memorial.

Cole would lead the column. At the rear were the rest of the soldiers, Houston limping with a wounded leg from the explosion at the church, checking his weapon and adjusting the gun belt around his waist. Henson was chewing gum, bracing a pump shotgun on his hip, an M-4 on his shoulder. He whispered to those around him: *For what we are about to receive, let us be truly thankful.* J.C. grimly held a Garand rifle. Bobby Sanchez had an Army .45 on his belt and touted an M-4. Hightower grimly held the strap of the M-16 on his shoulder. Eddie Hatcher squinted as he checked his pump shotgun. The men carried extra ammunition and wore Kevlar vests. Only the Chaplain was unarmed.

Cole motioned with his right hand and the procession marched out of the gravel parking lot of the Veterans' hall. One of the marchers behind the flag bearers held his own banner that he now unfurled to the cool winds: COME AND TAKE IT. The man at his shoulder unfurled a Gadsen flag.

The men marched at a steady, even pace. Cole surveyed the ground around them. They were passing through the neighborhoods of the East side. Armed members of the citizens' committee stood and watched the column go by, then fell in line behind, following the soldiers to Main Street.

Whole families stood silently on porches and watched the procession, the men taking off their caps and placing them over their hearts. The streets were lined with rows of small American and Texan flags.

On Main Street, Will and Sammy and the other Gunslingers stood by their bikes as the men marched past the storefronts and abandoned buildings of Parmer, Texas.

Cole made out a tall figure standing at the entrance of the Texan Café. He had once stood six foot five in his stocking feet. Now he slumped a bit under that, but he seemed to straighten when he spotted the approaching procession. He wore a long-sleeved pearl snap shirt of faded denim with a thick padded down vest over it. At his waist was a broad belt holding a holster with a .45 Peacemaker. A weathered black Stetson covered the steel gray hair of Roy Wallace. His thick, paw-like right hand held an Armalite rifle. His left hand stuffed the unlit stub of a cigar in his breast pocket.

Captain Roy Wallace stepped off the sidewalk, walking parallel to Cole at the edge of the street.

Armed men emerged from the side streets, following at a distance. The Gunslingers cranked their big bikes and rode to the front of the column, then slowed, waiting for the column to pass before again roaring past them.

The bikers and the citizens' committee had provided security for the McRae funeral. The Chaplain read the twenty-third Psalm. A bugler played Taps. Now the bikers flanked the marching column on this cool and bright November eleventh morning.

No band. No floats.

The Veterans Day parade was on schedule.

The column ascended a slight rise from which the men could see the flags and stone obelisks of the Parmer Veterans Memorial.

He was there.

Cole squinted in the morning sunlight, focusing on the stocky figure of Manny Rodriguez standing in a circle of stones, each stone bearing the names of those fallen in the wars the men of Parmer County had fought in. A bronze figure of an American bald eagle stood in the memorial's center. The flags of the old American union and the Lone Star state waved behind the circle of stones. The old water tower reading "Home of the Rangers" stood beyond the memorial. Manny's people, armed with Armalite rifles and shotguns, stood all around the stone obelisks.

The cousins were out in force.

As the marchers approached the memorial, the soldiers, save for the Chaplain, jogged to the front of the column. Cole was the point man, while the others fanned out, Houston, Henson, and J.C. to his left, Bobby Sanchez, Hatcher, and Hightower to his right. Sonny and Will and the other Gunslingers stepped off their bikes and flanked the soldiers. Roy Wallace and the Chaplain walked behind them. The townsmen moved in closer to the column, which had halted just outside the memorial.

Cole nodded.

The man carrying the wreath came through the rows of veterans, stopping next to Cole, who stepped within the circle and motioned the wreath bearer forward. The wreath bearer was a small, wiry man named Keith Atkins and he approached the bronze eagle and set the wreath in front of it. He stood at attention and saluted, then turned and walked back toward the column.

The wind whistled through the stone obelisks.

Rodriguez approached Cole. His right hand drifted to the holster at his side. He cocked his head and eyed Cole Landry, a Manny Rodriguez ironic smirk noting the completion of the Veterans Day ritual for this November eleventh. Rodriguez was wearing his uniform, complete with a padded jacket, a Sheriff's Department patch sewn on the shoulder. Cole couldn't tell if he wore a Kevlar vest or not.

Rodriguez, his eyes locked on Cole's, stepped toward him, paused, then slowly took another step.

"I'm coming closer, soldier, so you can hear me."

"I can hear you."

"Good."

Rodriguez silently glanced beyond the circle, surveying the men arrayed outside it. He nodded, held his chin between the thumb and forefinger of his right hand as if deep in thought, then sighed, dropping his hand to his side and lifting his eyebrows, as if to say, "How can I deal with these people?"

"It appears the soldiers are expecting trouble, Cole Landry."

Cole did not reply.

"You outnumber us a bit, but you have a lot of old men with you. Their day is over. *Your* day is over. The cousins are the wave of the future. And the future is *now*."

Manny Rodriguez nodded toward the soldiers.

"Bobby Sanchez should know better."

He shook his head in disbelief.

"But I suppose he's not the only one."

Rodriguez squinted, looking past Cole's shoulder. He noticed the hothead Henson was staring at him, grinning broadly.

Rodriguez's eyes shifted back to Cole's.

"You cowboy types always think you're in a movie. But this ain't the movies, *amigo*. This is real life, as they say."

Rodriguez paused a few beats, pursed his lips and said, "Connelly is dead."

"We know."

"I always liked him. He had a chance. He could have stuck with his in-laws."

Rodriguez shrugged.

"His boys... We are related, after all."

Rodriguez held up his hands, palms forward as if to say "What can you do?" He sighed again and said, "This doesn't have to be, soldier. No, it does not. Just give us the two crazy preachers and we will be even and walk away from all of this."

Rodriguez squinted and cocked his head and said, "He is alive, isn't he? Rojas, I mean."

"What's the plan, Manny? Get rid of any witnesses, kill the old man, blame last night on Rojas's enemies in Juarez? Then what? What about the Escobars?"

Rodriguez said nothing.

"Manny Rodriguez at a loss for words. Now that is something. What if I told you, Sheriff Rodriguez, that I know of a certain man in the DEA, name of Posey, and I hear he is very interested in you. Maybe *you* tried to kill Rojas. Maybe it was *you* who brought that maniac to town and he got out of hand."

Manny Rodriguez smiled broadly and chuckled. He lifted his right hand and wagged his forefinger at Cole.

"You can't bait me, soldier. Good try, but no, you can't bait me. I'm not biting."

Rodriguez paused.

"What about Charlie Bass? I forgot to mention him. I have word that something has happened to Charlie Bass."

Rodriguez pointed toward Will and Sammy.

"Did they, do it? If so, then they have my thanks. Problem solved. But we have a new problem. Well, two new problems, namely two crazy preachers. So, the terms have changed, Deputy Sheriff Landry. Charlie Bass is dead. That's good. The cousins will be happy. But this nasty business last night, that's something else. Now somebody will have to take the blame for that and I'm thinking maybe Charlie Bass's friends did it."

Manny Rodriguez looked from side to side and said, "A little closer, soldier, one more step. I want to say something that's, you know, really sensitive."

Rodriguez slowly moved his right foot forward and stopped, then his left foot. He spoke in a low whisper, leaning forward a bit as if he were confiding a deep and terrible secret to a close friend.

"Look, soldier, we can wipe the slate clean. Rojas would be gone. The crazy preacher is nothing to you, anyway. And we can get rid of the bikers, too. They have been nothing but trouble for both of us. We can start over. You should walk away from here and talk to the other soldiers and that half-assed committee. Hand over the preachers. Then the cousins will be satisfied, especially when Will and Sammy go down. All will be forgiven."

Cole smiled.

Rodriguez looked quite puzzled.

And Cole said, "You go to hell."

Rodriguez took a deep breath and looked around him. The wind had once more picked up, whistling through the stone obelisks.

The Rodriguez smirk slowly made its return.

"I killed him, soldier. I did it myself. And I enjoyed it. Yes, I did. All you old cowboys will go down. And your women, too."

Rodriguez stepped back. The smirk was now a broad smile.

"I killed him."

Rodriguez, still smiling broadly, raised his eye brows.

"I'm giving you a chance, soldier."

Manny Rodriguez's hand slid down to rest on his holster.

Cole made a feint with his left hand and Rodriguez reacted. He fired at Cole as the soldier was backing up.

*

Bodies of the dead and dying were in the street and around the stone obelisks. The obelisks were pockmarked by gunfire, shell casings strewn on the street and about the stone circle. Two of the bikes belonging to the Gunslingers were in flames, black smoke billowing into the wind. Along Main Street, shattered glass was scattered about the pavement and sidewalks.

*

[*News item for posting on Channel 12 website/Video for nightly news broadcast version/Video embedded at web site*]

Former Parmer County Sheriff Manuel "Manny" Rodriguez was taken into custody by DEA officers in San Antonio today. [*Cut to video of the arrest*] Rodriguez stands accused of managing a major narcotics-smuggling operation from Parmer County. According to DEA officer Leland Posey [*Cut to video of Posey*], Rodriguez was involved in a vicious power struggle within his own organization, known locally as "the cousins" (or "*Los Primos*"), a power struggle that led to a series of gruesome murders in Parmer and an attack on the church of the man known as *El Pastor*.

[*Cut to file footage of Rojas*] El Pastor, one Luis Rojas of Juarez, Mexico, a man loved and admired by many and, perhaps, feared by the cartels, had brought his ministry to Parmer. That ministry, centered on rehabilitating drug addicts and those involved with the cartels, may have threatened Rodriguez's position as the *jefe*, or boss, of the regional drug operation and thus, Rodriguez's political future. [*Cut to file footage of Rodriguez's past campaign for sheriff*] According to DEA sources, Rodriguez was positioning himself to run for a statewide office, perhaps a state senate seat, and from there, the sky was the limit for the popular and charismatic sheriff. Some political insiders say that Rodriguez, a man admired by his Hispanic base and respected in the Anglo community, could have been state governor.

[*Cut to video of Posey*] Posey: "DEA has reason to believe that former Sheriff Manny Rodriguez was being groomed by a major Mexican drug cartel to infiltrate the state government and use his influence to benefit organized crime. As a potential future governor, Rodriguez could have eventually run for a federal office, corrupting government at both the federal and North American free trade zone levels." [*Cut to video of Parmer*] Posey said that the DEA and other federal and state agencies had been "interested in" — his words — Rodriguez for some time. Cell phone video of Rodriguez shooting a Parmer County deputy sheriff, Cole Landry, during a bloody Veterans Day confrontation between rival factions in the area triggered a full-scale investigation. The video "went viral" on the Internet, attracting the attention of state law enforcement authorities. [*Cut to the cell phone video of Rodriguez firing at Landry*]

Since them, DEA agents and Texas Rangers have been involved in a thorough investigation of the Parmer County administration and its possible links to organized crime, resulting in a "purge," according to law enforcement sources, of Rodriguez's closest associates from the Parmer County Sheriff's Department and local government. Texas Ranger sources also say that Rodriguez may have personally executed a Mexican man involved in the drug trade outside a Parmer nightclub last year. At Deputy Sheriff Landry's funeral last November, local civic leaders called for action by both the Rangers and federal law enforcement. [*Cut to file footage of the Landry funeral*]

Today, the citizens of Parmer and Parmer County fear that rival drug gangs will fill the vacuum left by Rodriguez's arrest. [*Cut to street interview with Hector Comacho; Eyewitness voiceover on English language version; Camacho speaking in Spanish version*] Hector Camacho, a local business owner in Parmer, told Eyewitness News that Rodriguez's departure gives rivals affiliated with the Espinoza drug cartel an opportunity to seize control of an important drug transit route through Parmer County.

Meanwhile, rumors persist that Deputy Sheriff Landry, shown being shot in the cell phone video, survived the attack, his whereabouts unknown. Rodriguez supporters in Parmer and the state capital are claiming that the confrontation was a set-up orchestrated by a local faction known as "the soldiers" and their allies in organized crime, an outlaw motorcycle gang known as "the Gunslingers." [*Cut to replay of cell phone video; cut to video of motorcycle riders in Parmer*]

[*Cut to video of Eyewitness News reporter Marianna Lopez*] The people of Parmer remain divided over the charges against their former sheriff, with some defending Rodriguez's tenure as the county's chief law enforcement officer, while others are certain the charges are true — but people on both sides of the divide remain wary, fearing that the story of drug cartel corruption in Parmer County is not over. This is Marianna Lopez, Eyewitness News, reporting from Parmer. [*End*]

*

From his seat in the chopper, Leland Posey surveyed a panoramic view of sunset in the sprawling Dallas–Fort Worth metroplex. He had taken off from Parmer after holding a press conference on the continuing investigation of former Sheriff Manny Rodriguez and drug cartel activity in the region.

It had been quite a show and Posey was pleased with how he had played it.

Leland Posey saw below and before him a mass of shanty towns sinking into the shadows as darkness encroached on the ground below. Flotsam accumulated after the dam had burst.

The chopper approached the bright lights of the metroplex, flying east from Fort Worth towards Dallas.

From above, newer slums appeared to flow like spilled and coagulated blood from the decrepit, decaying bodies of both cities' poorer areas.

As the mob collected on the fringes and in the decayed parts of city centers, the wealthy had retreated to secure compounds guarded by checkpoints manned by private security services. Some commuted by helipads to the city centers.

Like many Anglos, Leland Posey was not a reflective man. He was a pragmatist who had made the most of whatever situation confronted him. The sea changes that had occurred in his lifetime went apparently unnoticed by Posey, who was not inclined to contemplate what seemed like the results of an irresistible force of nature.

The chopper veered to avoid the flight paths of airliners at DFW airport, then corrected to stay on course as it headed eastward to the heart of Dallas, a mass of illuminated glass and steel structures, daytime dying in twilight. The chopper touched down on a helipad at the top of a building near Central Expressway, the headquarters of a business conglomerate headed by a man of Indian extraction well known in the city as a mover and shaker in political and social circles. Posey was not here to speak directly to him but to two of his silent partners.

The chopper touched down and Posey stooped to make his exit beneath the still sweeping blades of the aircraft

A short Mexican in an expensive suit took him by the elbow and led him to a stairwell enclosing the executive elevator.

Espinoza and Escobar were expecting him.

*

They say that *El Brazo* died that night in the flames of the church. But many people do not believe this. They believe the man who supposedly killed him is another incarnation of the dreaded *sicario,* a snake that has shed its skin. Or that *El Brazo* lives and the story of his death is a tale meant to hide his continued presence among us, so that every mysterious death is attributed to him.

As for the man Rojas, known as *El Pastor*, he came back to the city of the dead and continued to preach, calling on the wretched to repent. He was killed somewhere in the city. That is the story, though the body was never discovered. He disappeared, like so many others, and the disappearers left no sign of him. As in the case of *El Brazo*, many people do not believe that he is dead, but that he lives and will someday show his face again in the city of the dead.

24

Reflections (The Chaplain remembers)

So, it is finished.
I've lived through the worst of it.
When I was over there and saw what was happening, I knew what the endgame was.
The world I knew is gone. Most of the things I've loved are gone. We've left a mess behind us. You'll have to make something new.
I don't have all the answers. You'll have to find them yourselves.

Epilogue

The Hum and the Hive

The sky was pale blue, turning to a glaring white as the eye traced its way to the blazing disk overhead. It was dry, so dry that the ground looked like a cracked and fissured moonscape, the far side of a satellite too close to the sun. What grass remained was brown and crisp and there was no wind, not even a wisp of movement as the planet orbited the center of its corner of an indifferent universe. Or so it seemed in the second year of the drought.

The man adjusted his sunglasses and stood completely still as if the lack of movement would prevent the heat from penetrating him further. There was no sound, just the eternal hum of the cosmos. He used the T-shirt he held in his right hand to wipe his torso of accumulated dust and sweat.

A ritual cleansing in a land of heat and dust.

The tank was a pool of shallow and rancid water. A blue heron stood on a spit of land, a hard and gray peninsula that jutted into the middle of the dying tank. The bird took no note of the man as he approached, standing still, looking like a weathered skeleton in an arid pit.

The man stopped and watched. He noticed movement in the cattails at one edge of the tank. A huge rat came out of the water. It stopped and looked at him before moving into a mound of brown weeds that were matted around the cattails, disappearing to who knows where.

The man squatted near the cattails and listened for the hum.

The heron lurched into an awkward flight that took it to the far side of the tank. The man stiffened, crouched in the cattails, and surveyed the banks of the dying pond. He braced his elbows on his knees, balancing his weight in his work boots. He listened and waited and watched and eased the pistol from his belt and clicked off the safety.

Were they coming?

But all he heard was the hum, the only vague constant as the Earth spun through space. And the man and the bird and the rat and whatever was coming were pinpoints on the spinning globe.

Then he saw the dog. It was brown and sinewy with a jowly face drawn by heat and hunger. And he saw the tight muscles around its shoulders and the ridges of the ribs that stood out on its sides. The dog gingerly walked over the rocks and the cracked scales of land on the receding edge of the tank and lapped up some of the brackish water. Then it looked up and saw the man squatting and looking at him.

The man clicked on the pistol's safety and stuck the weapon back in its holster. He shoved the T-shirt into his belt and draped it over the pistol and walked away from the tank toward a rise beyond it and the dog trotted up beside him as he passed.

The man reached the top of the rise and the dog approached him and squatted on its haunches. It wore a dried, cracked leather collar around the loose skin of its neck.

The man wiped his torso with the t-shirt again, then shook the t-shirt like a rug being cleared of dust and put it on. He started down the far side of the rise and the dog followed through a patch of mesquite and cedar and went home with the man.

*

The man sat on the back porch of a house in a stand of live oaks surrounded by withered pasture land. He had put a bowl of water and some scraps of food on the porch and the dog approached as if he had always lived with the man and lapped some water and ate the food, then plopped down on the porch.

The man rubbed his chin and said that dogs don't know they have to die.

He looked at the dog and the brute's eyes flickered, then shifted away. The man shifted in his chair, took the gun from its holster and set it in his lap.

Even memories die.

The man wondered whether it was the memory or the action that makes us who we are. If the memories fade or become distorted, does that make us something different? Maybe that's why so many try to forget. They want to be something different.

*

Remember the recording of the guy singing the Lord's Prayer after the Late Late Show? It ended with a dove against the background of a bright sunrise. I was always touched by that. The song. The prayer. Jesus never

207

seemed so real to me as he did then. Like he was standing there in our house. Momma used to let us stay up sometimes and we would bring our pillows and blankets into the living room and wrap up to watch an Errol Flynn or Randolph Scott or John Wayne double feature. The Late Show followed by the Late Late show. We might sleep through some of it, but I usually woke up to see the end and hear that beautiful prayer sung. And I'd wake y'all up if you were asleep and we'd slouch off to bed.

I dreamed last night I had pictures of the old house. I mean the inside and the outside. The hall to Momma and Daddy's room. The kitchen. Our old room we shared until Daddy built on that back bedroom. The hardwood floors that creaked and popped in the night. That deer head. The big deer Daddy killed that used to hang in the kitchen.

The trees. Pecans. Live oaks. Mimosa. A hackberry tree by the fish pond Daddy dug. A willow that Daddy had to cut down.

I was sittin there and sifting through those pictures and tryin so hard to remember.

They tore the house down.

The man's eyes opened and he sat up in the cot and looked around the room.

He didn't hear anything except the crickets outside.

He was breathing heavily.

*

The two of them had come a long way together.

They had lived much and remembered much and recited those memories to one another and to anyone who would listen.

The tall one was blind.

He carried a stick and tapped his way ahead.

Beside him walked a scarred man with one arm carrying a battered book.

They walked slowly up a steep rise and the scarred man gripped the blind one's arm and helped him.

They reached the top of the rise and the scarred man could see ahead in the shimmering waves of stark and burning sunlight a mirage or a shining city.

Acknowledgements

The author would like to acknowledge his indebtedness to Michael Fumento (for his Iraq war reporting), the late Charles Bowden (especially his book *Murder City*), Brian Mockenhaupt (his story on American military chaplains in Afghanistan) and Doug Colligan of *Reader's Digest* (writing on wounded Iraq veteran Bobby Henline). I am also indebted to the law enforcement officers and military veterans I have spoken to in recent years regarding their experiences. I owe heartfelt thanks to Chilton Williamson, Jr., Bill Crimmins, Adam Johnston, Tom Piatak and Derek Turner, who read and commented on this novel at various stages of its development. I extend a special thanks to my wife Stacy for her patience, forbearance, and advice. Finally, thanks to all the writers who brought me enlightenment, pleasure, and inspiration in a lifetime of reading.

About the Author

Wayne Allensworth is the author of *The Russian Question: Nationalism, Modernization, and Post-Communist Russia*, published by Rowman & Littlefield in 1998. He is a Corresponding Editor for *Chronicles* magazine, and his short story, *Man of the West*, was nominated for the 2000 Western Writers Association of America Golden Spur award. He has contributed to the following collections: *Exploring American History* (Marshall Cavendish, 2008); *Peace in the Promised Land: A Realist Scenario* (Chronicles Books, 2006); *Immigration and the American Identity* (Chronicles Books, 2008); and *Russian Nationalism and the National Reassertion of Russia*, edited by Marlene Laruelle (Routledge, 2009). He lives in Keller, Texas. *Field of Blood* is his first novel.